red asphalt

A Novel
by
Scott Cherney

ISBN 978-1-4357-1186-0

DEDICATION

To Don and Mike
Radio Gods
Thanks for the laughs when I needed them the most

CHAPTER ONE

LIP SERVICE

"What's that thing on your lip?"

It was the nicest thing Karen had said to me all month. Granted, it's not exactly the first thing that anyone wants to hear at the beginning of a brand new day. Somehow it just doesn't have the same ring as "Top o' the mornin' to ya!"

But for me, ever the tragic optimist in this farce we called a marriage, it showed Karen still cared. For one thing, she actually acknowledged my presence, which she hadn't for the most of that entire week. I was starting to believe that I could have walked around sans pants and nary a peep would she utter. The fact that she noticed anything at all gave me a microscopic piece of hope that we, as a couple, might actually survive. It wasn't much, but it was more than we had for quite some time.

Of course, what I had mistaken for true concern in Karen's voice was, in reality, only disgust. This fact became self-evident when I turned about to face her. She had yet to put her contacts in and had been wearing her severely rimmed, Mason jar lensed glasses, giving her that all too attractive comparison to Mr. Moto in drag. Her eyes, comically magnified behind the glass bricks she wore, were honed in on my mouth. Her face contorted into a mask of utter revulsion and her mouth froze in mid-EWWWWWW.

I could feel a tingling in my lower lip. With the tip of my tongue, I touched what seemed like a tiny BB had lodged just in the lower right corner. I rolled it back and forth, furthering my investigation process.

"Well, go look at it in the mirror. You're making me sick," Karen snapped

Ah, there it was. Karen's inner bitch had awakened, shooing away that single solitary piece of hope I held with the flick of her fingernail.

I stumbled into the bathroom with all the grace of a sterno bum while Karen dove out of the way as though I had leprosy, nearly falling backwards into the closet. Nothing boosts confidence like watching your life partner recoiling in terror as you pass by. I fumbled for the light and, even though my bladder was full to the brim, I gazed at my reflection in the mirror first. I figured could pee anytime. This could be serious.

I had a fat lip. It protruded slightly but it was evident that it was swollen. There was some discoloring with light pink and dark purple hues. In the center were little white bumps, not unlike pimples that had begun to take shape. I'd had cold sores in the past, even cankers, but this thing was more than an insect bite. Maybe it came from a Black Widow. Maybe it was filled with eggs.

"It's just a cold sore," I said, feeling Karen hovering nearby.

"Also known as Herpes, " Karen added accusingly. She obviously didn't mean the good kind. There was near-glee in her tone. To taunt me even further, she then asked, "Who have you been kissing?"

"Nobody in this house," I retorted.

She stormed out of the bathroom after exhaling a nasty sigh that filled the bathroom like a loud fart.

In retrospect, Karen's comment was snide to be sure, but it was also playful. Had my defense shields not been deployed, I might have recognized this instead of lashing out. My choice of comeback lines tilted the machine and, if it were up to Karen-and it usually was-there would be no replays.

"Do we have any lip balm?" I asked, knowing full well she was pissed enough to hit me with the nearest heavy object. My sharp tongue has both a hair-trigger and the capacity to set off anyone in the free world. If only I had the common sense to keep it check sometimes. Not receiving a reply, I headed for the kitchen to ask again.

"No, we don't have anything for your diseased lip," she spit. "Why don't you go to the doctor?"

"Why don't you?"

Good one. My groggy mental state had sufficiently dulled my wit. That's what I get for boasting. Now it was my turn to storm away.

"Oh, that makes sense. I'm not diseased."

"You could have fooled me," I muttered, knowing full well by this point that any clever banter was completely out of the question. Now we were reduced to arguing like kindergartners.

"What? Don't mumble."

"Don't tell me what to do! God, why does this have to be this way? This is so stupid," I groused, stomping back into the kitchen. "Shit. Look at the time. Where's the coffee?"

"I didn't make any. I'm sick of coffee. If you want some, you'll have to make it yourself."

"There's no time! I have to get ready for work. I can't wait for a pot of coffee to brew. Goddamn it!"

"Try 7-11. They have coffee. They might have something for that lip too."

"You're a big help, you know that?" I told her, pointing at my lip. "This is caused by stress, too, y'know. Small wonder, isn't it?"

"If you say so," she said so blasé you could have spread it on toast. She sipped her morning beverage of choice nonchalantly out of her kitty-cat mug.

"If there's no coffee, what is that?"

"Tea. Ever hear of it?"

"Does it have caffeine? If it does, I'll have some of that."

"Make it yourself. You know how to heat water, don't you? You just put it in the kettle and boil."

With that, she turned and walked out to the backyard. It was the last I saw of her that morning. It's difficult to tell whether her paraphrasing of Lauren Bacall was intentional or not. Delivered behind those lovely spectacles of hers, she came off more like Percy Dovetonsils, an old Ernie Kovacs character that she knew nothing about, therefore becoming my own private joke.

I didn't bother to heat up my tea her way, nor did I use the microwave. No, I just threw a tea bag in my cup and used hot tap water-the quickest method for anyone suffering a caffeine jones. After filling the cup and dunking a half-dozen times, I squeezed the bag for all it was worth and gulped the tepid liquid down in one gulp. Naturally, I spilled a third of it all over myself.

Oversleeping yet again as I had that morning cut my preparation time in half, turning this time of the day into something right out of Mack Sennett. I dashed to the bedroom to change into my uniform when I realized I had nothing clean to wear. Therefore, I wore what I had the day before which, considering the unflattering uniform combo of teal pinstriped shirts and tacky khakis, was no major fashion crime on my part. Next stop, back to the bathroom for a quick shave and a pee, nicking my face four times and dribbling down my leg respectively. Not feeling confident enough with one caffeinated beverage in my system, I made the gross error of trying another cup of tea, this time dumping the entire contents all over my pants which at least covered up the real piss stain . Not bothering to dry myself, I scrambled out the front door and into the car. I zipped off, then around the block and back when I figured out that I neglected to bring my wallet. On the way out for the last time, I caught my right shirtsleeve on the doorknob and tore off the cuff button.

Top o' the mornin' to me!

CHAPTER TWO

MORNING DRIVE

I was trapped. Given the general tone of the day thus far, there was no way around the realization that my morning commute would just flat out suck three ways to Christmas. Voila! Right again. I was literally smack dab in the center lane of traffic that was crawling at the speed of slugs. No way out to the left. No way out to the right. The only thing faster than my fellow traffic prisoners and me was Time.

Time. My archenemy, staring at me with blood red LED eyes from his dashboard perch, mocked me as usual.

"7:54,' the clock sneered. "Six minutes to go, Chico. It's almost eight o'clock…again. Eight. Ocho. I say ocho. You gonna say oucho when you're late for work again, my friend."

I popped Time in the face with the heel of my palm. I hate Time. Especially when he's right.

Sitting at a completely dead stop on the freeway is a crime against nature. In my dream world, it should happen only once in a generation, but realistically, annually would be nice. Weekly could even be a compromise I could live with. But daily...? Every single stupid day of every single stupid work week is just painful. Agony on an endless loop. This routine congestion of vehicles falls under the category of UNACCEPTABLE. I just don't buy it. It just doesn't wash. What could be the hold-up? Just move it along. Sure, it can move at a slower pace as long we were continuing to be MOBILE. The bottom line is to just fucking MOVE.

Surrounding me in this jam were the regular cast of idiots, the same stereotypes that I had grown weary of seeing way before this day began. Sure, different actors appeared in these roles from day to day, but the characters remained the same. There's the perky little receptionist who keeps checking her gooped up eyes in the mirror while bobbing her head to some insipid Top 40 ditty from the wacky Breakfast Buffet Crew on 94.5 FM-The Bomb! Then there's the bald punk boy with a goatee, tattoos, piercing and a black t-shirt with the logo of some obscure band like Testicle Maneuvers or Phlegmbot. Now a soccer mom in her mini van pulls up. She turns all the way around in her seat to discipline her nasty brood that she probably squeezed out every year for the past five, one at a time of course. Oh, and my favorite character type in all the world sat directly to my right-the yuppie from Hades in shirt, tie and SUV, yakking away on his cell phone while running his manicured fingers through his mousse laden hair and sipping on a skinny latte, half-caf, of course.

Phones. The bane of my existence. Whether they be cell, pay or just home, they are the Devil's Communicators. And cell phones.... what is this

13

obsession with constant interaction all of a sudden? Do we really have that much to say? What is there to talk about that you can't say in person? Nothing. Not now. Not ever. They are just a distraction, a diversion from LIFE.

Time decided to chime in.

"Oh my goodness…it's 7:55. Five minutes! Five minutes to unemployment! You know that if you ever get out of this stinking mess, you'll still be late! Five minutes! Cinco de Minuto, mi amigo!"

I couldn't be late again. As much as I hated that soul-sucking job, I was headed into the Danger Zone as far as tardiness was concerned. That's a sin, don't you know. Tardiness. Even if you were an honest to goodness bonafide saint here on Earth during your entire life, you would not be able to enter the kingdom of Heaven if you were had the stigma of tardiness on your permanent record. You may not go to Hell, but Purgatory is filled with people who just couldn't make it anywhere on time.

And I was certainly sitting in the foyer of Purgatory right then and there. Not a creature was stirring, not even a Hyundai. To add to my misery, the ditzy receptionist had the top of her VW Beetle down so that all could enjoy the crazy, kooky sounds of the wacky Breakfast Buffet radio show.

"It's a good lookin' Thursday, wouldn't you say so, Frank?"

"That it is, Beans. We got traffic and weather together at the top of the hour."

"That's right, Frank. There's also more great music ahead AND the semi-finals of this year's annual Breakfast Buffet Fart Contest."

"And you, my friend, could be in the Hall of Fame."

"Well, they don't call me Beans for nothin'!"

"We gotta hit a break. It's Frank and Beans on the Breakfast Buffet on 94.5…The Bomb! It's 7:57."

That was enough for me to roll my window up on the white Ford Escort station wagon that Healthfirst, the company I worked for, had provided for me to go to and fro, over hill and down dale while fulfilling my nefarious duties as a courier for this clinical laboratory. I flipped on my own radio, channel surfing impatiently as was my normal modus operandi.

Click.

"The Dow Jones Industrial average…"

Click.

"Ba-widdy-ba-di-bang-di-bang…"

Click.

"Metro police responded to a 911 call…"

Click.

"Zero down and zero payments for a whole year…"

Click.

"I'm Frank…"

Click.

"Illegal aliens…"

Click.

"Gridlock in Congress…"

Click.

"What would Jesus do…"

Click.

"Ba-widdy-ba-di-bang…"

Click.

Shut up

Shut up

Shut up

I turned the damn thing off. It was a mercy killing.

With the window closed, the car seemed smaller and was closing in as each moment passed. Perspiration dotted my forehead. My stomach whirled like a cheap carnival ride, forcing my rage up, up into my throat. I had to open my mouth or I would surely explode. I had to SCREAM....

But hold!

A van pulling slightly ahead in the next lane revealed an exit I'd never spotted before just ahead on the right. Suddenly, the entire parking lot of cars began to inch forward just a teensy bit, but it was more than we had moved for several minutes. But here I was, stuck in the middle and I had to get over in order to take advantage of this escape route. I flipped on my turn signal and made my move. This had to work, right? What could possibly prevent...

An obstacle.

The SUV and my well-groomed friend on the phone, totally wrapped up in his inconsequential conversation, was completely oblivious to anything outside of his selfish spectrum. Therefore, he kept pace with me, unaware I wanted to get over to his lane, as if he fucking owned it. When I moved, so did he. I even lowered myself to try to get his attention by waving my arm as though I had to get his permission. All this occurred while the remainder of this band of idiots that surrounded me began some forward mobility, causing me to lurch along spastically with the pack. All the while, this Mousse Head moved along oblivious to my plight. It almost seemed to be deliberate.

"You can't invade my space. I am a mover and a shaker. You don't matter. Only I do. Stay away now! This is MY lane!"

Frustrated and losing it faster than a speeding bullet, I tried to focus on whatever positive energy sat in some hidden reserve in my system. Visualize...see

myself driving right off the freeway…escape…escape…
Be the exit! Be the exit…

"Let me over, Shit for Brains!" I screamed
demonically.

Shit for Brains did not acknowledge me, no way,
shape or form. I did not exist in his world. Was it really
his world after all? Did I simply just cease to be?

"7:59, Chico! Sixty seconds to go!"

"Shut the fuck up!"

I jerked forward, thinking the sudden movement
might somehow catch Shit for Brains' eye. Nothing. The
SUV, acting independently of the asshole piloting it,
blocked me for the very last time because the exit had
just about…

Passed.

Bye-bye.

With both hands, I locked the steering wheel in a
death grip and shook ferociously. I wanted to pull it off
with all of my might and sail it across to the bastard to
my right. My head flailed madly with all the fury I had. I
opened my mouth and detonated.

"Motherfucker! You fucking shit for brains
MOTHERFUCKER!"

I started hyperventilating. Surely I was going
berserk at that very moment. Mad, I tell you! Not just
pissed off, but stark raving MAD! My head began to
spin. There was no way off of this carousel. Make it
stop…make it stop! Make it stop NOW! I have never
felt such fury in my entire life and I couldn't find the off
switch. What to do? What to do?

Just as rapidly, I seized control. Closing my
eyes, I took in a series of deep breaths. It was difficult at
first. My windpipe had closed off. I needed to focus on
the one thing in my life that meant anything at all to me.

Sarah. I thought of Sarah.

Just as suddenly, I was able to suck air into my lungs…and out again…in and out…in…and out…in…out. As my brain cleared, I knew at once what had to done. I opened my eyes and sighed one last time for good measure.

Shifting into park, I turned off the ignition and got out of my work car after pulling a blue aluminum baseball bat from behind the driver's seat. Because I was now a man with a mission, I strutted straight over to the SUV with single-minded determination. Others in traffic must have been baffled by my actions since they began to blare their horns in protest. I ignored them. What were they to me?

Shit for Brains was blathering inanely to his undoubtedly equally moronic companion on the other end of the line. I had no idea or interest in what he was saying. To me, it was just white noise.

I snatched the phone from his ear and stepped doggedly over to the guardrail that overlooked a housing development below. Glancing over my shoulder to the SUV, the shocked fuckhead froze in disbelief, looking completely lost without his toy. I then methodically pointed outward as if to right field, just like Babe Ruth silently announcing to the fans where he going to hit his next home run. I was calling my shot. Then, I tossed the cell phone up and swung my bat with all of my might. I batted that baby into 1001 itty-bitty phone pieces, spraying them all over Suburbia. It was a triumphant moment in my history.

My Shit for Brains buddy had not been impressed by what I had done. He flounced out of his vehicle and marched over to me. Then, grabbing me by the shoulder and spinning me about, he seemed prepared to exact some yuppie vengeance on me. Too bad for him. Instinctively, I jabbed the bat into his rock-hard abs, doubling him over since I caught him off guard. This placed his head directly in the batter's box.

"Shit for Brains," I snarled and swung away.

Connecting with full force, the Yuppie's head exploded into brown goo, splattering across the windshield of his SUV. I grimaced quizzically from what I perceived to be a very familiar smell. Timidly, I sniffed the bat.

"Whoa!" I exclaimed, recoiling from the suddenly identifiable stench. "He really did have *SHIT FOR BRAINS*!"

The blast from the car horn brass section awakened me.

Just a daydream.

Goddamn it.

The pack had begun to move and urged me to do the same. Snapping to attention, I pulled the car ahead, only to discover that this was not unlike false labor for we only scooted a couple of feet. I blew my stack again, this time sticking my head out the window-after rolling it down, of course.

"A foot! We moved a fucking foot! This is what you were honking about? Terrific! Sensational! Yee-fucking-ha!" I bellowed at the great unwashed amongst me.

As I turned back around to simmer in my seat, Time had inadvertently opened his mouth one too many times.

"8:00! It's 8:00 on the dot!"

I punched his face out.

"I've had it with you too!"

Grasping my hand in pain since I grazed the volume knob with my knuckles, I could see the dreaded SUV in my peripheral vision. I glanced over to see the yuppie, still on his goddamn phone, staring directly at me, shaking his head back and forth derisively.

HE was judging ME.

You go right ahead, pal, because I can judge too, you know…and I find you GUILTY AS CHARGED. And the sentence? Well, my well-groomed friend, you might consider the fate I have in store for you to be CRUEL AND UNUSUAL. You know something? You may be right. But as far as I'm concerned, it is also JUSTICE.

DEATH by lethal injection…

…of styling mousse.

CHAPTER THREE

SWIPING IN

Freeing myself from the logjam of motor vehicles and morons at the next freeway exit, I was able to conduct some fancy maneuvering through the streets of Stockton. I knew shortcuts that were legally dubious at best and probably shouldn't have been allowed to exist. But they did serve a primary purpose and that was to cut several minutes off my travel time. No one was hurt, inconvenienced or even the worse for wear with all the zigging and zagging through parking lots and neighborhood back streets and alleyways I performed like the proverbial bat out of Hell.

(I know I make a lot of references to Hell. You don't have to point that out to me. I may doubt the existence of Heaven but I most certainly believe in Hell. In other words, Hell yeah.)

Getting to work on time at this juncture was totally out of the realm of possibility, unless I could get my hands on a used Way-Back Machine. My main concern was to try not to be *too* late, a goal of 8:15, which I felt was both obtainable and feasible. It just wasn't very ambitious in the grand scheme of things.

After all, was it all really worth it? Of course not. But as much as I detested my job with every fiber of my being, that hatred was an unnecessary luxury at that moment because I needed to remain focused. I couldn't allow myself to be distracted by my true feelings, especially while stunt driving through North Stockton. One daydream and I might end up wrapped around a telephone pole. Not only that, the finish line grew oh so near.

Onto the home stretch of March Lane I swerved and exhaled in relief once I spotted the Weber Business Park sign where the Stockton branch of Healthfirst was based. Speeding into the parking lot like Steve McQueen on his best day, I pulled up to the loading zone and dashed to the employee entrance, expecting the worst.

Just as I had hoped, the lab was empty, save for one single, solitary employee, Elsie Prine, my sparring partner, who sat on her stool arranging petri dishes. Elsie was a microbiologist who had two years left before retirement. Her only joy in life seemed to be to make my life as miserable as possible. She would taunt, tease and generally poke me with a sharp stick without knowing when to quit. Even if she did know, she wouldn't have cared. It wasn't that she was nasty. Quite the contrary. She'd give you the shirt right off her back, a gesture both generous and nauseating all at the same time since she resembled everybody's image of a school cafeteria worker and who needs to see that topless?

Looking up from her work, she drolly asked, "Oversleep again, Calvin?"

"I don't oversleep."

"Maybe you're just under-awake."

"Tee-hee," I replied, finding my way to the time clock, my least favorite business tool of all time..

This useless hunk of metal had been my nemesis since Day One. Employees had to swipe their plastic personalized time cards just like an ATM at the grocery store checkout stand in order to clock in and out for the day. Not only was it five minutes fast, but it usually didn't work and this day proved to be no exception. First attempt at a swipe…nothing. Again…nothing. Two more times…nothing, nothing.

"Come on, you useless piece of junk!" I complained.

I tried again with no luck, so I smacked it. I had forgotten my previous injury from my radio punch-out but the instantaneous agony reminded me. I just didn't care. This monstrosity from the Devil's Workshop deserved to be hit and often. Elsie had strolled over and took my card away from me. She looked at me patiently..

"Slowly," she said, demonstrating that she could get it right the very first time.

"Lucky swipe," I grumbled

"Lucky at swipes, unlucky at love, " she smirked, standing way too close for my comfort, then sauntering back to her station almost seductively.

I begrudgingly thanked for her help with a snarl. The truth of the matter was that I truly had grown fond of Elsie over the years. (But don't you ever tell her.) I'm sure the feeling was reciprocated. She was one of the very few people in that place I could tolerate for more than five minutes at any given time. Though she may have been eccentric, at least she seemed sincere. Also, being around as long as she had, Elsie knew where all the bodies were buried so nobody could get anything over on her. If I wanted the straight scoop, I went to

Elsie. If only she hadn't been such a pest. Sometimes Elsie really creeped me out, especially when she said things to me with an underlying sexual theme. I had an unnerving feeling that she had a crush on me. It also didn't help that she smelled like she bathed in Boraxo.

In the break room, I noticed that no coffee had been brewed that morning, which certainly figured. I mean, why would anybody both to make coffee for other employees to consume? Oh, I don't know…common courtesy, perhaps? Nahhhhhh.

"I see there's no coffee," I called out to Elsie.

"I don't drink that swill. I have good coffee at home," she answered.

"Then why aren't you home drinking it?" I yelled back, emptying the brew basket filled with grounds from the day before.

Elsie had been right again. The office coffee service for the lab, in a word, blew. I could have brewed up a batch of compost and made a better pot of Joe with the crud they provided, which was some obscure Canadian brand. Still, caffeine was caffeine and this monkey on my back had been getting pissed off.

"Calvin?"

Even the hint of Terri Urbani's voice gave me an immediate gag reflex. It had the tone of a female Wookie that had just learned English, her jowls undoubtedly strangling her with each difficult breath. My revulsion to Terri must have been evident even though I had my back to her as she entered the break room. I could feel my nerves-and my sphincter- immediately tense up, causing me to physically jerk while I stood at the sink.

"Yeah?" I didn't bother to turn around, choosing instead to complete my coffee mission.

"You're late again," she stated, which in her case, was always the obvious.

I paused for a mildly dramatic sigh, but, again, all I could manage to say was "Yeah?"

"It's getting to be a bad habit."

"It's not a habit, Terri. It's called traffic. Look into it."

"We have to get here on time," she admonished.

Oh, how I wanted to toss the glass coffeepot that I held in my hand at her. I knew I could score a bull's-eye, right in the center of her enormous forehead. But, I restrained myself for understandable reasons not the least of which being that this useless slab of flesh was my boss, my supervisor, and my albatross.

"Yeah?" I said one more time, then finally turned to face her. "*We* have to get here on time? What time do you want me to pick you up tomorrow?"

"You know what I mean," Terri said flatly.

She seemed to be getting fatter as we spoke, as though her metabolism was in constant flux. Perhaps this had been due to the fact that her choice of wardrobe always included stretch pants, pants that cried out, "I-CAN'T-BREATHE!" Her enormous breasts pointed at me bulging beneath a pink blouse, held fast by what was probably the world's strongest brassiere. They seemed to be ready to attack at any given moment. Her Mardi Gras sized head appeared even larger with her haystack of flaming red hair that was piled as high as an elephant's eye. Her face, however, had grown smaller over time, beginning to disappear into a bog of blubber.

"Sure, I know what you mean. Do you know what I mean?" I asked, knowing damn well I wasn't making a lick of sense thanks to lack of sufficient go-juice.

"Why are you trying to pick a fight with me?" Terri asked damn near pathetically.

I tried not to give in, but the words just weren't coming. "I'm not…I'm…trying to get here on time, okay? I'm here now. If I could set the clock back and start over, I would. Since I can't, I'm here now. I fully admit it, I'm late, but here I am, raring' to go. As soon as my coffee's ready, I'll be out the door. Honest."

"Well, you're going to have to wait. Your reports aren't ready yet."

Call me dumbfounded, but I had to inquire, "Let me get this straight. I have to be here on time so that I can just…wait?"

"It's your job," Terri had the audacity to say before she waddled out of the room. Spoken like a true ineffectual supervisor. I heard her greet J.B. Linderman on her way out
and wondered if he would slip in her snail trail.

J.B. entered the employee break room with a sneer on his face not unlike the victim of a Dutch Oven. A roly-poly sort of middle-aged guy, J.B. always appeared to be on the verge of de-tox. To say that he perspired profusely would be an understatement. This guy sweated in the shower. I'd known him for probably ten years or more after we had appeared in a few community theater productions together. He had been with Healthfirst since its inception and was responsible for recommending me for the job, something for which I've never been able to forgive him.

"Hey, man, what's happening? What'd The Beast want? Was she lookin' for donuts?" he quipped.

"Yeah. In all the wrong places," I answered, completing the joke.

"Don't tell me you were late again."

"Yup."

"I asked you not to tell me that," J.B. kidded as he sat and rifled through a newspaper. "Ever think of leaving home earlier?"

"It's crossed my mind…every single day. Any other suggestions from the World's Oldest Living Courier?"

"Which way do you drive to work?"

"The only way I can."

Beat.

"Don't go that way."

Bah-dump-bump!

Everything was a vaudeville routine to this guy.

"Thanks, Uncle Miltie. You're a big help," I muttered, plunking down in a chair across from him after I finished prepping what passed for coffee. "I've tried every way possible. I've gone this way. I've gone that way. The best way is the only way."

"Sounds like you're going nowhere slow. You'd better find another way by next week."

"Why? What's next week?"

"Overtime justification."

Apparently, I had my head cocked to one side like the RCA Victor dog and I sure as hell didn't like the sound of my master's voice.

"You have no idea what I'm talking about, do you?" he smirked. "Healthfirst doesn't want to pay any more overtime."

"But what if I work overtime?"

"Then you have to fill out an overtime justification form to explain why you're late. Three guesses who gets to say yea or nay."

The hair on the back of my neck bristled.

"Not…?"

"Bingo! The Beast from the East! If she denies it, you don't get it."

"This is bullshit!"

"Sure it is. Didn't you read the memo?"

"No, I didn't read any goddamn memo," I barked, clomping over to the bulletin board. "There's nothing here."

"Well, Terri showed it to *me*," he said smugly, washing his hands of the whole ordeal. "She always does this. You know that. Every time a new policy gets handed down from corporate, she shows it to a couple of people in the hopes we'll all spread it around like a bad rumor. I guess it's too much trouble to post it on the board."

In the meantime, I stared at a sign-up sheet for an upcoming Tupperware party and declared, "I'm not doing it."

"That's all well and good, but I don't think you have a choice."

"Sure I do. I didn't read it. It's not posted. As far as I'm concerned, it doesn't exist. I'm not doing it."

J.B. leaned back in his chair and pulled off his clip-on tie. Opening his collar button, he looked out the window knowingly. He knew damn good and well was that no matter how right I really was about this matter, I'd be proven wrong. We called that *The Nature of the Business.*

Attempting to speak reasonably to Terri about this overtime fiasco just made matters-and our working relationship-that much worse. I tried to explain that the way she had laid my schedule out for the day, it was inevitable that I would be at least a half-hour late at the end of the day. I told her I understood that the company was cutting back because it didn't make any financial sense. Instead of forcing us to try harder, there needed to be a redistribution of duties so that we can all share the burden, not just a select few. What it really boiled down to was that she, being the supervisor of our department AKA the Lead Driver, would have to actually have to go out and drive. Terri wasn't having any of that. No, she had to stay at the lab and supervise from there. She couldn't run our department if she was on the road. What if something required her immediate attention? What if one of us had an emergency and no one else was there to help? What if her services were needed at the lab because she was, after all, a licensed phlebotomist herself?

Whatifwhatifwhatifwhatif...

"What if you tried to shit and your head exploded?" I screamed.

Okay. Not exactly Neil Simon. But I had the choice to either say that or attempt to wrap my hands around her swollen throat, which would have taken all morning.

"What did you say to me?" she demanded as she slammed the door of her office, which doubled as a supply room. Suddenly, I was claustrophobic being in an enclosed space with her. The air became thin, taken up by her monstrous girth.

"You heard me. Do you want to write it down for you so that you can accurately quote me on your incident report?"

"Jim's going to hear about this," she threatened.

Yeah, go to the Boss, Terri. Good tactical move. Jim Banner was the Heathfirst regional manager. While based at our lab in Stockton, his territory pretty much covered all of central California.

"Good. You go to Jim. I'll go to Rob Montoya," I countered by dropping the name of the company's human resources director for our area. En garde.

"You're arguing with company policy."

"How do I know that it's company policy?"

"What do you mean?"

"Prove it."

Confused, Terri dug through the in-box on her desk and found the memo. She handed it to me.

"There. What does that say?"

I narrowed my eyes ever so slightly and read; "It says 'Please post for all employees'. If it's in here, it's not posted, is it?"

"Uh..." she uh-terred.

Point. My advantage.

"THIS is why I'm so pissed off, Terri. Why is it in here and not out there for everyone to read? I don't necessarily disagree with the policy. It's business and I understand that. But you can't spring something like this out of nowhere and expect us to work it out amongst ourselves without any help from you. It's not right…and you're wrong."

She had realized her mistake, her error. Puddles formed beneath her widening eyes, releasing tears at last that rolled down her puffy, Campbell Soup Kid cheeks.

"I…can't tell you how sorry I am. Please don't say anything to Jim…or Rob. Please? I'll make it up to you, I swear. Anything you want, you can have. Would you like the day off…with pay? I'll run your route for you. Calvin, what can I do for you? Would you…" She pulled up her blouse, bra and all in order to offer her gigantic tits to me. "Would you like to touch my breasts?"

Terri arched her back and her now uncovered gargantuan boobs pinned me against the wall. They began to act independently of her own body, rubbing themselves against my face like two anxious puppies starved for affection. Their nipples brushed back and forth on my lips, hardening with each stroke. These bags of flesh grew friskier by the second, punching me across the face with increasing intensity. Her tits were pummeling me.

"Play with them! Play with my breasts!" she pleaded.

Well, that's disgusting, isn't it? That's what I get for being a boob man. If I were more interested in a woman's ass, I would have imagined that her huge posterior would have grown teeth and swallowed me whole. Suddenly, being beat up by two giant knockers doesn't sound so bad, does it?

That's right. I said I imagined it. For me to think of Terri Urbani in sort of sexual context would be, for me, justifiable grounds for suicide. As you can tell, I'm not very comfortable even speculating on such a topic, though I'm positive she and her slovenly husband engage in all sorts of fleshy fun, if their three horrid children are any proof. Call it a hunch. I also heard a story about Terri at the Healthfirst Christmas party before I was hired. It seems the event was just awash in alcoholic holiday cheer and afterwards, Terri drunkenly arrived at the apartment of another courier. She supposedly wore a trench coat with nothing underneath, wanting to spend the night. When she revealed her nakedness to her equally pie-eyed co-worker, he politely refused by vomiting all over her. At least, that was his side of the story. Maybe the truth of that matter was that Terri looked pretty damn good after a few dozen Screwdrivers and he bounced up and down on her all night like a giant inner tube. Ew. There I go again.

Anyway, the real confrontation between Terri and myself was brief and cut me to the quick. The memo had been read and initialed by everyone but me. The fact that it hadn't remained posted was my only arguable point. The memo had only been a week old while the sign-up sheet for the Tupperware party stayed on the bulletin board for two months. It didn't matter. I hadn't paid attention. Therefore, it was my fault. Debating the time issue went nowhere as well. Getting to work and finishing my shift on time were my complete responsibilities. Any mention of Terri cramming her fat ass into a work vehicle and helping us out was completely irrelevant, though it didn't prevent me from uttering my catch phrase loud as a bastard for all to hear.

"When is a Lead driver not a Lead Driver? When she neither LEADS nor DRIVES!"

On that note, I took my leave. Sometimes, I'm just too clever for my own good because, once again, Terri wrote me up for my actions.

The legend continued.

CHAPTER FOUR

HOT TALK

I never listened to the radio much before I start driving for the lab. Initially, it was frustrating trying to listen to any music station because there were never two songs in succession I could stomach, no matter what the format. I've nearly worn out my finger switching from station to station. While my work car came equipped with a cassette player, my own personal tape collection was too special for me to waste and I only used it sparingly, not wanting to burn out on my own music.

So, in an attempt to remain informed of the world around me that I was all-too-willing to ignore, I turned to talk radio. Sure, this forum wasn't exactly a microcosm of society, but it exposed me to a variety of opinions and issues, so it filled a certain niche. Unfortunately, talk radio created a whole new set of problems not the least of which was that I was just as choosy finding a talk show as I had been finding music.

The slant of any particular show had to achieve some sort of balance; otherwise it's the sound of one voice, one opinion, and one point of view. Here's the deal: I ain't no conservative. I ain't no liberal. I'm all kinds of things all wrapped up into one. A mutt, if you will. I refuse to be pigeonholed into one category and labeled for the convenience of others. So these people don't speak for me and I ain't havin' none of it, especially on a radio talk show. Besides, no matter what agenda the host of any given program might be professing, it always had an air of insincerity anyway. It's all about the ratings, baby and it doesn't matter what you say or even if you believe it yourself as long as you stir it up out there. I've discovered over the years that politics, sports and religion all bore me to horrors and I'll have none of them in my life or my ears. That cuts out a lot of potential airtime right there. All news, all the time puts the world into an even more monotonous spin, due to the repetitious nature of media. How many times can one listen to the same goddamn stories in one day? The search continued.

Sometimes I'd flip to the medical advice of Dr. Dan Devon. He grew tiresome almost immediately with his endless carping on the evils of circumcision. Dr. Dan could have circumcised himself with a simple haircut.

The pop psychology of Connie Sandler was totally out of the question with her sanctimonious agenda. Her dual life as a saint on the air and a slut off was way too much to bear. Hypocrisy is even crueler if one doesn't practice what one preaches, especially if one is in the business of preaching.

I traveled up and down the radio dial trying to find something I could at least pass the time away. There were so many nationally syndicated offerings-humorless "comedy" shows, financial gobbledegook, religious nutjobs, blowhards each and every one of them. The

34

local programming was even worse, bottom of the barrel blather about bond measures in the upcoming elections or heated debates over parking meters. It was like a high-spirited evening with an insurance salesman on Seconal.

But I found that I couldn't turn the goddamn radio off. Spending 90% of my time in my car on any given workday required some sort of stimuli. Silence just was not an option. Without suitable audio distraction, all there would be left for me would be the job itself and that was a confrontation I tried to avoid whenever possible.

Finally, I stumbled across a station out of the San Francisco Bay Area with a program whose host had been pretty much middle of the road. Sure, he was a pompous asshole, but at least he was a pompous asshole that I could somewhat tolerate. He had a varied set of topics and the occasionally interesting guest. And *The Don Olsen Show* fit right into my schedule, beginning its broadcast as soon as I got into the car for the start of my morning route.

"We're talking about work this morning. Do you hate your job? I certainly don't. I am one lucky son of a gun because this happens to be my dream job. I've never wanted to do anything else in my life and I wouldn't trade it for anything in the world. But that's me. What about you? This morning, I want to hear about what you do for a living. How do you make a buck? More specifically, how bad is your job? And if it is so bad, why do you continue to do it? I want to know. So do you, I'm sure. Give a call toll free at 877-555-8899. Fred from San Jose. You're on *The Don Olsen Show*. Good morning."

Fred, a nasally sounding yahoo, began, "Hey, Don. Thanks for taking my call."

"It's my job, Fred. What do *you* do for a living?"

"My job really sucks, Don. I work the Can-Do at one of the downtown supermarkets."

"The Can-Do? What is the Can-Do?"

"The Can-Do is the recycling center in front of the store. People bring in their cans, their bottles, what have you and stick 'em in the machine. Then when they're done, the machine prints out a receipt and they go inside for their money."

"And *your* job?"

"I empty the machines when they get full…and they fill up a lot. It's noisy. It's messy. It's sticky. Everything spills."

"Like what?"

"Soda pop, beer, juice, what have you. It stinks too. So do the people."

"The people stink?"

"Sometimes. You got your homeless folks who spend all day lookin' for recyclables and they're pretty ripe to begin with."

"I can imagine."

"Especially in the summertime."

"Sounds a festival of smells. Stinkapalooza. How long have you been working the Can-Do?"

"About two years now."

"That's a pretty long time doing a job you hate."

"Well, gotta eat."

"Yeah, gotta drink too which explains why your job is necessary, Fred. Look at it this way. You're helping the environment."

"Hooray for me. Maybe they'll erect a statue of me outta old beer cans."

"There you go."

"Thanks, Don."

"Take care, Fred. You see it's the Circle of Life. Every job is necessary. No matter how much you may detest what you do, it serves a purpose and someone has to do it. Is there a totally useless job? No, not this one. My producer thinks she's being funny. Look, Christine, if I don't work, neither do you, so there. Let's take another call. From Walnut Creek, Maria. Good morning. Don Olsen, KGY radio."

"Hi, Don."

"What do you do, Maria?"

"I work in fast food."

"The Golden Arches?"

"No. One of the other ones. I hate it. It don't pay well. It's hard. It's hot. The customers are so rude."

"Maria, I love fast food. I eat it all the time, probably more than I should. Let me tell you something. Some day, these places will all be automated. It's going to happen. When it does, those jobs just won't exist. People will be out of those jobs…permanently. That day is coming sooner that you might think. Until then, somebody has to work there."

"I wish it wasn't me."

"Well, until you find another job, do me a favor. Please don't spit on the food."

"I wouldn't do that!"

"Good! It's getting close to lunchtime and I don't know where you work. Thanks for the call. Next up, Calvin, from a daydream, Don Olsen, KGY. Good morning."

"Hi, Don" I said. "Long time listener, first time caller."

"Actually, you're not calling now either. This is all in your head."

"Thanks for putting me in my place, Don."

"No problem. So, Calvin, do you hate your job?"

"Yes, I do," I stated unequivocally, straightening as I spoke since I had finally been allowed put my two cents in with the rest of the world. It didn't matter a fig that it had just been make-believe.

"May I ask what you do?"

"Don, I work as a courier for a medical laboratory. I drive a company car through three, sometimes four counties per day, delivering reports and sometimes supplies to various hospitals, clinics and doctors' offices."

"That sounds…like a damn good job to me. You're not chained to a desk inside a tiny windowless cubicle. You're out there in the world, driving around all day on somebody else's dime and, on top of that, you're providing a great and necessary service," Don explained in what seemed so obvious to me to be false sincerity.

"I realize that. But…"

"There's always a *but*, isn't there? Go on."

"But…" I paused for dramatic effect. "…not only do I deliver, I also pick up."

"What do you pick up?"

Here it comes.

"Specimens. Bodily fluids. Blood, urine, sputum, sperm. Then there are the ever-popular pap smears. You can't forget those."

"Who could?"

"Exactly. Then there are the other items that the pathology department tests, assorted body parts from inside and out."

"What is the worst thing you ever picked up?"

Without hesitation, I answered, "Fecal fat."

"Fecal fat? Sounds like a good name for a rock band. What is fecal fat?"

"It's exactly what it says it is, the fat from feces. It's all whipped like a chocolate mousse and frozen in a sealed plastic tub. Even then, you can still smell it. In fact, as a tribute, I call my car the Fecal Fat Fiat."

"That's both amusing and disgusting. Do you have to transport larger body parts as well?"

"No, I'm rather fortunate in that regard. My co-workers have the pleasure of that experience on their own routes. Mercifully, I've been spared so far."

"Any accidents?"

"Oh sure," I grinned as I recalled an amusing anecdote. Damn, I was a good caller to this show, or would have been if I had used a phone instead of my imagination. "There is a jug that patients use to collect their urine over a 24-hour period. That's why they call these 24-hour urine containers. Well, I dropped one of the babies down a stairwell. It sailed down about three flights and just exploded on the bottom floor."

"Bombs away! So what happened?"

"You mean after I cleaned it up?

"Uh-huh."

"The patient had to start all over again."

"I'm sure he was a little…P.O.ed," he quipped.

"Good one, Don."

"Calvin, as nauseating as that sounds, I think you're underestimating what you do. Let's face it. You're saving lives out there."

"At the expense of my own," I replied soberly

"How do you mean?"

Again, I paused, but not for faux effect this time. This hesitation stemmed from the fact that this was to be a true confession. Since my first stop that morning was twenty-five minutes away in Modesto, it afforded me the opportunity to tell my story…and it was high time I did.

"Look, I don't take this job for granted," I told Don and the listening audience in my head. "I know how important it is. Every specimen represents a human being. I get that. It's been drummed into me from day one. It's just…this is not what I've wanted to do with my life."

"Didn't you ever say, 'When I grow up, I wanna pick up fecal fat'?"

"Hell no. Who would?"

"To tell you the truth, I'd rather not speculate."

"But Don, that's not the worst part about it."

"What's worse than fecal fat?"

"The drudgery."

"Drudgery is worse than fecal fat?"

"Yes. At least fecal fat is temporary. Drudgery is constant. It's the same places, the same faces, all day, every day. What about traffic? You think your morning and afternoon commutes are stressful? I'm on the road ten times more than your average driver and I've got to deal with everyone else on the road-good, bad *and* ugly. Then you throw in the time constraints. Be at point A at the same time point B and C need you and to get from A to B to C through traffic in the time you are allotted… Suddenly you're imprisoned in a maze of cars and doctors and patients and blood and urine and fecal fat and the clock keeps running and running until it runs you down. Then, it starts all over again, the same cycle and you realize that it is all about time. Get to work on time. Get the specimens on time. Bring them back on time. You only have so much time and then it hits you right between the eyes. This is cutting into *your* time and it is starting to get away from you. The clock had just about run out and you've still got things to do, things you're supposed to be doing. Don, I feel that I have a destiny to fulfill and I am running out of time! When will I be able pursue my own dream? I'm getting worried because as the clock keeps ticking, I can feel my hopes and dreams beginning to fade away. I'm trying to hold on but it's slipping away and so am I. Everything about me is slipping and sliding and…"

"Alpha base to Calvin!"

Oh dear sweet Jesus up above. The sound of Terri's porcine voice snorting over the car's two-way radio from Alpha base, the code name for the home lab, rattled me to no end. I had to gain some semblance of composure before she squealed again. Man, I felt like I just couldn't talk to her right then. I was just making a point. My point! My point in life!

"Alpha base to Calvin. Do you copy?"

I furiously grabbed the microphone and answered, "Yeah, Terri. What?"

On the other end, there was a dramatic…sorry, comedic pause.

"You're supposed to say 'over'," she said. This idiot loved formality. I considered it and her both complete wastes of time.

"Yeah, Terri. What? Over."

"Dr. Ferrari has a pick up. Over."

"Dr. Ferrari or Dr. Ferrara? Over."

"Ferrari. Over."

"Could you double check please? This has happened before. They're on opposite sides of town and I don't want to be sent to the wrong address again. Over."

"I know where they are, Calvin. Stand by."

"Over?"

"Over."

Wait for it.

"It *is* Dr. Ferrara. You were right. Over."

"I'm sorry. I didn't copy that. Over."

"You were right."

"Over?"

"Over."

"Uh-huh. Over."

"So, Dr. Ferrara has a pick up, not Dr. Ferrari."

"Over?"

"Calvin…"

"Dr. Ferrara. Got it. Over, under, around and through."

"Alpha base clear."

"Clear," I sneered, dropping the mike on the passenger seat.

Don spoke up. "She's a real treat."

"No, Don. She's a trick, a very cruel trick."

"Go ahead with what you were saying…"

"No. Maybe later," I grumbled, turning off The Don Olsen Show both externally and internally.

That interruption felt like a charlie horse in my psyche. I had to stop my interview with Don or I was afraid I'd spin off on my own axis. Lest you think I'd already passed "GO" on the Mental Monopoly board, I was fully aware I had just been role-playing and actually engaged in a rousing conversation with a radio talk show host. I found this self-analysis extremely beneficial, especially since I had rounded the corner to an epiphany that I sought desperately sought. At least I wasn't speaking out loud for all the world to see as I drove about town and city to city. I like to think I wasn't anyway. It was becoming a wee bit difficult to tell at that juncture. Very difficult indeed.

CHAPTER FIVE

MAKE UP

Picking up whatever Dr. Ferrara had in store for me that morning was not my idea of a good time. It meant that I had to travel to an out of the way, crappier part of Stockton in order to walk into an office that smelled of old yeast and deal with a nasty-ass nurse whose credentials I'm convinced were highly suspect. This additional trip broke up the flow of the morning, which was a hardship by itself without adding this insult to that injury.

My actual job began at Alpha Base when I would put my lab reports together which Terri had to pull off the printer and distribute to each driver. I would then stuff these reports, into envelopes addressed to individual doctors or facilities and arrange them in the order of the route to be delivered. Then I had to re-stock my various ice chests used to transport specimens with cold packs for refrigeration and dry ice for frozen goods.

Those that required room temperature had a separate chest all their own. Then, before I'd leave, I would check the dry erase board near the specimen-processing center for any additional pick-ups that would be called in.

Finally, off I'd go, first to Modesto at the Heathfirst lab (nicknamed "Beta") for anything that required rerouting or additional processing at the bigger facility in Stockton. On the return trip, I'd veer off to the sprawling megalopolis known as Tracy, the town of a thousand smells, including the dry poo-like odor of beets from the sugar plant in town, vinegar from the Heinz factory or rotting tomatoes from the same facility since that's where they made all that lovely ketchup. (I say ketchup. You say catsup. Let's call the whole thing off.) The only attraction that town ever had was an oncologist's office with a redheaded receptionist with big beautiful green eyes who, when she finally spoke, might as well have said, "DUH..." She could have been a living clock that would DUH the hour.

"The time is one o'clock...DUHHHHHHH..."

Who knows for whom the bell DUHS? It DUHS for thee.

I had never heard such stupidity in the timbre of a voice. Her eyes, so seductive to me at one time, resembled two VACANCY signs from the moment she opened her mouth.

The next leg of my journey took me to Manteca, which is the Spanish word for lard. 'Nuff said.

Nearing the end of my morning, I would have to journey to the south side of Stockton starting with the Gothic building known as the San Joaquin County General Hospital. From there, it was an ostensibly endless succession of offices and clinics, each more aggravating than the next.

None was more so than Dr. Ferrara's charming clinic and yeast farm off the beaten path and damn near out to Linden, an itty bitty lil' ol' farming community. This trip would add another twenty to thirty more minutes to my already crowded schedule that day and I was already behind thanks to the well fed Terri and Kismet. Had I not been so pressed for time, I might have actually enjoyed the ride through the orchards on what could have been a beautiful summer morning. Not a chance. I was addled and addled I would remain when Ferrara's nurse held me up even longer when she took forever to get off the phone and give me the blood I came to fetch. May the mole on her cheek eat her alive. (If it were a real mole, you see. Aw, forget it. If I have to explain it to you...)

Now up to a half-hour behind, the possibility I would be able to take a lunch that day became debatable. Some days, I'd truncate my lunch hour to remain on schedule even though it was guaranteed by law. But the route dictated all and it was either cut it short or fall further behind in the afternoon. To complicate matters, I had one more stop to make downtown and upon arrival, the traffic lights were all against me-figuratively and literally.

Ahead of me was a red Pontiac Firebird with a bubble-brained bimbo at the wheel. Each time the light turned yellow, she slowed to a crawl. Certainly she could have pulled through the intersection without a hitch, but she chose not to and, in doing so, decided for the both of us. After all, it was only a two-lane street and she was in front of me.

"You could have made that!" I yelled to no avail.

The BBB (Bubble-Brained Bimbo) decided to utilize her valuable time at the stoplight to apply her eye makeup. It figured. From the looks of things, she applied her war paint very thickly. My God. Tammy Faye

Bakker would laugh at her. Then came the lipstick. The light turned green in the midst of this major renovation. The BBB paid it no heed.

"Green are the GO lights, honey! It's in the handbook! C'mon! It doesn't cost anything to pay attention!" I called as I honked my horn.

The sudden noise seemed to startle her, causing her to jerk forward and swipe her cheek with the lipstick. She smudged her face when she turned to give me a dirty look.

"Serves you right! Let's go, Pocahontas!"

The BBB moved reluctantly, glaring at me in the rear view mirror.

"Don't look at me!" I warned. "Look at the road! I've got to turn here!" So did she, without a signal of course. "Oh, great. What are we, on a date? Get out of my way!"

Fortunately, I had another lane to use on this street and I did. Pulling along side, the BBB tried to assassinate me with her scornful painted eyes.

"A little impatient today, are we?" she croaked in a voice that will kill grass.

"It's called traffic, honey. Look…"

She sped away before I could deliver the punch line. That was uncalled for. I caught up with her at the next light.

"Aren't you going to apply another coat of spackle?" I asked.

"Leave me alone!" she snapped. "I'll report you to your company!"

"Go ahead. The name's right here on the door!" I dared.

"Or maybe a cop…"

"Aw, get over yourself. You're not that cute."

"I still wouldn't fuck you."

With that, she pulled away again at the green light. What a delightful young lady. All of her tricks think so.

My eyes glazed over like two day-old Krispy Kremes. I was forced to drive behind her again when then the lanes merged and, naturally, here came another series of red lights. I couldn't believe she had the unmitigated gall to don even more mascara. How could she see through all that muck? What if she wouldn't be able to see at all?

That last question prompted me into action. I rammed my car right into the ass-end of her Firebird. I heard her scream. With that voice, it was the smoke alarm of the damned. Vampires sat up in their coffins and said, "What the fuck was that?"

I shifted into reverse since our bumpers locked together in the collision and freed them. Now loose, I drove around to her driver's side to survey the interior damage. When I hit her car, the BBB jammed her mascara brush directly into her eyeball about ¾ of the way, puncturing it like toothpick to a grape. Blood sprayed out of her socket and over her steering wheel. With her one good eye, she turned to stare at me in disbelieving horror.

"Now nobody will want to fuck you…not even me."

The light turned green and the Firebird drove off, popping my daydream like a balloon, a lovely, cartoon balloon. It burst just like the eyeball of the Bubble Brained Bimbo. But, sigh, it never happened. It never happened at all.

Just to tickle my fancy just an eensy-weensy bit more, the last stop of the morning had closed early for lunch, making this trip downtown totally unnecessary. I sat in my work car, shaking my head so rigorously, it could have fallen off my neck. My bottom lip tingled from the stress as though it was filled with uranium. I suppose I should have taken that time to ponder the why of it all. But, I had a better idea.

LUNCH!

CHAPTER SIX

LUNCH PALE

As I had figured, that day's lunch hour had to be unnecessarily edited to fit into this time slot. I planned to spend it as I always had-at home. I certainly wasn't surprised to see Karen's car in the driveway when I drove up. Why wouldn't she be home? It wasn't as if she had anywhere to go or anything to do. She didn't work anymore and wasn't about to start any time soon. Besides, Oprah would be on in four hours and why take the chance to miss that?

I never ate lunch at the lab. It never appealed to me in the least. The less time I spent there, the better. I needed to ground myself by touching my own personal home base. Call it a security blanket if you wish, but coming home for a short period of time during a workday both centered and relaxed me, unless Karen was pre-menstrual, as she seemed to forever be. Coming home was a time saver too because I could load up my reports and supplies for the afternoon and get a head start. I just wouldn't swipe out for lunch and would write my time down on the clipboard that sat next to the time clock so it could be adjusted later. Hey, I didn't make the rules, but I could bend them in my favor every now and then.

But, somehow I just knew there wouldn't be any welcoming committee on the other side of that front door. If this were an alternative cartoon universe, there might have been a rolling pin with my name on it laying in wait for me. Still, I persevered and stepped inside, hoping for the best but expecting the worst. There was the missus, plopped down on the couch watching some daytime soap opera like *The Bold and the Restless* or some damn thing. I gritted my teeth, but at least, strived to be pleasant with a friendly grin only to be greeted in turn with a snide sneer.

"What are you doing here?" Karen asked without looking up from the light of the TV set.

I could see where this was going immediately.

"I live here," I replied.

"Don't expect me to make you lunch."

"I don't expect anything anymore."

At one time in our life, Karen would spoil me rotten with culinary treats on a near daily basis since she was a sensational cook. Many a time I would bask in some gourmet goodness she would whip up for my lunch. It had been no small wonder that I enjoyed coming home at that time. When we began to drift apart, the good eats were among the first things to go. Karen was my pusher. She got me hooked on her food, and then took it away, leaving me to salivate on my own as I tried in vain to make something substantial for myself in the time I was allotted for the mid-day meal.

"I don't even know why you bother to come home for lunch," Karen said, growing more agitated by the second with my mere presence.

"Why shouldn't I?"

"Couldn't you just eat something out for a change? Do you not want to spend the money? There's nothing to eat here."

"There's CHEESE!" I exclaimed, not readily aware that a dairy product could be so melodramatic. I marched into the kitchen and flung open the refrigerator. The thing is, I hate American cheese, but at least I knew for certain it was there. I looked. It wasn't. "Where the hell is it?"

"I ATE IT!" she shrieked.

Slamming the refrigerator, I threw my arms up in a grand gesture of absolute frustration. "Great! That's just great! Now I have to eat out!"

"That's what you should have done in the first place."

"What-and miss all of this?" I wondered aloud as I waltzed right out the same door I entered probably not sixty seconds before.

No wonder Karen watched her soap operas. Their plotlines-and dialogue-were better than the bad drama we were living out. *The Young and the Cheeseless*. If our show had been part of the daytime lineup, I would have changed the channel myself. As it stood, I didn't have it in me to cancel it once and for all. Apparently, neither did Karen.

Lunch became the two for ninety-nine cent hot dog special at the AM/PM. I had a water bottle in the car to wash down all that Oscar Mayer product down, so the price was right and yes, that was an issue. In between paychecks, also known as The Dead Zone, I had strict budget constraints. I pinched pennies so hard, Lincoln cried like a little bitch.

Cheese.

That wasn't even the problem, but somehow it became symbolic. I didn't know how. I didn't know why.

But I did know when.

I could always remember when.

High school, as you could probably predict, had been an extremely difficult period for me. My hormones were bouncing around my body like a pinball machine that kept tilting. Being the creative and awkward outcast I had set myself up to be, I naturally gravitated to the drama department, which I discovered to be the natural habitat for the creative, awkward outcast. It was within that sanctuary that I found the woman I wanted to marry.

Karen looked as though she just stepped off the set of thirties movie musical directed by Busby Berkeley. She had a star quality from an era from long before we were both born, almost as if she channeled the spirit of a long dead film legend. It was an exotic look indeed. Her amber tresses sat on slender shoulders, framing a face as dramatic as Greta Garbo's. Her long body was slight, but solid. There didn't seem to be an ounce of fat on her. Her penchant for vintage clothing accentuated her figure and her ethereal sensuality.

When I first set eyes on her, I felt like I hit been hit in the forehead with a wooden mallet. I was instantly head over heels, over the river and through the woods gaga over her. When we were introduced, I didn't hear a word she said. I could only stare. Love at first sight be damned. I was willing to take a blood oath.

Once I finally figured out how to speak again, the romantic beast in me sprung to life. I began to pitch woo at her almost incessantly, barraging her with flowers, poems, sonnets, for God's sake. I even serenaded her outside of her algebra class. I fell crazy in love with Karen before we went out on our first date. First and only date, I should add.

Though I was seventeen years of age and could have legally done so, I did not drive. Not only did I not have a car, I had neither a license nor even a permit. Instead I walked or rode my bike or took the bus or depended on family or friends for a ride. Right. I didn't date. But now what course of action did I undertake to take the lady faire out on the town?

I called a cab.

A taxicab in a town like Stockton is like a monorail in the Rain Forest. The sight of a cab driving down the street was as much an anomaly as a horse-drawn carriage. I, on the other hand, thought that it had an air of sophistication about it. How wrong can one delusional teenager be? From the look on Karen's face when I picked her up, I might as well have escorted her on the short school bus.

My choice of restaurants was equally lame. The Happy Steak, despite its cheerful name and the fact that it was the "Home of the Golden Spud", stunk to high heaven. If I'm not mistaken, I believe there was a nearby animal shelter in the same general vicinity as the restaurant, which would explain their curious selection of meat. Nothing could explain why I picked such a dive to impress a girl. Depress was more like it.

To say my behavior at this fine dining establishment was overbearing would be the understatement of the century, especially since Karen ended up leaving me long before dessert. Apparently, the puppet show I performed with the two baked potatoes wrapped in gold foil known as the Golden Spuds sealed the deal. The spuds were meant to represent the two of us. What drove her over the edge was probably a combination of the high-pitched voices I gave our characters and when I finished up my little skit by making the potato lovers kiss. I guess I should have gotten a clue when she wasn't laughing and covered her face with her hands. She excused herself to go to the rest room and, after a half an hour, I realized she wasn't coming back. In fact, our waitress had witnessed Karen's hasty exit out the back door.

Needless to say, this didn't stop me from trying to win her over. I had been relentless in my many futile attempts to get into Karen's heart the way she had gotten into mine. Alas and alack, she flat out told me if I didn't stop harassing her, she would have me arrested. I took that for a no.

I backed off. I backed all the way off and climbed into a shell that lasted the rest of my last year of high school. For several months that never seemed to end, I became so withdrawn and depressed that I quit drama and refused to attend many of my classes. Little did I either know or care that I was dangerously close to not having enough credits to graduate. If I didn't, so what? Suicide became a viable option. While I didn't pursue it, I did read the prospectus. I found that it took too much effort to do myself in. Instead, I turned my back on happiness and transformed into a teenage zombie. I merely existed and that was all.

The dark place where I had taken up residence throughout the remaining months of my second decade on this planet grew claustrophobic. This self-imposed imprisonment caused me to be introspective and, as a result, saved my life. I began to delve into my creative side out of a pure survival instinct and my tortured soul slowly healed.

Writing helped me more than any therapist or drug ever could. I started a journal I called *Myself 'til Now* and it was exactly what the title stated. Self. *My* Self. Self-analysis, self-help, self-serving, self-indulgent, it was all there. In the final days of my nineteenth year, I counted the pages, all 5442 of them. Then, I proceeded to read the entire journal in one sitting.

What I discovered about myself was that I was special. I don't mean in a feel-good, I'm okay, you're okay, we all shine on like the moon, the stars and the sun sort of way. I mean I was NOT like everyone else, but *extra*-ordinary. You see, I had been gifted in ways I couldn't even begin to fathom. And it truly was indeed a gift, one that it had been my destiny to pursue, nurture and share with the rest of the world. It was the gift of TALENT. Why else was my head so filled with dreams, an imagination that flowed through my bloodstream like lava from a volcano of creativity? Stories, characters, concepts all lived inside of my mind and they were busting to get out. No wonder I felt out of step with the rest of the world and its inhabitants. I was really was that guy that everyone talked about, the one who marched to the beat of a different drummer. That was me! What I came to realize was that I owned the drum.

This line of reasoning liberated me. I had enough of myself by then. Now it was time to get back to my life. It involved some baby steps at first, but eventually I left my cave and sought the light of day. Once I reached it and felt its warmth, I marched back into the world under my terms. Eventually, I took care of my scarred heart and sought the touch of female companionship. Much of my dementia seemed to be extreme sexual tension and I really needed relief. I managed to have a few, albeit unsuccessful relationships with members of the opposite sex. My needs were strictly carnal once I realized the current object of my affection had no idea what I was all about. No one understood me but me. At least I was getting laid.

I was bound to run into Karen sooner or later because Stockton, no matter how big it might grow, is and always will be a small town. It might as well be

Mayberry, California. The six degrees of Stockton is that everybody knows everybody, one way or another. Sure enough, she crossed my path fleetingly, once in the Weberstown Mall during the Christmas holidays and another time walking out of a movie theater. In the back of my mind, I almost dreaded running into her at all since I still had feelings for her and considered the possibility of a relapse back into deep depression. Fortunately that was not the case when I finally did see her. I was better off than I thought. I often wondered what her reaction might be. She could have fled in terror, I imagined, but somehow, didn't. In fact, she was quite friendly and, at the theater, I even made her laugh. I didn't see her again for another five years.

The acting bug had re-bitten me right square on the ass, so to satisfy this urge, I became involved in several community theater productions in the area. To tell you the truth though, I never much cared for the whole process. I knew I had some talent in this area, but it just didn't satisfy me creatively. In retrospect, I suppose I was just in it for the social aspects of it all. Just as my interest was waning, I had been appearing with the Tokay Players theater group in Lodi in a production of Tom Amo's British farce entitled *Bob's Your Auntie.* After one Saturday night performance, one of the audience members approached me. He was a triple threat-tall, dark and handsome with the goofiest smile I had ever seen, a combination of Stan Laurel and a gap toothed sterno bum. He shook my hand vigorously and tried to tell me how funny he thought I had been in the show, but he couldn't stop giggling. Eventually, he calmed down enough to speak which relieved me momentarily because he quickly grew unnerving and not just a little creepy.

"My girlfriend knows you," he said rather over-enthusiastically. "Here she is now."

Well, I don't have to tell you who THAT was, do I? Right. It was TV's Betty White. (No, I'm just kidding. I kid because I love.) Of course it was Karen looking as radiant as ever. Something about her demeanor had been different than before. If I wasn't mistaken, and I really didn't need that sort of embarrassment if I had totally misinterpreted it, but I could have sworn she was rather blatantly flirting with me, right in front her dopey boyfriend. He became easy to ignore since all he contributed to the conversation was his persistently inappropriate sniggering.

A week later, there was Karen in the audience again, this time with a female friend. She told me that she enjoyed the show so much she just had to see it again. And for a second time, she seemed rather taken with me. From my standpoint, I played it rather cagily, like I said before, not wanting to be proven wrong. This was Karen after all and not just any old high school acquaintance. Therefore, I showed great restraint, though I felt like I was having a stroke.

The following night, she reappeared, this time alone. Well, what could I say? I had to ask her if she wanted to join me in a bite after the show…of food, that is. She graciously and almost anxiously accepted.

That night, I discovered her ulterior motive. As difficult as it was for to comprehend, she had pursued me. I had represented a big mystery in her life that she just had to solve. Karen knew that I had fallen for her hook, line and sinker, even to the point of tying an anchor around my neck when she rejected me. It had been all too obvious to her that each time I saw her after the regrettable Happy Steak incident, I couldn't help but feel the same way about her. My love remained fresh after all that time as though the Ice Age had preserved it. I felt so deeply for her that I never could successfully mask it no matter how hard I tried. She had to know why.

What I told her was the most childish thing imaginable.

"That's for me to know and you to find out," I said, keeping my cards close to my chest.

I wanted her to chase me a little further…and she did.

Karen dumped her boyfriend and immediately took up with me. I don't think considered me too funny after that. She and I hit the ground running and never looked back.

Ours was the classic whirlwind romance. We were goofy in love, calling each other little pet names like "puddin'" and "lamby-kins" and laughed at the silliness of it all. We may have been kidding, but our love had been dead serious. We just could not keep our hands off each other and oh my blue heaven, did we ever fuck. Everywhere, anywhere, over here, over there, on the bed, on the floor, in the chair, against the wall, in the kitchen, in the shower, in the car, in her parents' closet! I was making up for lost time and she caught me right up to speed. Our passion was boundless and I discovered the true meaning of the words "making love". My heart had finally healed and Karen was my cardiologist. She was everything I wanted in a lover, companion and partner, the complete embodiment of my true soul mate.

Our love evolved into a state I had never felt before-complete TRUST. So, it wasn't long before I took her where no one else had been allowed before, into the secret world of my writing. It had been high time for me to revel to her the Real Me. Each piece of work I presented to her was a revelation to her. She finally understood me and what I was all about. She said that if I didn't fit into this world, then I just have to make a place for myself and she was going to help me do it. Karen had fallen for me this time and she loved me more than she had even loved anyone before. How could I not reciprocate? Finally, someone GOT me.

As far as my writing went, she gave me a great piece of advice and that was that I needed a good solid project to sink my teeth into and carry it all the way to completion. Karen told me that once I finished, it would be a total success. That would the strength of the faith that she had in me.

And once again, thanks to Karen, inspiration struck like a lightning bolt from Zeus.

Every year, Karen loved to dress up for the annual Renaissance Pleasure Faire in the Bay Area. This was one of those recreations of Merrie Olde England in medieval times in a forest setting. A whole village had been constructed and populated with brave knights, damsels in distress, busty broads and lusty lads, all of which had regular lives during the week as accountants, video store clerks, software engineers and bank tellers. It was kind of like an outdoor historical version of a *Star Trek* convention.

I had resisted attending because it all seemed too geeky even for me. But Karen insisted I accompany her. It was the last year the Faire would be held at Blackpoint Forest in Novato, which she claimed was the perfect location for this and couldn't be missed. She even made a period-appropriate shirt for me, which she whipped up in a snap. She had always sewn her own costumes for the yearly event and to create one for me was no trouble at all. She looked absolutely fantastic. Shakespeare would have gone into re-write if he had seen her.

Once we arrived and wandered about, I totally agreed with Karen. Blackpoint Forest could have easily passed for Sherwood. It all helped to create the illusion and fantasy that took over whoever wished to participate, as if Dungeons and Dragons suddenly became a reality. What I didn't expect was the overwhelming air of bawdiness about the whole affair. I became so overwhelmed with passion that I took m'lady into the forest and ravished her.

The carnal passion that overwhelmed me that day unlocked a door within my soul that caused my spirit to run free like a wild stallion and I became consumed by a flood of creativity I had never known before. 'Twas right then and there in the middle of the woods that I finally found the muse I had been searching for my entire life and my magnum opus was born…

…and it's name…

ABRACADABRA.

My love for Karen had such a positive residual effect on me that I had been   re-born. Confidence, so far out of my reach before, had been handed to me on a silver platter. I banished insecurity from very being. I was well on my way to becoming the person I was meant to be. So, without a single doubt in my mind, I made the important decision of my life.

We were driving home from the Ren Faire when I pulled the car off the main highway and drove up a country road. I told her I wanted to watch the sunset with her. We got out of the car and walked up a hill. When we reached the top, I kneeled, professed my love to her and asked her to be my wife. Of course she accepted. What did you expect?

I arranged so that we could be married in an untraditional setting on the stage of the Tokay Players Theater. A retired judge with body odor performed the civil ceremony. So, on a beautiful April afternoon, we became Mr. and Mrs. Calvin Wheeler. We spent our honeymoon at a friend's cabin in Lake Tahoe, where we made love morning, noon and night. In between, I somehow had enough energy to begin *ABRACADABRA.*

It began with the old writer's game called What If. While taking in the revelry that was The Renaissance Pleasure Faire, I wondered what would happen if through some wrinkle in time, the entire festival would somehow be transported back to the Elizabethan era. How would these weekend warriors, those who worked in cubicles in their real lives, stack up against the real deal, the Knights of the Round Table? With that as a starting point, I formulated the plot of what I thought at first to be just a short story. As it grew, it became a novel, a huge step from the shorter pieces I had been writing up until that point. Then it kept evolving, not being able to be contained within one volume. A series seemed more appropriate and from that, the possibilities became infinite. Of course it could be eventually adapted to the big screen but only I could imagine such a thing, so I would have to write the screenplay as well. This was my Treasure of the Sierra Madre. I owed it all to Karen. She gave this gift to me. With its completion, I would be able to pay her back. Most assuredly, we would live happily ever after.

On our return, we set forth the major task of moving into a new set of digs. Previously, we had been living in her apartment, but my mom had offered us one of her rental houses for dirt-cheap as long as I kept up the maintenance. This grand gesture was a shot in the arm since the price was absolutely right. It was a cute little two-bedroom place complete with both front and back yards. On top of everything else, it had also been the house I grew up in. My folks raised their two sons-my older brother, Jason and myself-there in what used to pass for a suburb right near Oak Park and just down the street from Billy Hebert Field, home of the Stockton Ports minor league baseball team. Jason and I shared the same bedroom that eventually became my office and Karen's sewing room. Some might have called it a starter house, but for me, I was perfectly content right there for a long time. Sure, the neighborhood was populated with miscreants, malcontents and mutants, but that was a given. This was Stockton, after all.

The thing is, money was tight back then and it became readily apparent that the first romantic illusion to evaporate would be that we could live on love. Karen worked full-time as a bank loan officer while I reluctantly registered with a temp agency, working here and there but not full-time just yet. Karen and I both agreed that I needed time to work as much as I could on *ABRACADABRA* while it remained fresh in my mind. After all, I had never written anything longer than a short story before and my journal didn't exactly count. With such a monumental task ahead of me, I couldn't be distracted by the common restraints of menial labor until I felt far enough along to be able to put *ABRACADABRA* aside and work on it periodically until it was finished. This was a luxury we could barely afford, but we were able to squeak by.

It wasn't long before Karen began to change her tune, as she felt miscast in the role of primary breadwinner. As much as I reassured her that this was only fleeting, the less she was convinced as time passed. I tried to explain to her that art just couldn't be rushed-the old Michelangelo ploy. For me to be employed on a normal 9-to-5 basis would prolong the completion of my work and potentially jeopardize it altogether by interrupting the process.

She scoffed. She did. She actually scoffed.

Suddenly this woman was a stranger to me. How could she, of all people, fail to comprehend the gravity of this situation she was putting me into at that moment? Was she suffering form amnesia? Did she forget whom she married? Did she think that after all we had been through that I was only kidding, that I wasn't serious about my craft at all and believe it to be merely a frivolous hobby that can be picked up and tinkered with like a model airplane? Was she expecting me to change into something I was not? Did she not "get" me after all?

For some couples, the dreaded money issue is a constant. It can be a minor speed bump or a major crevasse for a relationship. In our case, it became an expanding sinkhole, growing wider and more treacherous by the day. Here we were, not married a quarter of a year already, teetering on the edge.

Karen became cold and indifferent. She'd lost her luster. The confidence she once had in me evaporated quicker than a puddle in the Sahara. It wouldn't be long before she resented me altogether. Needless to say, this reflected in our bedroom too, which soon became No Man's Land.

Our main problem was the inability to talk to one another. We knew how to fall in love with each other. We just didn't know how to make that love last. We wouldn't discuss anything. She would close up like a clam with an impenetrable shell. I, on the other hand, was afraid to ask because I didn't want to know the answer. My own fear was doing us both in and I'm sure that of all the things Karen resented about me, she probably hated the cowardly side of me most of all. Frankly, I wasn't too fond of it myself. So we hid in our own separate silences, causing far more damage than if we had engaged in shouting matches from dusk to dawn every single day of the week.

I couldn't blame her. How could I? I loved her with all of my heart and it killed me to make her feel this way toward me. I began to doubt myself as I hadn't for some time. Maybe I just wasn't mature enough for marriage. Maybe I didn't deserve Karen. Maybe I was just a delusional fool after all. Maybe…just maybe…

The maybes ate me alive. As a result, my writing suffered at a very crucial part of the *ABRACADABRA* story. My engine stalled and I couldn't even put two sentences together. The goddamn thing just sat there like a big steaming pile of dung that stunk up the place and my marriage as well. The quandary I suddenly found myself in drove me back into the dark abyss. Karen was everything to me but now I felt as though I as betraying myself. It was a vicious triangle-Karen on one side, *ABRACADABRA* on the other and me, right in the center. I had to choose wisely. The Lady…or the Tiger?

But…

What if the Lady was the Tiger?

The implications of this dilemma I found myself in began to overwhelm me. I spent every waking moment on this most important of all decisions to the point that it became a tortuous obsession. I ached inside and out. But within this constant pain came the most exquisite pleasure I could imagine. I reached an epiphany within my bruised and battered soul that was-

YES!

I never had to face this problem before! Did I know why? Because I never had someone like Karen in my life before. She was my true love, my soul mate, the other half of my whole being! And she was my muse, for had she not been responsible for putting me on the right road for the creation of *ABRACADABRA*? Had she not lead me to that place within myself which physically, mentally and spiritually allowed me to be the person I was always meant to be? With Karen, I became a man, not just any man, mind you, but my own man.

The clouds parted inside my head and my mind cleared. My decision had been made.

I chose the Lady and, more importantly, my marriage. As soon as I could, I sought full time employment. There had been no justification for my actions-or inactions, as it were. She didn't need to shoulder the responsibility for our marriage all by herself. What I brought to the table was a mere pittance and it was high time I righted that wrong. I had to make it up to her and show what I was really made of.

Besides I could still work on *ABRACADABRA*-or *ABCD*, if you will-but only on a limited basis. After rereading what I had already put together, I believed it was strong enough to survive, more so than the damage my marriage was experiencing. Besides, as long as I was able to work on it now and then, I could have what I crave most-my cake and the ability to eat it too.

How naïve of me. Little did I know that I just attached a price tag to my soul and placed it on the card table for the next garage sale. *ABCD* sat gathering dust while I dove into the job pool with water wings that I had once used as testicles. The search was on and quite an extensive search it was. I had no discernible job skills, unqualified and inexperienced at, well, everything. I'd scan the want ads not finding anything I wanted or could do. From one disastrous interview after another, I accomplished nothing more than humiliation. Though I had a few more temp jobs and one part time gig that I thought was right up my alley, it seemed I was destined to be a minimum wage earning nobody for the rest of my born days. However, from out of the blue, I ran into J.B. Linderman who told me about Healthfirst and the rest, as they say is history…extremely boring history…

Now gainfully employed, I fully expected this to be the panacea to my troubles at home. It most certainly was not the case. Karen had softened only slightly, but it was obvious our relationship had tarnished. Our sex life made cameo appearances, mostly on my part. For us, infrequent was not two words, to paraphrase an old joke. It became annoying to us both when I couldn't control my ejaculations. The more I worked at it, the less interested she got. I was topping the sixty-second mark, a personal best in those days. She was fed up because I let her down yet again. I became too ashamed to even ask for her assistance.

Why did our most passionate moments become such anguish all of a sudden? To think of what we used to be able to do for one another. Jesus! We were animals! Many a time we were driving somewhere when she would unzip my fly and make the time pass on those long road trips that much sweeter. I once took her on top of a Mercedes in a parking garage one night. And one time…oh my God…on a carnival ride at the California State Fair, she straddled…

"Alpha base to Calvin! Alpha base to Calvin! Do you copy?" Terri warbled over the radio.

Fuck! What now, stupid cow?

"Yes? Over."

"Hi, Calvin. This is Terri. When you come back from lunch, I have some supplies that need to go to Jackson. Over."

"I wasn't coming back. I already picked up my reports and I'm leaving from here. I have to make up time I lost this morning. Over."

"Well, I have some supplies that…"

"…need to go to Jackson. I heard you the first time. You're killing me, Terri."

"I'll see you when you get in. Alpha's clear."

"Or you won't. Clear.

I dropped the microphone to the floorboard, not bothering to attach it back to the radio. Then I grasp the steering wheel with both hands and rammed my forehead against it.

Ow.

CHAPTER SEVEN

AFTERNOON DELIGHT

What annoyed me most about going back to the lab was the negative effect it would have on my afternoon run. Everything led up to that time of day for me and I didn't want anything to ruin it. And, truth to be told, it was the only thing I could actually look forward to these days for more reasons than one.

After lunch, I would journey up to Jackson in the Gold Country of California's Mother Lode where Healthfirst had a drawing station. The hour-long drive took me through some beautiful countrysides and I'd relish each and every one of them since I knew 101 different ways to go. I could vary my journeys and never allow them to become stale. This also afforded me the luxury to kick back a little, listen to some music and reflect on whatever was on my mind, usually *ABCD* after I picked it back up again. The cherry on top of the afternoon dessert was that the surrounding foothills took me out of radio range, cut off completely from Alpha

Base and the rest of the world. I had ME all to myself. I grew very protective of this time and did not want it compromised by a stupid cow whose only lot in life was apparently to piss me off as much as possible. The more she held me up, the more she would screw up my afternoon. The more she would screw up my afternoon, the more darts I would toss at her picture in the game room of my mind.

Greeting me upon my triumphant return to the Alpha Base were J.B., in full tilt Dangerfield mode, and Jessica Stubblefield, another driver who walked a very thin tightrope between being very hot and very aggravating. When she didn't get on my nerves, I wanted to get on her bones. J.B. had been entertaining her with more jokes he had downloaded off the Internet. Here's to the World Wide Web-keeping comedy alive for every office clown from here to Sheboygan and back again.

"Hi, Calvin. Howth it going?" Jessica lisped in her sexy, lispy cartoon-like voice.

"Just ducky," I replied as I gathered the supplies Terri left for me.

"Supplies! Supplies! Supplies!" J.B. added ala Gomer Pyle.

"Yeah. Shazam," I groused. "Is *It* here?"

It would be Terri AKA The Beast, The Stupid Cow, The Big Load, et al.

"No. *It's* at lunch."

"Again?"

"The word is STILL," J.B. rimshotted.

Jessica laughed at our comedy. I only wish I could have done the same.

"You know what this is, don't you?" he started.

"It's the Nature of the Business," we finished together.

"You guyth are a riot," Jessica chuckled. "You okay, Calvin? You don't look tho happy."

"I haven't been happy since *It* became our lead driver," I explained, not looking at her.

"Calvin, I don't know why you didn't take that job. You could have, you know" she reminded me.

"Yeah, well, I turned it down."

"You'd be better at it than Terri. I'm therious," she said, taking my arm.

Jessica was compassionate to the point that you just wanted her to just go away. She meant well, but she was also a crisis junkie, leaping from one problem to the next without a let-up. I was not about to be her next cause celebre.

"I don't want to talk about what I could have done, Jessica. Okay?"

I looked into those big green eyes of hers that sat inside what was undoubtedly an empty head. I found her attractive in a way that I knew I could have some good dirty fun with but would have to kill her afterward because she'd want to talk…and talk…and talk.... Jessica was a wisp of a thing, near dwarf status, but solid as a rock because she worked out constantly. I guarantee you she had the perkiest butt in the state of California, not bad for a woman in her late thirties. You could bounce a quarter off that ass…and maybe even make change.

"Look, Terri ith my friend, but she thuckth. Thith morning, I almotht kicked her ath mythelf."

"Yeah?" I said, suddenly interested. "You could have lost a shoe."

"Tho what. I was pithed. Gueth what? Sheth changing my route."

Jessica had been driving the same route since she started, not six months after J.B. began.

"Really. How come?" J.B. wondered.

"Haven't you heard? Sheth changing all of them," Jessica told us, J.B. and I staring at her in rapt attention.

"Why the hell is she doing that?" J.B. demanded.

"She sayth everyone hath to rotate their routeth every thix monthth tho that we can fill in for each other when we need to," Jessica explained.

After a pause, J.B. could only say, "That's stupid. We don't have to switch routes to do that. We could just cross-train, but I guess that's too logical."

To which I added, "She'd better not touch my route."

Jackson. The Foothills. The Mother Lode. Sanctuary. Sarah.

The top 5 on my own personal endangered species list.

"Well, Terri thaid sheth gonna change everybodyth," Jessica warned.

"Over her dead body," I said, never more serious. I snatched up my supplies and started to leave.

As I headed out the door, I heard Jessica ask J.B., "Whath wrong with hith lip?

Shit fire.

My lip.

I had completely forgotten about it since morning. As if I didn't have enough on my plate now, the jig was up. Since no one had mentioned it all, I put it out of my mind. But, Jessica had to open her mouth and my secret identity was forever blown.

"Clark Kent! Why, you're actually...Simplex Man!"

The rear view mirror in my car revealed that the swelling had increased to Maurice Chevalier size. Was there any end in sight? How big could it get? Would it have the ability to grow hair and teeth and eventually, a mind of its own? Could I, as its host, ever hope to

70

control its evolution? When would it become the dominant factor and make me its slave? But what if just as it opened its eyes and set forth to rule the world, it reached its peak, drying up in the open air and hanging lifeless from lip like a piece of dangling pork? No longer Simplex Man would I be. Now, I would be known as…The Human Turkey!

As it was, it was a big fat fucking lip.

Now more self-conscious than ever, it became essential at this point to cover up this malady the best way I knew. If it meant tucking under my upper lip all day, so be it. Anything to hide my shame. I hoped that I wouldn't accidentally bite it off and swallow it whole. Even that seemed like a viable option. I didn't care what I did as long as Sarah didn't see me in this sad sorry condition. That was critical.

The time had come to focus on other matters or else the afternoon drive that I so cherished would be wasted on asinine obsessions like my diseased lip, my diseased job or my diseased marriage. Whatever was giving me grief had to be left in Stockton. The best way I knew how to accomplish that task was to break into The Collection.

The Collection was my traveling music, several dozen cassettes of a wide array of eclectic, eccentric sounds that relaxed, stimulated and inspired me on my longer driving trips. These tapes were stored in a shoebox under the driver's seat so as to be easily accessible. Whatever tape I would pop in would open a portal to my imagination and reawaken my muse. She would guide me into the world of dreams and fantasies that gathered in my brain.

The majority of The Collection consisted of instrumentals, primarily motion picture soundtracks with composers like John Barry, Bernard Herrmann, Ennio

Morricone and Jerry Goldsmith. Many of these were from obscure films, some of which I'd never seen like *Puppetmaster* (music by Richard Band)*, Flashpoint* (Tangerine Dream)*, Crimes of Passion* (Rick Wakeman) and *Johnny Handsome* (Ry Cooder)*.* Not seeing the films actually kept me from having any pre-conceived notions and I could enjoy the music on its own terms. Then there was the assortment of New Age works, which I also listened to unashamedly. There had also been a Yanni tape in that bunch. I make no apologies. They all served a purpose.

A mere ten percent of The Collection consisted of a varied selection of pop, rock and old standards, which I would only break out, given the right mood. Radio had burned out almost every song I had ever loved with endless repetition, so these treasures were only for special occasions. What special occasions those might be I never really clarified for myself.

There were several reasons I had nothing but cassettes, by now becoming as extinct as the dinosaur known as the 8-track. For one thing, my work vehicle, where I spent most of my time, had a tape player. The Collection itself had been growing by leaps and bounds for years and some were now out of circulation. I was able to pick up many of these for extremely cheap prices in outlets, bargain bins and thrift stores. Convenience and frugality aside, I felt no obligation or any inclination whatsoever to eliminate The Collection and replace it with CDs even if they were more prevalent. Cassette players and tapes were still being produced. It isn't always necessary to upgrade. Technology is a goddamn bully that likes better than to throw its weight around and force society to make rash lifestyle decisions. We have a tendency to immediately toss out the old to embrace the new even if it isn't necessarily for the better. We're only going to be able to retain what we have if we fight to keep it, if for once we just say "No". Giving in makes it all slip through our fingers and fall into the black hole of history, something that is becoming less and less important by the day. When we submit to the onslaught of technology, our lives become increasingly trivial and the past is nothing more than a nuisance. It is all forgotten in the wake of the new. Our shortened attention spans will be the end of us all because we won't care. Nothing will matter. It's all disposable anyway.

I am very passionate about The Collection, even it is only a shoebox filled with cheap plastic. Principle is everything.

For my afternoon underscoring, I chose a compilation of George Winston piano solos. My mood, bordering on melancholia, seemed to be calling in this long-distance request to the radio station in my sub-conscious. At times like this, George always delivered.

The sun-baked foothills that lay ahead in the horizon led me to Jackson. They provided the proper visuals for this, the most therapeutic of all possible drives in my repertoire. A sense of relief came over me for I knew that I now had The Big Valley to my back and could escape into the womb of the Mother Lode. Yes, I was headed for the place where legends where born and bred, the land where folks from all walks of life flocked to in search of that most precious metal… GOLD. Those days were long past, yet the memories of that historical time gave the land a vibrancy that resonated within me each time I visited. For me, those haunted hills were still filled with riches beyond my wildest imagination and that's what stirred my creativity like a sluice box.

I had driven the Jackson route for over two years. In fact, I had pioneered the very first route for Healthfirst when they opened a blood-drawing station in this uncharted territory. That was me, a regular Kit Carson with a saddlebag full o' pap smears. At first, I didn't want to go. It seemed too much of a long haul day after day, especially when the pressures of time, always a factor on this job, became an issue. But once I realized what leaving the urban squalor behind felt like and I could revel in the grand change of scenery, I made it work. It may not have been paradise, but it sure as hell wasn't…well, Hell.

The lack of direct communication with Alpha Base while out of radio range afforded me a luxury that I had been craving-a modicum of freedom. Up there, I had some semblance of solitude and breathing room. It gave me invaluable time, time otherwise lost and wasted. I actually had time to think…and dream…and create. Once I found this inner peace, *ABRACADABRA* sprang back to life and again became foremost in my mind. Ideas and concepts for my pet project had really begun to take off in this period. I certainly couldn't write while I drove, so I dictated my thoughts into a mini-tape recorder and transcribed them when I got home. This was a win/win option for a lose/lose situation, thereby it into a win/lose. Or was it a lose /win? Who gives a shit? I made this happen. I turned a negative into a positive. I created my own rainbow.

And at the end of this rainbow, a treasure…
Sarah.

But, I had to block her image from my mind at that moment. The anticipation would have been too distracting. Besides, after I would laid eyes on her, she would be all I would be able to think about all the way home. I have to divert my attention elsewhere and pre-empt my destiny any further.

I had to concentrate on *ABRACADABRA*. With my head fairly relaxed by then, I still needed to jump-start my creativity due to the amount of anxiety I carried around like so much excess baggage. First I had to say goodbye to George Winston and break out the Big Guns. By that, I required nothing less than what I consider to be the finest piece of music of The Collection, Gustav Mahler's Symphony No.1 conducted by Leonard Bernstein with the New York Philharmonic. I had loved this piece from the moment I heard it back in junior high school. When I began work on *ABCD*, I found that I would play this whenever I would write. Whether by coincidence or divine fate, I discovered that deep within this glorious piece of music the entire saga of *ABRACADABRA* sitting like a vein of gold, ready to be prospected by the likes of me. Now was as good a time as any to play it again, Sam. After all, they do call this the Gold Country, don't they?

With my dear old friend Gustav loaded and ready to fire, the next course of action was to re-visit another acquaintance of mine. I hesitate to call him a friend as well since, most of the time, I want to beat him to death with my shoe.

Yes, it's time once again for *The Don Olsen Show*.

CHAPTER EIGHT

THUS FAR

"Good afternoon. Don Olsen, KGY News Talk Radio. Welcome to a very special *Don Olsen Show*. Yes, just like TV, we have our own very special episodes as well, as in 'Tonight, on a very special *Will & Grace,* Will discovers his testicles are not his own' or whatever. Therefore, today on a very special *Don Olsen Show,* our guest is our old friend and sometime adversary, Calvin Wheeler. At long last, Calvin is finally going to break his silence with us and let us in on that mysterious project he's been teasing us with for so long that, frankly, many of us were beginning to wonder if it ever existed at all. Are you ready to spill the beans, Calvin?" Don Olsen began the non-existent afternoon portion of his mediocre talk show.

"I'm ready for some bean spilling, Don," I replied confidently.

"Give us a little background first, won't you, Calvin? By day, you work in what you consider to be a go-nowhere, do-nothing job. Yet you say you aspire to greater things. What might those greater things be?"

"Well, to put it succinctly, I wish to be a successful writer."

"That's certainly a lofty goal. So what's stopping you? Just go ahead and write. I've heard it said that you write anywhere."

"Thanks, Don, but I'm way ahead of you. I'm here today to tell you about a project of mine that's been seven years in the making and now, I'm ready to reveal it to the world. In all modesty, I assure you that this creation of mine is going to be a guaranteed bonafide hit."

"After seven years, it damn well better be. Otherwise, you just wasted the better part of a decade. How old are you, Calvin?"

"I'm 34."

"That's almost 20% of your life on one single solitary project. Do you think it's worth it?"

God, what a rotten bastard. I can't say this banter didn't help pump up my brain cells because it did. This constant badgering helped keep *ABCD* fresh in my mind so I would never lose my enthusiasm for it again. As grateful as I could be for my sparring partner's help in keeping me on my toes, I still wanted to punch this loudmouth in the throat. If I actually ran into him on the street, I probably would do that very thing. The best thing about it is that he'd never know why.

"It is worth it. Totally, " I said with utter conviction.

"So you say. What is this, a book?"

"In essence, yes, but it also much, much more. As far as I'm concerned, I feel like I've created an entire universe."

"Well, that's quite a claim. Let's not keep everyone in suspense any longer. What is the name of this opus in question?

Taking in a deep breath, I admitted to the world, "It's called *ABRACADABRA.*"

Hearing its name uttered out loud was like opening a window to a brand new spring day. I couldn't believe that I finally divulged my greatest secret to anyone besides Karen. An unfamiliar yet welcome sense of pride began to swell within me.

"So let me get this straight," Don asked, rather confused. "It's all about candy?"

Well, so much for my sense of pride.

"What?"

"I remember *ABRACADABRA* when I was a kid. I loved it! What a great candy that was…taffy filled with peanut butter, wasn't it?"

"That's Abba-Zabba!" I corrected angrily.

"Oh yeah! Do they still make that?"

"How the hell should I know and why the hell should I care? Look, if you're going to interrupt me with whatever idiotic comment pops into your brain…"

"Hold it right there," Don said in all seriousness. "May I remind you that this is *The Don Olsen Show*, not *The Calvin-Who-Talks-to-Himself-in-the-Car-Show*? But, I'll tell you what. It's your serve. I'll shut up if you just tell me the story."

"Do you promise?"

"I swear on a stack of Abritron rating books."

For some reason, I took him at his word. At last, I could begin my beguine.

"*ABRACADABRA* is a tale of magic, right here and right now. It's the story of how the ancient past of swords and sorcery collides with the world of science and technology right before our very eyes. Wizards and warriors clash with demons and aliens in the final battle to decide the eternal struggle of good versus evil-and only one can be victorious. This is an epic in every sense of the word. It spans not only the ages, but also every dimension and universe in order to tell this tale. One might call it everything but the kitchen sink. I prefer to call it a very rich stew. If it has only one message to convey it would be this: Magic is everything. Without it, there is nothing"

Don didn't say a word. I mistakenly thought he was suitably impressed.

Wrong again.

"Gosh, I'm sorry," he apologized. "In the radio business we call that 'dead air'. Not on my end. I meant on yours. Would you mind telling me what the hell that was?"

"What do you mean?" I asked in measured tones, controlling the urge to drive into a tree.

"Well, is that it? After seven years, I would think you would have more than that. Does this grand saga have an actual story?"

"Of course it does!"

"Good. Fire in the hole. Hurry up. We're losing listeners as we speak."

Frustrated by this buffoon's acerbic commentary, I sucked in another breath and blew out my growing anger. Then, to shut Don up once and for all, I turned off his microphone in my head. I popped Gustav Mahler into the tape deck as I began my magnum opus.

Behold.

ABRACADABRA

Synopsis

The annual Renaissance Faire is in full swing deep within the forests of California's Sonoma County. Populating the festival are normal everyday people with normal everyday lives who don medieval costumes and characters as they recreate the days of Merrie Olde

England. One such gentleman is Fred Muggs, a janitor by vocation but every summer, becomes the legendary Merlin the Magician, reading fortunes for the fairgoers and entertaining the crowds with various magic tricks and hocus-pocus. In researching his character in the off-season, Muggs had discovered an ancient book of magic spells that he purchased at a garage sale and decided to add this to his repertoire this year. During his own particular stage show, "Merlin" reads aloud from the tome, little realizing what damage he has caused. The janitor/wizard had opened a portal in the fabric of space and time to another dimension, releasing a marauding army of vicious demons to invade our world. Led by General Woraxas, the Eater of Souls and his lover, the psychic vampire known as Dulee, the demons tear through the Renaissance Faire, leaving carnage in their wake. In the midst of unrelenting chaos, another visitor enters through the portal, the warrior queen called Kala. Unable to halt the onslaught of the demon hordes by herself, she flees to safety with several survivors including Fred "Merlin" Muggs. Interrogating a captured demon, Kala learns that Woraxas has led his minions in search of Solan Kryne, the evil sorcerer imprisoned in this dimension and whose release threatens the entire universe. Not keeping them in the dark any longer, Kala reveals all to the small band of humans she has rescued. The world we have come call our own is actually contained within the realm known as Enatar, the creation of aliens from a dying galaxy that have attempted to start anew. Enatar consists of three separate dimensional circles, which we have come to interpret over time as Earth, Heaven and Hell. Combining the concepts of both magic and science, circle number one is Karn, home of the overseeing protectors of Forevertime, the lifeforce that keeps

*everything in balance and protects all of Enatar. The
second circle is Borgus, the land of Cr'So, the black arts
that corrupt magic in the pursuit of pure evil. The third
and final circle is Montei, the Earth that the Enatarans
created in their own image. Solan Kryne, master of
Borgus, once attempted to seek control of Montei but
was thwarted by his brother and Kala's father, Torsius
the Bold who stopped the demon lord by encasing him
within a jade orb. Torsius remained on Montei to live
out his remaining days with his wife, Melayna Ro in a
trailer park on the outskirts of the East Bay. Since this is
where Woraxas will be heading, Kala asks Fred for his
help to find her parents and warn them of the imminent
danger that lies ahead. Unfortunately, they are too late
as the battle of the trailer park leaves a beaten Torsius
and Melayna Ro captured by the demon horde along
with the jade prison that holds Solan Kryne. In order to
free their evil master, the demons head for San
Francisco, a place that the Enatarans had made a living
breathing entity on its own that keeps Montei in balance
with the universe along with other specific positions on
the planet. The demons force Melayna Ro to drain the
soul of San Francisco to release Solan Kryne and
nurture him to life once and for all. Once at optimum
strength, Kryne will overcome Montei and once in his
grasp will challenge all of Enatar itself. In Paris,
Torsius seeks out Amod de M'dau, the werewolf
magician and keeper of the Janus Stick, the mystical
staff that is the source of all the power of the Karn and
the key to Forevertime. The Karn Council made Amod
the Guardian of Montei after his father, Terramayne the
Joll died by the sword of Woraxas in the Borgus Civil
War. Raised by his human mother in Europe, Amod
grew to be a champion of Montei in times of strife,
battling demons that threatened its very existence, even
becoming cursed as a werewolf along the way. The*

Janus Stick could defeat Solan Kryne, driving he and his legions back to Borgus, closing the dimensional portal behind them. Torsius and Amod join Kala and band together with the other survivors to attack Solan Kryne and his army on the streets of San Francisco. Locked in a final struggle atop the Golden Gate Bridge, Amod loses the Janus Stick to Kryne who in turn destroys the mystical key. Now Forevertime is broken. Montei's past, present and future collide and everything becomes everything. Dinosaurs roam the earth with spaceships flying overhead. Nazis engage cowboys and gladiators in mortal combat. Medieval knights meet gangbangers. Chaos has run rampant over Enatar as the three circles have become as one. As such, they will cancel each other out and become nothing at all. The only hope lies within the small band of the Karn and the power of absolute magic if Forevertime is ever to be restored again.

And that was that. I managed to get the entire story without a hesitation, pause or even a single, solitary "uh..." For the first time in a longer time than I could ever hope to calculate, I felt rather proud of myself.

I heard Don clear his throat almost impatiently. He must have found a way to turn his mike back on.

"Well, that is just positively…uh, what's the word I'm searching for? Fascinating? No, that's not it. Interesting. No, that's not it either," Don insulted.

The pride I felt began to melt like cheese on the planet Mercury.

"You seem to be a little underwhelmed," I spoke through grinding teeth

"No, I would say I was just…whelmed."

He pushed the wrong button this time.

"Look! You asked me to tell you about *ABRACADABRA* and I did. What else do you want from me?"

"I guess after all this build up, I'm expecting the Next Big Thing. All I'm hearing is the Same Old Stuff."

"Meaning…?"

"Meaning that this ain't all that, mister. I've heard all before…and better."

Stupid fool. Now that he put me on the fence, I really had to go on the defense.

"As usual, you don't know what you're talking about. This is gold. Pure gold. It's not my fault if you're so ignorant that you can't recognize it."

"Maybe you're not selling it right."

"I don't need to sell it. When *ABRACADABRA* is finished, you'd better believe it'll sell itself," I promised. This was beginning to hurt.

"Then it is doomed for failure, my friend. You can't just say, 'This is great. Go out and buy it. You'll see' You have to convince people. You have to present it in some sort of coherent, accessible form so that people can comprehend what the heck you're talking about. Sounds to me like you really don't know what you have," he explained, driving the point home with an even more pronounced glib tone to his voice that made my skin crawl.

Fighting back tears and choking back emotion, I spoke very deliberately, "You're wrong, Don. You couldn't be more wrong. I do know what I have. Laying it all out in the open for the very first time has convinced me of that. Now I know for sure. So I say to you and to the world without any qualms whatsoever that *ABRACADABRA* is The One. This is indeed IT. This goes so far beyond just a story, Don. This is way beyond a mere franchise. This is the definitive saga of the ages. Within the very fabric of *ABRACADABRA* are infinite possibilities. I'm talking films, TV series, books, spin-offs, comics, games-an entire universe centered on this one single concept! This will be bigger than *Star Wars, The Matrix* and *The Lord of the Rings* combined! That is not an idle boast. That, my friend, is a fact. This is my true calling in life. It is what I was put onto Earth to do. This is why I've had to endure the most menial of existences so that I could devote myself wholeheartedly to accomplish this mission. This is why time-MY time-is so very precious to me because I need the time to finish and rest assured, I am going to finish. This is all about magic, Don. You have to believe in magic. Life without magic is life without meaning. Magic gives us hope. Because there has to be something else, doesn't there? Otherwise, it's all just Forevertime."

Again, Don was quiet on his end until he spoke solemnly, "Now *that's* a sales pitch. Our guest has been Calvin Wheeler. He is the creator of *ABRACADABRA,* coming very, very soon. We'll be back after these messages. Thank you, Calvin."

"You're welcome, Don"

I smiled, relieved in the knowledge that I stated my case passionately and admirably. I was also glad I didn't have to put up with Don the rest of the day. Why should I? He served his purpose. The interview was over.

Still, an air of uncertainty hung over me. There was a key element to *ABRACADABRA* that I had neglected to tell Don, the main reason its completion had been delayed for what seemed forever and a day.

I didn't have an ending.

Try as I might, I just hadn't been able to end my saga properly. I must have come up with 1500 possible conclusions and each had been worse than the other. When I finally thought I had a handle on it, the entire story would slip through the cracks and the premise became more absurd by the word. I wanted to avoid the clichés as much as I possibly could, but they have some kind of gravitational pull that were always working against me. The more I tried, the more I fell on my face. When I tried to sacrifice certain elements to make the ending fit, the whole structure fell apart like one big game of Jenga. It just wasn't right. I had to convince myself that an ending would come to me and I would if it was perfect. I wouldn't have to force it into place at the expense of the whole thing. It would fit like a charm.

But until then, the clock continued to tick. The longer it took to find an ending, the more I could feel *ABRACADABRA* begin to slip out of my grasp and into limbo.

Limbo. How low could I go?

Some questions are better left unanswered.

CHAPTER NINE

FOOT HILLS

The two-way radio snapped, crackled and popped with static. Through that electronic mess, I could barely make out someone garbling my name, making me feel like I had made a getaway-not a clean one, mind you but a getaway nonetheless. You can't catch me! Nah-nah-nah-nah-nah! The feeling was particularly sweet knowing that the voice I heard calling me had been the Beast from the East. No callbacks now, Terri. I am too far away. Go have another doughnut. Or seven.

I began my descent into Jackson proper. What a refreshing change of pace this had been after leaving a world where the biggest contribution to urban development was the strip mall. Jackson and the surrounding area seemed to be resisting the clock, as if blissfully out of step with the times. I like to think that this came not out of ignorance but by choice. Sure the area was growing by leaps and bounds, but there were boundaries. At least they made an honest effort to preserve their heritage. Maybe it's because they had a heritage to preserve. It was as if they were saying, "We've seen the future…and you can have it!"

I always felt at ease when I reached the city limits that I couldn't help but smile at the townsfolk. Somehow, I believed they were smiling back…and waving like I was a returning conquering hero. Grandma on her front porch, watering her zinnias, waved. Mr. Johnson sweeping out in front of his hardware store, waved. The twins, Missy and Cissy, eating their sno-cones, cherry and lime respectively, waved. And at the cemetery, dearly departed citizens of Jackson's historical past, prospectors and pioneers alike, rose from their graves and waved too, carefully so as to avoid further damage to what was left of their bodies (some assembly required). And I of course waved back. Hard to believe I had just been there the day before. They must have all missed me.

All was not entirely sweet harmony. I still had my insufferable duties to perform, but without that pesky stress that I had earlier in the day back in the "Big City". Sometimes, environment is everything. First order of business once I hit town, check in at the Heathfirst drawing station. It was like a cavalry outpost in the Indian nation. Here I would drop off any supplies, pick up any new reports that came over the wire and check for any pick-ups I needed to take care of in the area. Also I had to endure the potential onslaught of Thelma Praline, the sole Healthfirst employee in the entire county.

Thelma had been born into this world a nasty bitch, had fully accepted it early on and wore the title proudly. There was no way possible in heaven or earth to please this woman whatsoever and she let everyone know it. Thelma sat in judgment of the entire universe and would pass down the harshest of sentences, which would be her total disdain for just about anyone who crossed her path. She could count on one hand those she gave even one shit about and still have fingers left over. For some reason I never could fathom, I managed to attain favored digit status. I don't know how I came to get on her good side because it was impossible to imagine her having a good side. It turned out to be a fortunate place for me to be since I had to put up with her five days a week.

Though she was white trash to the nth degree, Thelma and I had a common ground that we could readily tread together: an utter contempt of anything and everything that was Healthfirst. Naturally, she had no love lost for anyone in the company, certainly not at Alpha Base nor any other base for that matter. No, Queen Thelma sat on the throne inside her doublewide with her thumb permanently pointed down. Off with their heads? Off with their balls was more likely. Her rantings and ravings wore me down but I put up with her rhetoric and she with mine. I agreed with her most of the time or at least gave a good impression that I did. Who knew what would have set her off? Therefore I felt it best not to bring up that I might soon be transferred from the area. I was having hard enough time suppressing the probability of that potential low blow without Thelma's ragging on about it relentlessly.

The drawing station sat at the far end of Jackson in a tri-plex that Healthfirst shared with two other offices, one a realty, the other a podiatrist who wanted nothing to do with our lab services. This was fine with Thelma since she said he was "a sneaky little gook bastard". Did I mention she was also a racist? I thought that was probably a given.

As I pulled into the parking lot, I saw the Woman of the Hour herself standing out the side door of the drawing station, hooving on a butt. Thelma smoked as though she had R. J. Reynolds stock options and constantly smelled like a poolroom, always a big plus for a healthcare worker. The origins of her raspy voice undoubtedly stemmed from years of huffing and puffing. She could have been another one of Marge Simpson's sisters-Patty, Selma and Thelma. I'm sure her lungs were coated with enough tar to pave a freeway off-ramp. She barely crested the five-foot mark, which had her both short and mean, a perfect combination for a mountain woman ala Mammy Yokum. I always wondered when she put down the corncob pipe and took up cigarettes instead. Her face, weathered by years of a bad attitude, gave her the look one of those apple dolls, a Braeburn in the last stages of preservation. This puny, shriveled up little nothing of a woman, this emphysema patient in training, this beef jerky with legs was undoubtedly formidable enough to snap me in half like a matchstick.

As I unloaded the supplies I brought for her, she wandered over to my car.

"Hey, Thelma. What's the good word?"

"Shit," she laughed evilly. She loved that joke and I set her up for it every time.

"Still working on your first pack of the day?" I asked.

"Nope. I just cracked open a new carton. You got all my supplies there, smart ass?"

"I suppose."

"Did Her Blubberness give you any Sharps containers?" Thelma referred to the covered plastic buckets used to dispose hypodermics. Did you notice she had her own pet name for Terri? Don't you feel the love?

I looked through what I brought and said, "Uh…just one."

She sighed with a breath straight out of Marlboro Country then griped, "She is such a stupid bitch. I need more than one Sharps container. Why is she rationing me?"

"Why ask why?" I asked anyway, walking inside with an armload of goodies. "Maybe you're just cursed."

"So are you," Thelma added, once inside. She handed me a scrawled note on a post-it. "You have to go to Pioneer today."

"Is that why Terri was trying to get a hold of me on the radio?"

"You betcha. It was my idea, actually. I wanted to give you fair warning."

A trip to Pioneer added another half hour to an already tight schedule. With adverse road conditions or ongoing construction delays, it would take even longer. This would cut into all-important Sarah time.

"Well, that was damn decent of you," I said, flipping through some additional reports she had put together for me to deliver.

"If I didn't think you were worth a shit, I wouldn't give a shit myself."

"Thanks. It's nice to know my worth."

"How's Mama?" Thelma asked. When she took an interest in my personal life, it always set me off-kilter. Sincerity didn't fit he profile. Now, the Mama she referred to wasn't my mother. Translated from her country-speak, she meant my wife, my "old lady", therefore, Karen.

Not willing to give an inch, I lied. "Oh, she's fine."

"She get any job leads yet?"

"Nada. Nada thing," I answered, regretting that I ever let her in on my troubles and woes.

"Well, I'm sure glad my old man's working. Too many goddamn bills and not enough hours in the day. 'Sides, if he was unemployed, he wouldn't be pulling his weight and I'd have to kick his ass to the curb," she blathered as if I cared. I didn't.

"Oh, you wouldn't do that, would you?"

She stared directly at me, completely stone-faced. "You've known me for what, two years now? Do you really think I would think twice about it?"

"I guess not."

"Damn skippy. I barely tolerate him as it is," Thelma grumbled. No, she wasn't kidding. Her current "old man" was husband #4 on Thelma's hit parade. I always wondered if he knew he was sitting so close to the precipice. Maybe he was fully aware of his situation and prayed to fall to his death.

Why I felt compelled to open this can of worms, I'll never know, but I posed the following question knowing full well this would lead to an uncomfortable answer. Given the nature of our usual conversations, I chose to ask it nonchalantly and almost mockingly. Still, there was no easy way out once the words spilled out of my mouth.

"Thelma, you ever really been in love?"

She looked as though I spoke to her in Swahili. Her walnut textured face crinkled up even further than usual. With skin that pliable, there's always a risk it won't snap back. But, what could have been mistaken for irritation at this sudden invasion of privacy appeared to have touched her feminine side, a difficult shot from any angle and I wasn't even aiming. Her expression actually warmed with a fond memory, probably the best one in her collection.

"Yeah, a couple times. I guess I loved my husbands, at least for a spell. But, to tell you the truth, there was just one fella that really rocked my world. He was a trucker, drove cattle trucks across the states. Big barrel-chested guy by the name of Sam Bollinger. Was he good lookin'… Damn! He had himself a head of red wavy hair that I'd just run my fingers through for hours at a time."

"Did he ever tell you to stop?"

"Hell no. He'd get mad if I did. Oh, he could make me laugh, that crazy son of a bitch. We'd only get to see each other about once a month because of his job but we sure knew how to cram a lot into a weekend. As soon as Sam would hit my front door Friday afternoon, I'd hand him a glass of J & B on the rocks and let the good times roll! Then before we'd know it, it'd be Monday morning and I wouldn't see him again for another month. I asked him once to do something for me and I didn't think he'd go for it."

"What was that?"

"I wanted a picture of him stark naked blown up to poster size on the ceiling above my bed. I'll be goddamn if he didn't do it."

I smiled, appreciating her honest recollections of her friend Sam. I was pleasantly surprised by both of our reactions.

"Why didn't you marry this guy? This one might have actually worked out."

"I wanted to. I had really given it some thought. We'd still have the same arrangement as always because of his work. We wouldn't have had the time to get on each other's nerves. It would've been a sweet deal, let me tell you. In fact, I was going to pop the question myself, but…it didn't work out."

"What happened? Did you get cold feet?"

"No, he up and died on me. He had a heart attack driving up in Oregon, ran his truck right through a video store. It was closed though so nobody got hurt, 'cept'n him, of course. Yeah, goddamn it. I guess I should'a asked him to marry me before. Yeah, should'a, would'a, could'a…It just didn't work out… Ol' Sam, he was a good man."

Thelma turned away to put away the supplies I brought in the cabinets above her. I wouldn't say she was crying, but the sweet memories ended up with a sour after taste.

"Do you still have that poster above the bed?"

"Oh yeah!" she chuckled rather roughly. "My ol' man would love that! Maybe I'll put it back up there to bug the shit outta him."

Thelma turned and rested up against the sink with her hands tucked into her lab coat. She gazed down the hallway to the window in the front office in what would be considered a forlorn expression for her. Thoughts of Sam Bollinger and what might have been probably filled her head. All of a sudden, her melancholia had been shoved out of the way by the nastiest sneer imaginable as the front door opened.

"I'll be with you in a moment, sir," Thelma called out in a coldly polite fashion. Sometimes, it just hurt her physically to be civil. "Shit. Not that asshole again."

My curiosity aroused, I just had to see who this asshole in question might be. There in the waiting room stood what some might refer to as a giant. If he wasn't seven feet tall, he was damn close. He fit the description of an atypical biker with unkempt, shoulder length hair framing a shrub-like beard that was badly in need of pruning. He didn't look as though he had seen the light of day since the year before for I had never before seen such a sickly pallor on another human being. I've seen Goth kids with more color. To make matters worse, he was covered in tattoos, which ran up his sleeveless arms in a most nauseating fashion. Tattoos are bad enough as it is, so commonplace these days to be positively mundane. To see them on ghastly pale skin is particularly hideous. They become not so much tattoos than varicose veined comic strips.

"Who's this guy?" I inquired.

"Oh, just the biggest pain in the ass in the world. He runs a tattoo parlor in his trailer park. The stupid shit got himself a nasty dose of hepatitis, probably from one of his own dirty needles. He has to come in here every single week to get his blood work done. Now get this. The first time I stuck 'im, he fainted, fell right outta the goddamn chair and onto the floor."

"Jesus! What did you do?"

"Oh, I have smelling salts. I crammed the bottle under his nose and he jerked so hard, he cracked his head on the chair!" Thelma laughed. She enjoyed a good chuckle at someone else's expense, especially if there was pain involved. "Now he just sits and quivers and pees his pants every time he comes in. Stupid fucker's afraid of needles and he's a tattoo artist, for Christ's sake."

"That's funny, " I smiled.

"Yeah, you'd think so, wouldn't you? To me, he's just a big goddamn pussy that I could live without," she sighed as she walked out to her desk.

As I finished putting my reports together, Thelma returned with the Pale Giant.

"Okay, you know the routine, " she said impassively.

"I sure hope I can get through it this time," the Giant said in an uncharacteristically high-pitched tone.

"Uh-huh," Thelma replied, wrapping a tourniquet around his meaty, decorated right arm and began to search in vain for a vein. The Giant began to twitch. "Hold still!" He froze in obedience as Thelma grabbed a needle.

"Uh…hang…hang on a s-second, ' the Giant stammered, his face beading with sweat almost instantaneously.

Thelma stared him down for exactly one second.

"Are you ready?"

"Uh…yes, go ahead," the Pale Giant gulped.

Thelma moved in again.

"Wait!" he cried.

Thelma slapped the needle down in the tray and shoved a latex finger in the Giant's face.

"I don't have time for this shit today! Either we do this or we don't. I really don't care. What's it going to be?" Thelma demanded.

The Pale Giant cowered at the vicious barking of this angry pit-bull in a lab coat.

"I'm…I'm sorry. Go ahead. I'll just…look away."

"Do it," Thelma snapped.

The Giant turned away, scrunched his eyes closed and bit his lower lip as Thelma jabbed him with a needle and drew his blood into a glass vial. A tiny, whiny moan started to emanate from deep within the Giant's very being. I wondered if a pack of dogs had gathered outside the door, answering his call.

Without a word, Thelma finished and pulled the tourniquet off his arm, leaving a cotton ball on his tapped vein.

"Is that it?" the Giant asked hopefully.

"Uh-huh," she uttered, taping the cotton to his arm to stop any further bleeding.

"Whew, that wasn't so bad. Sorry I'm such a baby," the Giant apologized. He looked toward me. "She's tough. She doesn't let me get away with anything"

"Okay, you're all done," Thelma said, dismissing him.

"See you next week," the Pale Giant waved goodbye as he stomped back to his tattoo parlor in the clouds.

"Not if I see you first, you big fuckin' pussy," Thelma spoke under her breath. She noticed me grinning. "And you. Don't you have somewhere to go?"

"I couldn't miss the freak show," I giggled.

"Well, y'know, you could be the star attraction with that lip of yours."

Uh-oh. Bus-ted.

A sense of shame suddenly enveloped me and began to wreak havoc through my entire body. This humiliation was a virtual wrecking ball, crashing and smashing everything in its wake. It destroyed my very foundation within nano-seconds. Finally, it careened to the top and broke off the thermostat in my head and my face boiled over. I felt myself burning up and I was sure my face flamed red. Such was my disgrace at knowing that I fucked up. I let myself completely down. I did not hide my lip as I promised myself I would. Stupid...stupid...stupid...

"C'mere," Thelma ordered, indicating that I follow her.

Stepping over to the sink, Thelma opened the side cabinet to reveal a treasure trove of drug supplies, given to her by various pharmaceutical sales reps who would drop by periodically. It wasn't as if this were a doctor's office nor could Thelma write any prescriptions. Maybe in their eagerness to make a buck, they were ill informed. Thelma wasn't about to tell them otherwise because she enjoyed the free goodies. Reaching up, she grabbed a couple of small tubes and handed them to me.

"Here. This'll get rid of your cold sore for you."

"Thanks," I said humbly, accepting the gifts. "Does it look that bad?"

Thelma got up on her tiptoes and examined my lip with a strained squint.

"It's gross, but it's not a prizewinner. I've seen worse."

"Thanks a heap."

"Put that stuff on it. It should clear up in a couple'a days. If it doesn't…well, that's show biz. I need a cigarette," she said, heading out the side door again.

I grabbed my reports and followed her out the door, placing the two tubes of lip medicine in my pocket. Thelma had already fired up another Salem by the time I reached her. She exhaled her first long drag out toward the wilderness outside.

"I'm leaving at exactly 4:00 today. If you're not here by that time, I'll put everything in the lock box here for you," she exclaimed, kicking the metal box next to the side door with her foot.

"Okey-dokey. Thanks again for the medicine," I told her as he headed for my car.

"I'll put it on your bill. You already owe me big time…and I'm gonna make you pay, one way or the other," Thelma called after me.

Whatever that meant.

Such was the wit and wisdom of one Thelma Praline, all sound and fury, signifying nada.

Nada thing.

CHAPTER TEN

SARAH SMILE

I had decided not to slather my diseased lip with the sample medicine until after my visit to Sarah. Now that the jig was up twice in the same day, there was no way I would be able to forget this time-the most important time of the day. I knew I could hide it from her, temporarily at least. I sucked that side of my lip into my mouth, clamped it down with my teeth and left it there. When I spoke, I could turn to the right and lower my head a touch, concealing it further. I could pull this off. After all, I was a damn good actor. I wasn't about to blow my cover this time. She wouldn't see it. She couldn't see it. Please, dear Lord, don't let me fuck up again…

This was all I could think about the entire ten-minute ride into Pine Grove. I needed to focus and not allow for any more until I reached my destination. Therefore, I put off the rest of my deliveries and pick-ups until after my visit with the fair Sarah.

So, fine and dandy. I suppose you think you need an explanation. The only thing you want to know at this point of the story is:

Just who might Sarah be?

I have to preface this by assuring each and everyone (including myself) that it had never been my intention to ever fall in love again, especially in such a juvenile fashion as a schoolboy crush. It happened anyway. I'm a creature of habit. Unrequited love must be part of my programming. After all, look how long I pined for Karen and I bagged her, didn't I?

Maybe the pain and sorrow I had been harboring during this difficult period with my wife caused me to react in this manner. After all, it had been made abundantly clear that Karen was my chosen one, my true love, my partner for life. When it all began to crumble, it just confused me. If she truly was The One for me, then I had to maintain some desperate hope that all would be well again between the two of us, no matter how much it was killing me. A psychic actually told Karen that I was her soul mate. Then this had all been pre-destined. The stars don't lie, do they? It was all going to work out, right?

Wrong. It was all wrong. It had always been wrong. Having to admit that horrible truth was tearing me...us apart. No wonder I felt so vulnerable. So often had I wandered about in such a zombie-like state of mind. My heart had been ripped out of my body and the whole world was playing "Keep Away" with it.

It had been the first day in late winter that offered a sneak preview of the spring to come when I drove up to Dr. Wilkins' office in Pine Grove. Though I was a useless member of the Undead, I had my routine down pat and performed it as always. Walking up to the receptionist's desk, I introduced myself as I always did.

"Healthfirst Lab. Do you have anything for me to pick up today?" I asked without a hint of humanity.

The crow in human form behind the desk didn't have the decency to look up from whatever mundane task she had been performing.

"I don't know," she sighed. Damn, I was such an imposition to this crone. Then calling out, she screeched, "Sarah! We got anything for the lab?"

Sarah? I thought the nurse's name was Betty or Barbara or Boom Boom or something innocuous. Maybe this was somebody new. I turned nonchalantly when I heard footsteps behind me.

Had this been a Bible story, I would have been struck blind at that very instance by the appearance of the absolute angel that walked toward me. Never before or since have I ever been witness to such radiance. It was immediately apparent that she actually glowed from within her very soul. I could have warmed myself by simply standing near her. If I had to speculate, I would say Sarah was probably in her mid-twenties, though to me she just appeared as ageless as a delicate porcelain figurine. Her dark eyes, bereft of mascara, widened with almost stark earnestness, the like of which I had never encountered before. She smiled, revealing a slight overbite that I found quite enchanting. Sarah might have been of Hispanic or Mediterranean origin. I could easily imagine her as a lovely senorita attending Mass at the town mission, a simple scarf around her head, holding a candle and clutching rosary beads as she stepped into the adobe church at sunset.

She wore a nurse's uniform that seemed to be of another era, almost a retro throwback to standard medical garb from the 1950s. No scrubs for this girl. I found her get-up to be quite charming and wished that she had topped it off with a starched Florence Nightengale cap. Sizing her up physically became a bit of a task since it was difficult to assess what lie underneath her conservative garb. It was readily apparent that she was short in stature and her calves, the only parts of her legs she exposed, were a bit thick. She might have been a tad overweight but I really couldn't tell. Even if she had a few extra pounds, so what? From what I could ascertain, Sarah was a natural beauty and someone who wouldn't need to be concerned with what society dictated to be the standard body type of the moment. She wasn't an emaciated twig with hair that passes for the Hot Babe du Jour, the kind that does not turns me on but does indeed turn my stomach. There was nothing fake about this woman whatsoever. She did not have to be processed or manufactured or even improved upon. Sarah was 100% organic. However, I had to recognize that she had some minor imperfections about her. They made her more human in my eyes and not the mythical creature I could easily have believed her to be. She could never live up to that image and nor would I ever expect her to. I had to see Sarah as she really was, faults and all, just to make her, in my mind, obtainable.

To say I was merely smitten would betray my heart. I plunged straight into love at first sight that afternoon. I just couldn't help myself. It was her fault. If she had not been so pleasant, so warm, so damn nice, I would have walked away thinking this was just a beautiful woman. But, once she greeted me and spoke only a few sentences, I knew Sarah was the absolute embodiment of a saint here on Earth. It was a true pleasure to just exchange small talk, which was all I could manage like the goofball I was capable of being. My own history bears me out on this.

With just a smile and a friendly word, Sarah had awakened something in me I believed to be lost. Hope. Hope that I would get through all this. Hope that all would come to pass. Hope that I would overcome whatever obstacle lay in my path so I could conquer my fears and become a champion. Hope that someone like Sarah really does exist in this world of ours. Hope that I could make her mine.

Let's just say, she made a good first impression.

As I hit the tiny burg of Pine Grove, I thought of what Thelma said about her friend Sam. Should'a, would'a, could'a… She missed out because she waited too long. How long was I going to wait for Sarah, especially since my time was running out? Was it possible to lose her before I actually won her heart? Was I going to blow another chance…maybe my last real chance? I had to block these thoughts. It hadn't happened…yet. I had to remain in the present.

Pulling into Dr. Wilkins' unpaved driveway, I parked next to a red GMC pickup and sat staring at the office. At one time, it had been a three-bedroom home, the kind that would look perfect with a white picket fence. But now, like many a country office, it was now just a place of business. I found it necessary to take a moment before I went inside, mustering up a bit of courage. I have to admit that I felt a little timid seeing Sarah, so, to ease my nerves, I played out a possible scenario in my head before I ventured into the office.

I step inside, but I see no one. As is my regular course of action, I head directly to the kitchen to take any specimens left for me in the refrigerator. Sarah sneaks up behind me and taps me on the shoulder. When I turn about, she puts a finger to her lips, signaling me to be quiet. Then, taking my hand, she leads me silently into an examination room and closes the door. Smiling broadly, she throws her arms around me and pulls my down to her beckoning lips. We kiss softly, then with increasing intensity as we open our mouths and dance with our tongues, passion escalating by the second. She then pulls away, breaking our embrace and hops onto the table. Unbuttoning her white nurse's uniform with one hand, Sarah spreads her legs open at the same time. Suddenly, she spins about and kneels on the table, pulling her dress up to reveal white garters holding up her stockings and nothing else underneath. Lowering her head, she turns to face me, gesturing for me to take her right then and there.

A patient, exiting the office, let the screen door slam shut behind him, knocking me the hell back into consciousness. This local yokel in XXL overalls just gazed at me curiously while heading to his pickup as I acted as though my mother just walked into the bathroom and caught me with a copy of *Barely Legal* and a tube sock.

"Holy guacamole…whew…" I gasped, trying to compose myself. I nervously grabbed my specimen bag and started to get out of the car when I brushed up against the bottom of the steering wheel. It seemed I had given myself an obstacle, one that was poking out of my pants like a pup tent. I decided to give myself another minute or two. When the blood began to flow in my brain again, I reminded myself to tuck in my lower lip. Fortunately, that was all I had to tuck.

Dr. Wilkins' nasty-ass receptionist pretended like she didn't recognize me when I entered, even though I had been there five days a week for the past two years. Such is the nature of the Nastius Bitchius.

"Hi, how are you today?" I charmingly inquired, my head cocked rather jauntily away from my oral malady.

No reply. No loss. I strolled to the kitchen nonchalantly, looking about for any trace of Sarah. Not seeing any specimens inside the fridge, I stepped back out again to confront Miss Crankypants USA.

"Excuse me. Could I possibly speak to Sarah please?"

In a tone that would curdle dairy products within a five-mile radius, she sighed, "She's with a patient. You'll just have to wait."

"Do you think she will be long?"

She stared at me with such disdain; it must have drained her supply. Reluctantly, she then picked up the phone and pushed an extension.

"Sarah? It's that guy from the lab. He said he needs to speak to you right away."

She hung up before Sarah could speak. What's wrong with people? There's no call for such rude-ass behavior. Naturally, she exaggerated to make me look bad since I interrupted whatever pitiful project she had been doing, like picking her teeth with a paper clip.

My growing hatred for this idiot was doused as soon as Sarah walked into the room, the same place she and I had occupied in my mind a few minutes before. She seemed genuinely pleased to see me.

"Hi, Sarah," I spoke, my voice reaching an upper register which, combined with the slight lisp I had from my tucked lip, made quite a combo.

"Hi. What can I help you with?"

How sweet. What could she do…to help me? Run away with me for starters…

"I'm sorry to bother you when you're busy. I didn't say I needed you right away, just when you were finished with your patient," I explained, giving a verbal shot to that creep on the other side of the office. However, I became a little self-conscious of my patented lip suck technique, which probably made me look like Senor Wences' fist. I tried to compensate by jerking my head about nervously. Now I was just a spastic marionette. "I didn't see anything in the refrigerator for me to pick up. Did I miss something?"

"No, not at all. We didn't have anything today, but thank you so much for checking."

"That's what I'm here for. How are you?" I asked, trying to stretch out the conversation.

"I'm fine, thank you. And you?"

Thank you for asking. God bless you for asking. Nobody ever asks about me.

"Good. I'm good," I said, bobbing my head around spastically. The more I moved, the blurrier I got she couldn't focus on my mouth.

"I'm sorry, but I have to get back."

The eminent Dr. Tom Wilkins sauntered out of the other examination room and nonchalantly stopped between the receptionist and the two of us. He was the new version of the simple country doctor, a younger model that just couldn't cut it in the big city. Therefore, now in the latter part of his forties, he had nowhere else to go and tried to lord it over anyone in his general vicinity. Wilkins used intimidation as often as his stethoscope, a fucking bully if I ever met one.

"Mrs. Quigley needs a follow-up," he said, and then whipped about like the pompous douche bag that he most assuredly was. "Sarah, are you finished with Mr. Phelps?"

"Not yet, doctor"

I hated the way he made her subservient.

"Could you do so please, provided you're finished with your…laboratory retriever," he joked. Oh, how the Algonquin Round Table would have loved him!

His little pun sure cracked up the receptionist, causing her to snort like any other pig. Sarah grinned, then looked at me with a slight pained expression, knowing full and well that this jackhole had just insulted me.

"Yes, Dr. Wilkins," she replied.

Dr. Giggles peered at me over the top of his bi-focals and blathered, "You know, I'm very unhappy with your company. You people are over billing again. I imagine it'll take a federal lawsuit to take you people down a few pegs, which is perfectly fine with me."

Not changing my expression, I told him, "I really don't know anything about that, doctor. Like you said, I'm just a laboratory retriever."

"Perhaps I should just find another laboratory," he dismissed. "Sarah, Mr. Phelps please?"

Wilkins strutted away in an attempt to be the cock of the walk when all he could really be in this world was just another prick.

"I'm sorry I bothered you, Sarah," I apologized.

She placed her hand on my shoulder. My heart stopped.

She…touched…my…shoulder…

"Don't be. I'm glad you did," she assured me. "Sorry. I have to go."

"I know," I gulped and headed for the door. "Bye, Sarah."

"Have a great day," she called to me on the way out.

Hopping into the driver's seat, I stared at my wrist and gave myself a second to reflect.

Have a nice day.

"Have a *great* day," Sarah corrected, ever so pleasantly.

Yeah, have a *great* day.

Now *that* is what I call HOPE.

CHAPTER ELEVEN

TRAFFIC SCHOOLED

T alk about a dose of strong medicine…just what the doctor ordered…and I don't mean Dr. Wilkins, either. No sir and m'am, I mean Dr. Wheeler, yours truly, your humble narrator, your partner in crime. My prescription for my number one patient (also me) was a single dose of one Sarah Knott and call me in the morning. One brief encounter with Sarah perked me up more than any vitamin, exercise or caffeinated beverage. My spirits were lifted so high they lifted me off the ground. I could have flown back to Stockton. Oh, what she brought out in me. It had to be a chemical reaction. Total bliss achieved with just a smile, a kind word and the face of an angel…my angel…my angel of mercy. Isn't that what they used to call nurses? Sarah was the total embodiment of that title. A moment with her was pure inspiration. And she…. touched…my …shoulder…

I had my new muse. She reminded me of whom I was supposed to be, what I was supposed to be doing and who I was supposed to be with. She became my goal, my benchmark, my quest and I had to win her. That's what all this was about. Winning. With her, I could be the grand champion with the finest prize in all the world. To prematurely reward her, I had created a character for her in *ABRACADABRA* and with it, adding another dimension that elevated the story into a higher level than ever before. Sarah became Sera, the gypsy witch who helps Amod de M'Dau once he is befallen by the curse of the werewolf. It is she who helps Amod both survive and cope with his malady, then winning his heart in the process long after he and Kala had gone their separate ways. Thanks to Sarah's inspiration, this was a major step for both *ABCD* and me. With this injection of new blood, my life and my work could meld into one. Now my fate seemed a lot more secure and I had the necessary strength to go on once again.

I don't recall much of anything else that afternoon. The fact that my job had become so routine was a mixed blessing for I could perform my tasks without thinking. Picking up and delivering does not require a lot of gray matter activity. Normally, I would have cursed that thought, wanting more exercise for my cranium, but the delirium I felt from the spell Sarah cast over me made me grateful for the commonplace for a change. I performed my duties like a good little drone. I barely remembered to return to the drawing station to pick up whatever specimens Thelma left for me in the lock box before I headed down the hill again to The Big Valley.

Regaining consciousness only slightly, I began to question my giddiness. What exactly was going on here? Sure, the first time I caught sight of Sarah, I had been thoroughly stunned, but I didn't get all goofy like I had this day. I giggled when I left Pine Grove that afternoon. Sometimes it just burst out of me almost as though I had acquired Tourette's Syndrome. I hadn't giggled since before I reached puberty. What was it? Sarah and I shared a moment, but it wasn't a particularly significant moment really. We had no exchange of thoughts or feelings, just pleasantries and truncated pleasantries at that thanks to my lip and the eminent Dr. Wilkins, Quack Extraordinaire.

She did touch my shoulder though…but come on, that was so platonic…wasn't it?

Finally, a thought occurred to me. That day had been the very first time I had thought about Sarah sexually. In fact, it had been the first time since Karen that I thought about anyone else in over seven years. I guess I had a lot of tension built up since my wife and I had not fulfilled our marital vows in too long of a time to mention. I hadn't so much as even masturbated that entire year. When I had before, my only thoughts were of Karen and my fantasies were filled with our greatest hit packages. When I started to resent her in return, I ceased to think of Karen in such glowing terms. Ultimately, I had suppressed my desire altogether. No wonder I was depressed. There had been no release for me whatsoever.

I could honestly own up to the fact that I was actually horny. Sure, I needed to let go, but man, did this ever please me by itself. It pleased me that I needed some pleasure. Yes, I could afford myself some pleasure. I deserved it. I was going to please myself!

Again, I giggled.

What a goof.

I flipped on the radio, punching dials nonchalantly until I stumbled across Stevie Wonder singing *For Once in My Life*.

I saw myself strutting down the main street of downtown Jackson in a seersucker suit, singing this happy tune with the whole town turning out to see. Sarah, in a flowery sundress saunters up to me as the entire populace of Jackson fills both sides of the street, cheering us on as I sing how I have someone who finally needs me. Sarah smiles and nods her head in agreement, holding me even closer to her. I lead her to a four-poster bed, sitting in right in front of the Jackson Hotel at the end of the street. We hop onto the bed and face each other on our knees, then lock lips like there's no yesterday, today or tomorrow. We break and wave to the cheering throng as they push the bed down the road and up over the pass away from them. We say goodbye to the good folks of Jackson as we roll off into the sunset, even bidding farewell to all, even the highway patrolman that we pass…

Oh shit. That guy's not part of the song.

Immediately, I looked at the speedometer. It read eighty miles an hour. Eek. Behind me, I spied with my little eye an honest-to-goodness CHP pulling away in a puff of dust from the dirt road where he was parked with lights a'flashing. This Chippie was on my tippie. I slowed the vehicle down in a flash to 70-65-60-55-50, but it was too little, too late. I had to pull over and I did.

Panicking only moderately, my mind conjured up several possibilities; chiefly among them was to play innocent and dumb. There was the remotest chance ala a snowball in hell that I could have gotten off with a warning. I just couldn't afford a ticket. It hadn't been my first that year. Maybe if I had showed him a little leg…

The officer, a stout fellow that Jack Webb would have cast in one of his television shows without hesitation, hunkered over to the passenger window of my car. No fool he, knowing he might be a potential target for any oncoming vehicle wanting to clip a highway patrolman for shits and giggles. He gestured for me to roll down the window and he meant now, mister.

"Hi. Is there a problem?" I asked innocently and as dumb as a bag of dirt.

"License and registration please," Officer Friendly said without answering the stupidest question of his day.

"Uh, sure, officer," I replied, pulling the driver's license from my wallet then opening the glove compartment. Several errant cassettes from The Collection fell to the floorboard in a bad recreation of an old Fibber McGee and Molly bit. I fumbled through the chaotic mess of papers and documents and finally found the car's registration and insurance card, even though he hadn't asked for the latter. Perhaps my cooperation would bode well in my favor. I handed all three items to the nice man in uniform.

"Can I ask what the problem is, sir?" I tried again.

"Wait right here," Officer Friendly ordered as he strolled back to his patrol car.

Sca-rewed.

That was me all over. There was no way I was going to get out of a speeding ticket, so I had to face the goddamn music and take it up the whoopee pipe like a man. Naturally, this gave me no solace. I slowly dissolved into what had become my natural state of depression and self-pity. I grabbed the steering wheel as I found myself sinking at too fast of a rate. Then to stop my free fall, I shoved my forehead into the top of it and held on for dear life.

Goddamn it to fuck anyway. Why was I my own worst enemy? No wonder I couldn't sustain any measure of happiness in my life when all I seemed to do was sabotage every effort with rampant acts of carelessness. How could I be so reckless? Sure, this job meant so little to me, but look, it was all I had to keep myself afloat. It served a purpose and that was my eminent survival. I knew damn well that another ticket would be a blotch on not only my driving record but also my insurance and probable grounds for disciplinary actions from Healthfirst. They could have fired my ass with the collection of tickets I had been gathering. Why was I so flagrantly putting myself in jeopardy? Did I want to start all over again? Was I aware of how much time and effort it took to get this fucking job? Wouldn't that take even more valuable time from my precious *ABRACADABRA*? I was on the brink of losing it altogether as it was. I couldn't manage to lose anything more at all at this point. I didn't have that much left.

"It's not the end of the world. Over," a tiny little compassionate voice reassured me from the two-way radio.

"Leave me alone!" I snapped. Catching myself, I realized that this voice came from nowhere and, therefore, non-existent. So I kept myself in check in case the CHP caught me talking to my imaginary friends. He might have to break out the pepper spray.

My hyperventilation started to activate again. Surely, I was having an anxiety attack. After a series of deep breaths, I calmed down almost immediately and rationality soon entered my thought patterns. I had blown it big time and committed a traffic offense. I was in the wrong and I had to pay. The decision to keep this news from Terri and everyone at Healthfirst was a no-brainer. I could have taken care of the whole thing including the fine, the point on my driving record, the whole string cheese incident with a simple eight-hour traffic school class. That would have been a perfect solution if I hadn't already taken advantage of it two months before. Oh well. I didn't commit murder. I drove over the speed limit. I'd take responsibility for my actions. Period.

The fine officer returned to my car and informed me that he clocked me on his radar scanner traveling at a rate of seventy-eight miles an hour in a fifty-five zone. He wrote me a ticket for only seventy and warned me to slow down. To drive this point home, he stared at me for what seemed to be five seconds of extremely uncomfortable silence. If I had cracked wise at him, I honestly believe he would have shot me. He told me to have a nice day. Not a great day, mind you. That was simply way out of the question.

Another stunning defeat in a day in the life of me.

Irony was not one of my best friends by any means, but it certainly was my constant companion. Not much time had passed since the days when I didn't drive at all. As a matter of fact and record, I didn't get my driver's license until I reached the age of twenty-seven, just before I got together with Karen. There are reasons for this and none of them will make any sense.

When I reached driving age, I took the required high school courses, yet never applied for a driver's permit. It just never occurred to me. Besides, I had an endless supply of rides I could bum from anyone and everyone I knew who already had a car. If not, I had my bicycle or would even ride the bus. The only possible explanation for my behavior was that I didn't want the responsibility of an automobile. It meant I had to further my development and achieve my rightful place in society as a mature adult. By not driving, I had stunted my own growth.

My folks sure as hell didn't help. Everything revolved around my brother Jason who drove as soon as his feet could reach the pedals. He had a voracious appetite for anything on wheels. By the time he turned twenty, he had owned almost every variety of motor vehicle possible including a go-cart, a pick-up truck, a convertible sports car, a van and even a motorcycle. With my dad's help, Jason even had a brief stint as a drag racer. Naturally, with all that horsepower at the disposal of a teenager with a need for speed, he had quite a few run-ins with the law. The folks stood at his side every time he fucked up, but it began to wear them out both emotionally and financially. When Jason got busted for stealing a motor home, they finally gave up and he had to face the music all alone.

So, by the time it came for me to get behind the wheel, they pretty much just ignored me altogether and I let them. I wasn't in any hurry. My experiences in Driver Training pretty much confirmed that. It only made me nervous.

I became a royal pain in the ass to any of my friends or family members who would haul my sorry ass around town. On the other hand, this also involved a lot of waiting around on my part. I grew to hate being so dependent on others. Instead of taking matters into my own hands, I just ended up not going anywhere unless I could get there on my accord. It made sense to me anyway.

This also meant that I dated very little. Sometimes, a girl with a car would be willing to give it a go, but how pathetic was this after all? Here was a guy with no car let alone a driver's license who still lived at home. Come on, ladies…doesn't that get you all hot?

I could always call a cab. I even tried it a second time after the disastrous night with Karen. Episode number two had an even better ending when my date found a ride home from the restaurant with our waiter.

Circumstances in my family caused me to finally relent. My dad suffered a massive heart attack and I ended up driving my mom to the hospital. I had no trepidation whatsoever. She needed me and I came through. All I did was get behind the wheel and drive, then continued to do so from then on. I ended up having to drive Mom every place because she herself did not drive. Why should she? She had my dad. Jason had disappeared off the face of the earth so no one could rely on him. That left me. This was the trade-off I had to make in order to use the car. What didn't dawn on Mom was that I had been carting her around illegally. I had no license. After three years of treading on the thinnest of ice, I broke down and entered the ranks of the legitimate.

When Karen and I got together, I had to drive her four-speed every once in a while and I hate stick shifts. Automatic transmissions were made for people like me who just wanted to put the car into D and go. No messing with a clutch. No first, second or third bullshit. If I could have the car drive itself, I would. I could just sit in the driver's seat and operate it like The Clapper. Clap, clap…turn left…clap, clap…turn right…clap, clap, clap, clap…The Clapper!

Believe it or don't, I don't really care, but it is indeed a fact that I actually taught traffic school at one time, one of the fine jobs I held in search of normal employment. I had answered a want ad in the San Francisco Chronicle asking for actors and comedians to conduct weekend classes that were approved by the State Department of Motor Vehicles. The purposes of these daylong programs were to allow drivers with minor traffic violations to eliminate these infractions from their records. By minor, that meant anything from speeding to making an illegal turn and things of that ilk.

In California, as well as in other states, those who committed these crimes against nature received a point on their records, a red mark that would cause the insurance company to jack up the rates of the ticketed drivers. An accumulation of points gave these miscreants the extra-added bonus prize of having their licenses suspended or revoked altogether. Traffic schools offered the option of a deadly dull eight-hour course that was usually taught by an ex-cop or ex-DMV associate or ex-interesting human being. These blowhards would blather on endlessly in the most monotone and straightforward manner possible about seat belts, traffic signals and the always-hot topic of who has the right of way. Lucky attendees might even get a movie like *Your Friend, the Turn Signal* or *Buckle Up for Fun!* No way would they show one of those classic teenage car-crash gorefests from high school driver training classes like *Red Asphalt.* Those days were long gone in the wake of political correctness, as they probably should, I suppose. But you know, a little splatter film would have perked those classes up, especially before or even after the lunch break.

Some entrepreneurial genius came up with a brilliant plan to sub-contract these classes and make them a little more tolerable by hiring entertainers as instructors. The content would basically be the same only presented in a much lighter and sometimes whimsical tone. This made the mandatory eight-hour length a bit more bearable and the response was outstanding. Soon, this form of traffic school became the preferred option over the deadly dull regular classes. Business boomed and a whole slew of new classes opened throughout the state. A wide variety of alternatives became available. Some schools featured comedy while others offered incentives like free pizza and ice cream.

Still more were specific for gender or sexual orientation. The end result was still the same. After eight hours of class time, the point on the violator's driving record would be erased. Of course, there was still the cost of the fine, the fee for the class itself and the waste of a perfectly good Saturday.

Intrigued by the newspaper ad, I applied to this company that called themselves the unfortunate name of the Ha! Ha! Traffic School and, much to my surprise, they hired me immediately after what was probably my most awkward job interview ever. I was so cautious of what these people were offering that I felt damn near paranoid as the words *too good to be true* kept running through my head. But something about me must have impressed them. With only a single day's training, I became a top banana traffic school instructor for an excellent rate of pay. Unfortunately, classes were only held on weekends, making this basically just a part-time job. But, it was something that I felt, if it worked out, could lead to bigger things. Was I funny? Well, I wouldn't have been with what I was given to work with. Along with the lesson plan, the company offered me a series of stale old jokes and puns that would have made a four year old cringe.

For example:

This guy was driving down the street and knitting at the same time. A traffic cop noticed this and pulled along beside him.

"Pull over!" the cop yelled. "Pull over!"

The guy calmly looked at the cop and said, "No. Socks."

Yuck.

I wisely decided to come up with my own material.

Through the use of various characters like a strict prison warden, a dim-witted, donut-munching cop and a zombie-like DMV employee, I was determined to turn the class on its ear. I even performed a traffic safety puppet show. I provided all the necessary information I was required by law to give since I had been monitored periodically by the State to make sure all of us were toeing the line.

For once, I really enjoyed my work. I finally found a niche and an acceptable outlet for my talents. The best thing about it was the response. My students were extremely receptive and downright appreciative of my work. To put it succinctly these were basically eight hour-long one-man shows-and I was the producer, director, writer and star. Since they were booked all over Northern California, I felt as though I were on tour. They had become so successful and satisfying that I had even entertained the idea of branching out on my own eventually, maybe even starting my own little company. This could have been my side-business as I put together my writing career.

But once again, just as I found a path I could walk, Fate stuck his foot out and tripped me, causing me to fall flat on my face.

One Saturday that I was due to teach a class in Turlock, I had unfortunately overslept. Traffic school started promptly at 8:00 AM and I didn't leave Stockton until 7:30. Travel time to this particular venue would have taken at least an hour so there was no way in hell I would have made my deadline. It became necessary for me to speed so that I didn't get too far behind. I virtually fly down Highway 99 with the hope that I could reach whatever remained of my class by at least 8:15 and miraculously, I almost made it. However, just inside the city limits, the Turlock Police nailed me for running a stop sign. My hostility toward the ticketing officer was way over the top. He forced me to sit in my vehicle for almost twenty minutes while he ran my license and plates, then methodically wrote out my citation with all the graceful penmanship of one of Jane Goodall's gorillas. I arrived at my destination, a conference room in a local motel as usual, at ten minutes to 9:00. Only a handful of students remained and they were none too pleased no matter how I tried to win them over. I even came clean about my predicament that morning, including the traffic ticket. They could not have cared less. Naturally, because I have all the good fortune of a hemophiliac in a razor blade factory, a Department of Motor Vehicles inspector had monitored the class that morning. When it seemed as though I would pull a no-show, the inspector contacted my boss, Stan, at the Ha! Ha! front office. I called Stan at the first break in the class session. He ordered me to refund the remainder of the students their money, then fired me without taking a breath. With the inspector watching over my shoulder, I returned the money to the students who remained enduring all the ball busting that came with this humiliation. Sure, they had sacrificed their weekend for absolutely nothing. But they failed to see what I had to give up. At least they had the opportunity to come back again. Not me. So ended my traffic school career and the last time I appeared before any sort of audience.

Because coincidence does occur in this wacky world of ours, J.B. called me not two days later, informing me that Healthfirst had an opening for a courier position. By the end of that week, I had been hired. Now I was driving for a living.

Oh, and as for that ticket I received in Turlock? I managed to get it removed from my record. All I had to do was go to traffic school.

CHAPTER TWELVE

SWAN SONG

Arriving home that evening, I slipped in through the back door as to avoid Karen and retired to what was now my room, the same space I used for an office. Yep, separate beds, separate bedrooms, damn close to separate lives. Whatever goes around comes around since this was the same room I'd shared with my brother.

With the eight-year difference in our ages, sharing a bedroom was a dicey proposition for Jason and myself. My older brother had always been my tormentor, taking his raging hormones out on his younger, pre-pubescent sibling with a vengeance. He made it abundantly clear that this was his room and I only slept in it because he let me. Beyond that, I was forced to vacate the premises at his discretion. Sometimes, when he finally let me back inside, he would keep me up to all hours of the night by keeping the lights on and his crappy heavy metal music blaring, never giving me any peace, let alone any privacy. When Jason left the nest, I felt like France after the liberation. I transformed that room into a Fortress of Solitude, even to the point of securing it with my own lock and key. It took a judicial order for anyone else to enter which really fried my dad's taters. Mom really didn't care one way or the other. I had claimed this territory as my own and remained there until I moved into Karen's apartment years later.

Now here I was again, sharing the same goddamn bedroom all over again, this time with Karen's sewing machine. I suppose I should have been grateful she had been so lethargic that she had given using it altogether. She never entered that room while I was home. It's hard telling what she did when I was working; though getting her off the couch during her "stories" appeared to be a major effort.

Oddly inspired by the day's events, I worked on a new scene for *ABCD* involving a character based on Dr. Wilkins. I had this striking image of Woraxas, wreaking havoc near a hospital when he suddenly spies Wilkins attempting to hide and pleading for his life.

"Please! Leave me alone!" the miserable excuse for a doctor whimpered. "I'm unarmed!"

Woraxas smiled wickedly as he stood before the helpless physician and extended his arms toward him. Suddenly, Woraxas flailed both of his appendages apart in a grand gesture, as Dr. Wilkins' own arms were torn from his body.

"You are now," Woraxas laughed maniacally.

"No!" Wilkins railed, blood spraying out of both arm sockets like a grotesque lawn sprinkler

"O Physician, heal thyself," Woraxas chortled as he sauntered down Market Street in search of new mayhem.

A knock on my bedroom door took me by surprise.

"Yes?" I asked with odd formality.

Karen popped her head inside as though she was intruding in her own home.

"Hi. Can we talk?" she asked rather nervously.

"Sure. Come in. I'm a little…taken aback. I didn't think you ever wanted to talk."

She sat in her sewing chair and grinned in such a way that suggested she had either bad news or gas. Since she was too much of a lady to expel the latter, the former seemed to be the logical choice so I just braced myself.

"This isn't working," she said after a sigh.

Uh oh. I was right. This was The Talk, wasn't it?

"No, it isn't," I agreed.

"I think it's time we both went our separate ways."

"Meaning…?"

"I'm leaving."

Those two words hit me with all the force of a punch to my kidneys.

"I have an opportunity to go to culinary school," she continued.

Culinary school? I wondered. Is this the same woman who ate all the American cheese? I tried to keep my thoughts to myself, but I couldn't help some of them leaking out and registering on my face.

"What? What does that look mean?" Karen demanded.

"Nothing. I'm just…taken further aback I guess. Culinary school? Since when?" I inquired.

"Since…for a long time. You wouldn't know because we don't talk."

I could only imagine how she came to this decision. She might have gotten the ideas from all those TV ads that are broadcast during the daytime hours. I surprised she didn't want to learn to be a long-haul truck driver.

"Calvin, I have to do something with my life. I can't if I'm with you."

"Thanks," I grinned sardonically.

She stood and paced in a very short space in the room, making her look like a shooting gallery bear. "You know what we have here is not working out. This is bad, Calvin. We sleep in different rooms and this place is just not that big."

"I know, I know,' I relented, not wanting to look at her anymore, but forced myself anyway. "What was it, Karen? What made you give up on us so easily?"

"It's never been easy."

Pow! Another body blow!

"Then what was it?"

"I don't know," she said, sitting again. She began to fiddle with her hair. "I guess…you're like your book. It's just seems you're never going to finish it. You just re-write and re-write and it never ends. It's still the same story over and over again. It never gets any place…just like you. You still don't know how it's going to end, do you?"

I shook my head reluctantly.

"Well, I need an ending and I feel that I have to end this for the both of us. If I don't, I'm going to wind up hating you for the rest of my life. I don't want that to happen."

Not really wanting to hear the answer to this, I asked this anyway. "Do you hate me now?"

She gulped. "A little…"

Now it was my turn to gulp. "I see."

"I'm sorry," Karen said almost under her breath.

"So am I," I added, knowing full well in my heart that I didn't hate her at all. The mere thought of it was unimaginable. "When do you want to leave?"

"As soon as I can."

"Can't wait to get out of here, huh?"

"Calvin…"

"Karen…"

We locked eyes as if we were engaged in a staring contest. There was no way I was going to blink first. I searched her eyes for answers but I just couldn't read her. This pained me even more since I always could in the past. Suddenly it seemed unfathomable that we had once been of one mind. Now we had drifted so far apart that we barely recognized one another. As much as it hurt to admit it, this was the right course of action.

"Look," I said, standing before her. "Stay as long as you want. Take your time. I'm in here most of the time anyway so there's really no reason to rush."

"Okay. Thanks. I was just going to move in with my folks for the duration and, to tell you the truth, I wasn't really in a big hurry to do that. Besides I could use the extra time," she sighed in minor relief.

"Sure."

What a swell guy. I could have charged her rent so that I could pay my speeding ticket, but, hey, why be a dick?

Even though the general tone of our dialogue was certainly tragic, a sense of calm began to fall over me. As we discussed the dissolution of our marriage here, I found myself oddly sedate because it dawned on me that this had been the only civil conversation Karen and I had in too long of a time. I began to imagine us having one last night together, kind of a grand finale. This was we could prove to ourselves that were a great couple at one time and getting together was not a mistake. Even though it just didn't work out for the two of us to stay together, we still could provide closure to our relationship. It would serve to heal most of the wounds we had inflicted on each other so that we could move on without regret. After all, we had a mutual agreement here. Karen may have brought it up initially, but I heartily concurred.

Therefore, I instantly formulated plans in my head for one last date. We'd start with dinner at Mylar, the scene of our first date-version two. For old time's sake, I would have preferred The Happy Steak, where I took her the first time out, but unfortunately, the Home of the Golden Spud had gone out of business long ago. Mylar in Sacramento was a wee bit more upscale. The absence of a salad bar was a big clue. From there we would take the long way back home, stopping out on the Delta and park our car on the levee like we used to. There we could sit and look at the stars as we'd exchange our hopes, dreams and the futures we could have without one another. Finally we could end up back home and, for the first time in a long time and the last time forever, we could make love like we always could. I remembered that I hadn't even kissed her face since Christmas, her lips, the summer before. This would be so good for us, so cleansing.

I hesitantly asked my wife out on a date.

"Would you…like to have dinner with me?"

"Oh, no thanks. I'm going to a movie with Cynthia," she replied nonchalantly.

A wave of disappointment washed my relief and my plans away like a sandcastle in the surf.

"Well, couldn't you cancel? I mean…don't you think we could, I don't know, seal the deal with a meal?" I half-heartedly joked.

"Seal the deal? There is no deal. We're splitting up."

"Okay, I'm just trying to lighten the mood. I just thought maybe we could go to Mylar."

"Mylar? In Sacramento? We went there once and it wasn't very good then."

"You never said anything before."

"It never came up. Besides, you seemed to like it and I didn't want to hurt your feelings."

"I see you got over that."

The Evil Karen started to emerge.

"What's the point, Calvin?"

"Excuse me for trying to end what we had on a high note. I only wanted to show you that there were no hard feelings."

Her face contorted in melodramatic horror.

"No hard feelings? Of course there are hard feelings! Why do you think I want us to break up?"

"Because…because…because, because, because!" I blathered in frustration. I'm surprised I didn't add, *"because of the wonderful things she does."*

Regaining her composure, Karen apologized, "Calvin, I'm sorry. You mean well, but I don't think this is a good idea. It would be awkward and we'd probably end up the same way we are now, only worse. I didn't mean what I said about hating you. I just know that I don't …love you anymore. That said….I don't want us to be hurt each other anymore either. Does that make sense?"

"Uh-huh."

"I have to get ready," she said as she turned to go.

"Yeah, you don't want to be late for your movie," I told her as I walked to the door. "I hope for your sake that it's not a love story."

I slammed the door behind her. So much for civility.

I plopped back down on the sofa and sank back into a sea of depression. This time, I slipped a few more leagues under the sea. I passed Captain Nemo in his submarine, the Nautilus, and flipped him off

From the other room, I could hear Karen talking to her father over the phone.

"It has to be this weekend, Dad. I just can't take it here anymore," she demanded.

Karen left the house not fifteen minutes later to meet up with her friend, Cynthia. At one time, she was *my* friend, Cynthia, but as time wore on, she gravitated over to Karen's side and stayed there. I wasn't too disappointed over this since Cynthia was about as interesting as an old shoe, but not nearly as attractive.

When the coast was clear, I ventured out to the living room. Karen had been such a homebody she had staked out that room as her personal territory. I'm surprised she didn't pee on the TV to claim it as her own. She couldn't. That baby was *mine*.

I polished off a frozen potpie of unknown origin that I discovered sans box in the back of the freezer. Without any directions to follow, I had to estimate the correct heating time and after two attempts, I ended up with an overcooked bowl of beige goo. I had no reason to actually enjoy such a meal nor was that my purpose. Sustenance, no matter how meager, was my only goal. It wouldn't have mattered if I had been fed intravenously. I wondered what my future ex could have done with this mess at culinary school.

Television was even blander than my dinner. Since I wasn't in the mood for indiscriminate channel surfing, I switched it off after less than hour. I sat back in what used to be Karen's grandfather's easy chair and pondered the wreckage of what was our marriage. Soon, that even grew tiresome since it offered the same thing the TV had-more re-runs. I played the same memory tapes that I had during my lunchtime, except with the sex edited out this time through. All I could dwell on were the low points of our marriage in a retrospective compilation I called *Where We Went Wrong.*

Needing fresh air, I took the kitchen garbage out and stood in the shadows of my driveway, gazing up at the sky. For an apparently clear night, it was virtually starless. As always on an evening in Stockton, the sound of a siren loomed in the distance. Traffic had died down to an intermittent series of vehicle sounds stemming from the nearest main thoroughfare of El Dorado Street not three blocks down. The world appeared peaceful. Of course, was it half-empty or half-full? In the mood I found myself in, I felt like the Earth was dying ever so goddamn slowly, just fading away to nothingness.

A skinny kid I had never seen before in the neighborhood strolled down the street with one those teenage gaits that suggested he really wanted to have some balls. They just hadn't dropped yet. He almost swam in his extremely baggy wardrobe of an extra large T-shirt and jeans from the Stupid White Kid collection. He crossed over to my side of the sidewalk and right by my work car, parked as usual at the curb in front of my house. All of a sudden, this little rat bastard hocked up the biggest loogy he could and spit on the hatchback window of my car.

I snapped awake, shocked by what I had just witnessed. I stood out from the shadows and yelled, "Hey! Come here!"

The kid seemed to be startled by this sudden outburst but his dull voice betrayed his feelings if he had any.

"Huh?"

"Not *huh*. Here. Come over here right now," I ordered stomping over to my car.

"What?" Mr. Innocent replied, shuffling over yet keeping his distance.

"What? What do you mean what? Clean this up!" I demanded.

Shrugging his shoulders dispassionately, he

obliged. Removing his shirt, the skinny little nitwit wiped the goo from the car window.

"What the hell is the matter with you?" I asked almost rhetorically.

"Nothin'."

"Nothin'? So you spit on my car for nothin'?"

"I guess."

"Don't do it again."

He shrugged again.

"Awright."

With that, he turned and continued down the street, shirtless.

More confused than ever, I watched him and didn't close my mouth for almost a minute. I shook my head back and forth so much that I almost gave myself a headache. As the little fucker turned the corner, he stopped on last time and returned my gaze. Once again, he hocked up another one just for me, letting it fly in my general direction. Then, he disappeared.

Jesus Horatio Christ. How did I become such a punching bag in this world? From the beginning of that morning right up until the last part of the night, I had been hammered almost relentlessly. Were it not an everyday occurrence I would have been able to cope more than I was able to at this juncture. If only I had the answer to this simple two word question: Why me?

Sorry, Sarah. I just couldn't manage to have a great day after all.

CHAPTER THIRTEEN

THAT'S THAT

The traffic gods decided to cut me a modicum of slack the next morning and afforded me the passage to arrive to work on time. I needed a small victory like this to start a new day on a positive note if at all possible. With a point in my favor, I was ahead for a change.

Just to give the day even more promise, the medicine Thelma had given me the day before already began to work its pharmaceutical magic. What had been a lump of diseased meat only hours before transformed into a slightly discolored nothing. By the next day, it would be gone the way of all, well, flesh.

Naturally, this lucky streak came to a crashing halt as soon as I entered the lab. Since the time clock had been set up next to Terri's office, there was no way to avoid her if she had been sitting at her desk when I swiped in.

"Hi, Calvin," she greeted in her singsong, cellulite encased voice.

"Good morning, Terri. Do you see what time it is?"

"It's five minutes to eight. You're not supposed to check in early."

"But did you notice that I'm not late. I'm early. See the difference?" I offered.

"You're still not supposed to..."

"I know! Sorry. I thought maybe you'd give me a little credit here for showing up on time."

I could feel my stomach tightening in knots that would make a sailor envious.

"Yes, that's good, Calvin, but that's what you're supposed to do. I'm just saying you can't check in early, that's all," she rationalized in a way that would have made even Mother Teresa want to knock her block off.

"Well, so much for that good morning," I groaned, starting for the break room. I caught Elsie out of the corner of my eye rolling hers in dismay.

"Calvin?"

When I turned, I was almost shocked to see that Terri had actually mustered up enough strength to stand on those massive stumps and take two laborious steps to her office doorway. Surely she would need a nap after that.

"Yes?" I said, biting my cheek so hard I almost drew blood. I had to. I couldn't stand talking to this ignorant baboon any longer than necessary. Even self-mutilation was more pleasurable than having to listen to Terri's inane babble.

"I need you to ride with Jill on Monday," she told me.

Jill. Dear sweet Jill. Dear sweet boring Jill. Dear sweet boring stupid Jill.

"Why?"

Duck! Here comes the bombshell!

"Well, since you're going to be taking over her route, I need you to learn it," Terri spoke as though I was privy to this information even though this was the first I had heard of it.

"What do you mean? When am I taking over her route?"

"Monday," she shrugged her shoulders, quite an effort on her part to manipulate all that bulk.

My thermostat had just been turned up.

"Since when?" I challenged. "This is the first I've heard of this."

"Oh, that's right. You weren't here. Everybody's switching. We want to make sure everyone knows each other's routes in case one of us has to fill in. We're going to
do this…"

"…every six months," I finished her thought.

"Then you do know about it."

"Only through office gossip as usual. Why is this happening so fast?"

"We were supposed to start next month, but corporate wanted this in place right away. Everybody who was here yesterday afternoon got to choose their new routes."

"Everybody but me. I was in Jackson…on *my* route doing *my* job. This isn't fair."

"It doesn't really matter. It's still the same job with the same hours. Besides, it all pays the same."

I detested her more than any other human being on the planet at that moment.

"It matters to me. I didn't get to choose yesterday, so I'll choose right now. I'm staying put."

"You can't. J.B. took your route."

Ow. Something had just pounded me right between the shoulder blades. Whatever it was knocked the wind right out of me.

"What?" I asked, my voice considerably lower.

"Calvin, I'm sorry you have a problem with this, but you're getting all worked up over nothing. It's really not important."

Through slit eyelids, I glared at her. "Don't ever assume what you might think is important to me."

Terri folded her massive arms over her gigantic tits defensively as if she was ready to draw her weapons.

"Calvin, you're riding with Jill on Monday and that's that."

"That's that," I repeated and marched back to the break room. The pain in my back that I felt earlier became obvious. It had been caused by a knife, thrust into me by my old buddy, old pal, old chum, J.B. Blood didn't flow from my wound. All it did was open a new vein of depression, causing a chain reaction through my system that boiled up all the remnants of depressions gone past. It all swam though me like a big depression soup. Depression? You're soaking in it.

Sarah.

Not fifteen minutes later, I pulled into my regular gas station on West Lane to refuel for the day. All of the islands were full with the exception of one lone pump that I would have to make a U-turn to occupy. Just as I spun my car around and angled into place, a brown Econoline cut me off and stole my spot.

Outraged, I maneuvered back the other way in an attempt to eyeball this thieving asshole. As he got out of his van, I could see that he was just another angry white guy in a short sleeve, button down shirt with a cheesy tie. He looked up to return my gaze, even fiercer than mine. He made the international dramatic gesture of "What?"

"Didn't you see me backing in?" I yelled.

"No and I don't care," he retorted.

We locked eyes. It was like looking at my reflection in the mirror. He *was* me. I wanted to get out of the car and kick my ass.

I let him win this one and only round since another pump had opened up for me. I dashed away so that this one wasn't stolen from me as well. I stopped short when I spied J.B.'s vehicle at the same island. I drove over to the restroom area on the far side of the parking lot and parked. I grabbed the microphone from the two-way radio.

"Calvin to J.B. Calvin to J.B. Do you copy?" I spoke professionally.

"Yeah, I copy. What's up?" I heard him say. In fact, I saw him say it.

"Nothing's up. Everything's down…down and dirty."

"Please repeat. I'm getting some interference," he returned.

"Yeah, I know the feeling. Listen, I just wanted to tell you thanks."

Even from across the lot, I could sense his confusion.

"Thanks for what?"

"Thanks for being such a good friend," I spoke in the most condescending voice I could.

"Calvin, you're breaking up," he said, straining to listen. There was a lot of static on the line and not just from me.

"Negative. I'm *cracking* up."

I saw him staring at his mike in confusion.

"I don't read you."

"That's okay, pal. I read you…loud and clear. Over and out," I finished, then spun my car over next to his and stopped.

"Hey!" I called to him, catching his attention. "Like I said, thanks. Really. Thanks a lot…buddy."

"For what?" he wondered.

"For everything. For nothing. Enjoy my route."

With that, I squealed away like an unrepentant teenager, in search of another gas station, one that didn't serve the likes of anyone like him.

Bastard. Son of a bitch. Buddy fucker.

This betrayal was so beyond my comprehension. I could not begin to fathom how he could actually commit such a deception. This kind of shit happens to executives at a corporate level, not to lower rungs of the ladder like us. We, the bottom feeders, are supposed to appreciate the small things in life because for us, they are few and far between. We should cherish things like friendship and try to hold onto them since we're told that it's lonely at the top. Therefore, at the bottom, all we have is each other. Once we turn on each other, what's left? Does anyone really want to be King of the Bottom?

As is perfectly evident, I was not exactly a social butterfly and could really only consider one person to be anything close to what would be considered a friend. That would have been J.B.-or at least that what I believed until that morning. We were kindred spirits, able to deal with the rest of the world on a superficial level, but really only able to relate to a select few. He too had been a loner most of his life, crashing and burning through one disastrous relationship after another. The mutual admiration of each other's talents and similarly narrow outlook on life gave us the common grounds to hit it off almost immediately. It wasn't like we were the best of chums. We still remained aloof, as was our nature, but sometimes a guy just needs another guy to talk to and he was that guy. Little did I know that he harbored a jealousy of me and coveted what I had. Hah! Totally green of envy…of me…and what I had! Again I say Hah!

J.B. would fill in for me when I would take the day off, so he got a good idea about what my route was all about. He'd always complain about the long drive but would concede that at least the scenery was "nice". He sure fooled me. He was speaking right out of his ass since now I knew that he wanted the Jackson route. Maybe that wasn't all

that he wanted.

Sarah.

Oh my God. No. Nonononono. No way. This can't be happening. Sarah wouldn't have anything to do with that fat fuck. No, she's too good for him. She couldn't insult him or be mean to him at all. No, she's too good. She'd be kind and gracious and as good as she always is…AS SHE ALWAYS IS…

But what if that fat fuck tried to force himself on her? Have his way with her? HIS FAT FUCK DISGUSTING WAY WITH HER? She'd try to resist but he'd grab her wrists as she struggled to break free? Then he'd smack her back and forth and back and forth across her face, her beautiful face until she'd fall to the floor. Sweating the way that all fat fucks do, he'd drip all over her with his fat fuck sweat, drenching her in his vile fat fuck secretions. He'd pull his fat fuck pants down and attempt to find his fat fuck dick that he hadn't seen since his fat fuck childhood. Then he'd lay on top of her and try to fat fuck her…try to fat fuck my Sarah…

NO!!!

GET OFF OF HER, YOU FAT FUCK!

I'd stand in the doorway, broadsword in hand. Startled by my presence, he'd rise from atop of her, fat fuck pants around his fat fuck ankles, drenching her in a shower of his fat fuck perspiration. I'd draw my sword

136

with both hands and slice forward with all of my might. The blade would strike his fat fuck gut and cut it open from one end of his size 46 fat fuck waist to the other. He'd open up like a meat filled piñata, releasing the entire contents of his fat fuck organs over the floor. He'd fall to his fat fuck haunches; still living but whining in fat fuck shock. Staring at me in fat fuck disbelief, I would return that pathetic fat fuck look with the bottom of my foot. I kick him squarely in the center of his fat fuck face, busting open his fat fuck nose and smacking out several fat fuck teeth, one of them embedding in the sole of my shoe. He'd fall fat fuck face forward into a pile of his fat fuck self and would be no more.

Yeah. My friend. My pal. My buddy.

Do you know what a buddy is?

J.B. told me one time that a good buddy was a guy who went downtown to get two blowjobs, then came home and gave you one.

Keep 'em laughing, funny boy, because when you do, they won't be able to see who you really are.

Hardy-har-har, you fat fuck.

CHAPTER FOURTEEN

ROAD RASH

Due to the intensity of this revenge scenario that had played out on the main stage of the theater of my mind, I had inadvertently driven way off course and ended up on the northeast side of Stockton. I had locked myself into a trance and, quite honestly, put myself and anyone else on the road in potentially great danger. In my anger, I had blanked out.

My old traffic school lessons popped into my head. I could hear myself lecturing my students on the subject of maintaining one's cool.

"You must take responsibility when you are behind the wheel of an automobile. You are the captain of the ship. You are in charge. You are in control. Therefore, you must keep yourself in check. Don't let your emotions get away from you. It can definitely affect your driving. If you lose control of yourself, how can you expect not to lose control of your vehicle?"

Forty pair of attentive eyes would be focused on me as I'd continue my dissertation on road rage.

"You have to understand that you do not have a right to drive. No. In the eyes of the law, it is a privilege and as such, can be taken away from you if you abuse that privilege."

Oh, my. How sanctimonious can we get?

"But, look, we're all human beings. We all have bad days. There are times when we are simply P.O.ed. Your boss yelled at you. You and your significant other are not getting along. The IRS is breathing down your neck. There could be a million and one reasons and sometimes, all of them at the same time. BUT you have no right to take it out on the rest of the world with your car…or your truck…or your van…or whatever you drive. That, my friends is assault…with a deadly weapon."

There would actually be a hush in the room after that monologue. Maybe I got through to them. Maybe they were just embarrassed for me.

Obviously, I had never taken one of my own classes so these words fell on my deaf ears. Do as I say not as I do, I'd rationalize. This just made me another hypocrite in the world. With this truth staring me in the face, my short-lived career as a traffic school instructor has just been negated, just another zero to make my life continually add up to nothing.

I needed to get back on track, so I took Highway 99 heading toward Modesto and floored it, still stewing in my own angry juices. Attempting to blow off some steam by driving it off was a total contradiction of what I used to teach, but that was not my concern. I had a raging mad-on and I had to get rid of it somehow.

Unfortunately, the road ahead of me had not been clear. In the fast lane, being the wrong place at the wrong time was an elderly gentleman in a Mercury sedan, traveling way below the speed limit. Semi trucks occupied the other lanes and there was no way around him. Naturally, in the crazed state of mind I found myself in, this brought me back to the boiling point once again. It became necessary for me to encourage him to pick up the pace, right on his rear bumper.

"Excuse me, sir? Sir? You are in the FAST lane. You're supposed to drive FAST. Why are you driving SLOW? LET'S GO! TOO SLOW! LET'S GO! Would you like a PUSH, HMMMMM????"

I slowly accelerated my vehicle so that it could kiss the rear bumper of Old Man Driver. From fifty to fifty-five to sixty to sixty-five to seventy in mere seconds, I could see him grasp his steering wheel in a death grip. We locked fenders and I pushed the outside of the envelope even further as I took Chuck Yeager here for a blast from the past.

"Mach one!" I cried.

The sound barrier broke as we screamed down Highway 99.

"Mach two!" I bellowed as the glass from the instrument panel exploded into a thousand shards.

Sparks sprayed from all sides of our conjoined cars and I laughed as only demons can. Old Man Driver was frozen in fear. It was all he could do to keep his Mercury in control. The stupid old fart! Didn't he know that I was in control?

"Mach three!" I cheered as I slammed on the brakes, separating our vehicles and Old Man River was set free.

As if shot out of a cannon, his car was propelled on its own and at even greater speed, veering off to the right and onto the off ramp of an overpass. Up it flew like a raging comet as Old Man Driver and his Mercury ignited into a giant fireball and launched into space, sailing into the heavens like an authentic Mercury astronaut. Jetting skyward toward the edge of the earth's atmosphere, Old Man Driver suddenly exploded into a Fourth of July display.

Observing the spectacle from below, I led the crowd in a chorus of "Ooh! Aah!"

Back on Earth, Old Man Driver had grown weary of my tailgating and pulled over to the next lane at his first opportunity. He glared at me when I passed, muttering some old man drivel, though I could read his lips enough to make out the word "cocksucker". He shook his head at me in disdain.

I plummeted even lower than before when I realized what had just transpired. Guilt weighed me down to such an extent that I could feel the pull of gravity pinning me to the driver's seat. I reflected on what a fine human being I had turned out to be. What right did I have to take my frustrations out on Old Man Driver? I had hoped he…oh, fuck him. He shouldn't have been driving so goddamn slowly. If you can't handle the freeway, Pop, then stay the fuck off the road. My empathy levels had been exhausted.

There were other matters to attend to that day. First order of business was gasoline because at that point, I had about a fart's worth of fumes left in my tank. The red warning light had been trying to get my attention the entire time I was in La-La Land. Filling my tank at the next station, I considered praying for spontaneous combustion.

I didn't bother saying goodbye to anyone on my morning route. I tried not to be too pleased that I would no longer be seeing this collection of feebs, cretins and assholes on a regular basis. Good riddance to bad rubbish. Besides why should I try to put a positive spin on an obviously detriment to my general well being?

"So, Calvin, what's next for you?" Don Olsen asked me just after the news, traffic and weather at the top of the hour.

"Well, Don, it appears that I'll be moving on to browner pastures. While it won't be any hardship to leave this part of the world, I will be saying an unfortunate farewell to my beloved Gold Country. My days will be occupied in one place and one place only and that is livable, lovable Lodi."

"Lodi? As in 'Oh Lord, stuck in Lodi again'?"

"The one and the same. To tell you the honest to God truth, I really don't know what to expect."

"Who knows? You might actually grow to like it," Don went on, trying to be helpful in his smug insincere radio talk show host way.

"Don, don't even. Why would anyone go to Lodi if unless they had to go to Lodi? I have to go to Lodi and I don't sure as hell want to."

"Oh, Lodi's a charming little town and, hey, it is wine country, isn't it?"

"That comes in mighty handy for a guy that drives for a living," I grumbled.

"If you call that living."

"As always, you're a big help, Don. Get ready to push the dump button. Eat shit and die."

On the way back to the lab at the end of that morning, I drove past my house just in time to see Karen unloading some packing boxes from her car. Carrying too many at one time, she dropped them, scattering the cardboard on the lawn. I considered stopping to help her, but decided to drive away instead. I caught sight of her in my rear view mirror. Somehow this image seemed to sum the whole thing up.

My destiny had been chosen for me and I had to live with it. Karen was leaving. My route was changing. It was my last day to see Sarah.

Funny. The day was just half-over. It sure as hell wasn't half-full.

CHAPTER FIFTEEN

SO LONG

A red rose is my signature flower. It has served very well over the years. I've used it as an introduction, an invitation, an apology, a sign of gratitude and, in this case, a fare thee well.

While purchasing said flower at an over priced florist, I grabbed a fistful of note cards in order to write a personal message for the rose's recipient. I sat in the parking lot of the floral shop pondering this issue and took pen in hand to jot down the perfect sentiment.

I began:

Sarah-
Let's not say goodbye.
There's nothing good about it.

That was laying it on a bit thick.

Next.

Sarah-
Thank you for…
What? Thank you for what? Letting me be myself again?
Sarah-
You are the brightest nugget in the Gold Country.
Nugget? Oh God no! How lame is that?
Sarah-
Hope to see you again soon…and thanks.
Thanks? Again, I had to ask, thanks for what? And what if I didn't see her soon? Then that would be a lie, wouldn't it? Some writer I was.

What was I trying to say here? I needed her to understand but first I had to understand it all myself. Ay, there's the rub, matey. It was far too soon for both of us. After this day, there would be no chance for us at all. Fate would keep us apart permanently unless I wrote something that could somehow keep that door from being locked and perhaps even keep it propped open. That's what this was-a goddamn doorstop. The card had to compliment the rose, conveying a message without, well, put honestly, scaring her away. If I came on too strong, she might get the wrong impression, one that might make me out to be stalker material. I couldn't express a declaration of love on a tiny little card unless I wrote in the miniscule handwriting of the truly insane. Besides, I knew goddamn good and well that the reality was that this was just a big schoolboy crush. But, I knew in my heart the potential it held. It happened before with Karen and I would make certain that lightning would strike twice. So, a total confession would be absurd because these true feelings come with time but what was it I just didn't have, hmmm? TIME! Okay, that was a given. I had to be concise, yet suggest ever so suitably an air of mystery.

I closed my eyes.

Sarah is filling out paperwork at her desk when I walk into the office, rose behind my back. She smiles affectionately, letting me know instantly that she is pleased to see me. Rising from her seat, she steps over to greet me when I present her with the lovely flower, a red bud about to bloom. At the sight of it, she positively glows with both surprise and delight.

"My favorite," Sarah smiles so sincerely. "It is absolutely beautiful."

Instead of handing it to her, I brush the rose across her right cheek, then back down again. Then, I slide it slowly down the nape of her neck, causing her to narrow her eyes as if the bud is kissing her on its descent to her chest. I outline each of her full breasts while she sighs at its touch. She takes my hand and pulls the flower up to her mouth. She kisses the top of the bud, then again on each side ever so gently. As a final gesture, she parts her wet lips and takes the entire bud into her mouth.

YOW!

I shook myself into consciousness and excitedly write down my perfect message.

Sarah-
Thank you.
Calvin

Suddenly, I knew why I was thanking her. The answer was not esoteric after all. This simple message left the door wide open for her. If she wanted to know - and why wouldn't she-I would simply have to tell her.

"Thank you for being you. Thank you for your kind words, your kind eyes and your kind smile. Thank you for making my afternoons up here something to look forward to. Thank you and goodbye."

When I would turn to go, I was hoping to hear one single, solitary word from her.

"Wait."

In fact, I was counting on it.

Having allotted ample time for the flower purchase, I could now make my last regular trip to the foothills at my leisure. That was important to me. I needed to bask in the pleasure of this long drive and take it all in. The thought of losing it all was a sad, sorry situation all in itself without becoming melancholy about the whole thing. I wanted this to end on a high note and remember how good I really had it up there, not how miserable I was going to be to have it taken away from me. I was going to enjoy myself. Ain't no doubt about it…or so I thought.

"Alpha Base to Calvin."

The Voice of Doom.

"Alpha base to Calvin. Do you copy?" Terri blubbered again over the two way.

Reluctantly, I answered her.

"Go ahead, Terri."

"Calvin, is your pager working? Over."

I checked the pager I wore on my belt. Preoccupied with the recent turn of events, I neglected to turn the stupid thing on.

"Uh…I guess so. I don't know, " I lied blatantly as I corrected my error.

"Maybe you need a new battery. Over," she offered.

"I guess I do. Anything else?" I asked hopefully.

"Yeah, I need you to come back. You didn't take your reports. Over," she replied.

"Yes, I did," I said nervously, frantically looking about the car. I couldn't go back. There'd be no time… Shit. She was right. I hated it when she was right. It was out of character for her. "Okay, look, I'm already in Lockeford. It's Friday. A lot of those offices are closed by the time I get there. Can't they just go up Monday with the new driver?"

"You know better than that," Terri scolded.

Frustrated, I barked, "Leave 'em on the counter! I'll be right there!"

I tossed the microphone at the glove compartment and fumed. For once, I wasn't mad at Terri, but I sure was pissed off at myself. I had been getting so forgetful, so incompetent that I couldn't even do my phony baloney job. My sub-conscious had begun to betray me as well. The autopilot that got me out of most of my jams at work went on a walkabout. I supposed he had been bummed too. He didn't want to leave the hills either.

The clock read 12:55. I had wanted to be on the road by 1:00 anyway, so this wasn't much of a setback, but enough to make me nervous. While it was true that many offices were closed Friday afternoons, Dr. Wilkins kept his open until 2:30. That was the deadline I really needed to meet.

Not five minutes later, I stopped abruptly at the curb near the back door of the lab. I flew inside with all the grace of a pregnant pelican, grabbing my reports and making a very hasty exit when I heard someone calling my name.

It was Julie, an attractive but bland blonde phlebotomist who usually never gave me the time of day even if my watch was broken. We had worked together for almost three years and I don't remember speaking more than two words to her. I knew nothing about Julie just as she knew nothing about me, not unlike most of my co-workers. I probably wouldn't have recognized her away from work other than the fact that she had a nose that resembled a big toe.

"Are you calling me?" I asked, out of breath.

"Yeah. God, are you in a hurry or something?"

"Do ya think?" I snapped.

"Cheesh. Having a bad day, are you? Must've been that five minute drive back from Lockeford," Julie said smugly, knowing full well that Lockeford was at least twenty minutes away...without traffic.

"Must be. Gotta go," I conceded and turned to go again.

"Wait a sec. I need you to take a stat out to County."

Translated, I had to transport blood for immediate testing to San Joaquin County Hospital-in the opposite direction in which I was heading.

"No frigging way."

"Yes frigging way. Come on. I'm really stuck."

"I'm really sorry. I have to go the other way. That's northeast. County is southwest. Have Terri take it, " I suggested.

"She's at lunch."

"Of course she is. No, I can't, Julie. Gotta go."

"Come on" she pleaded. "The way you drive, you could drop this off and still be in Jackson by, oh, 1:30."

"Cute. Sorry. Can't."

"You mean won't."

"Can't. Won't. Bye."

With that, I slammed the back door shut just in time to run smack dab into Jim Banner, the regional manager. This guy defined the term "straight arrow". He could have been a poster boy for *The 700 Club*. Damn, he was clean. Pat Boone looked like Marilyn Manson next to this guy.

"Calvin! Whoa, big fella! You're off in a flash," he laughed.

"Yeah, as usual, Jim. How are you?"

I switched over to my good ol' boy mode. Considering my accumulation of fuck-ups as of late, it wasn't in my best interest to have the Big Boss see my dark side.

"Good. I'm good. Say, there was something I was going to ask you…"

Again, my timing was thwarted, this time by Mr. Clean. I was hoping he wasn't going to quote me some scripture, not that he ever would, but the way things were going…

"Darn if I can think of it now. You look you need to be on your way," he offered.

"I do, but if you remember what it is, give me a call on the horn."

"I will do that very thing. Have a safe drive and please give my best to Thelma."

"And I will do that very thing. Bye, Jim."

I almost leapt back into my car and zipped to the quickest possible exit out of the Healthfirst lot. Just as I turned onto March Lane, the radio crackled.

"Alpha Base to Calvin," Jim called.

Almost, but not quite. Thanks a heap, God Boy.

"Yeah, Jim. Did you jog your memory?" I spoke good-naturedly into the mike.

"I did. Sorry about that. I need to send a printer up to Jackson with you. Apparently, Thelma's is on the fritz."

So am I, Jimbo, I said to myself. Fortunately, I hadn't gotten very far, having just stopped at the first traffic light.

"Uh, my only hesitation is that is that several doctors close early on Fridays and I won't have time to hook it up," I explained, trying to get out of this if I could.

"Oh, Thelma can hook it up herself. She's handy that way. I've got the printer right here so if you can just come back…"

150

I bit my lower lip, not very mindful of my recent cold sore. I'm surprised I didn't start chewing it like a wad of Hubba Bubba.

"Not a problem, Jim. I'll be right there."

And I was, just like the good Healthfirst employee I could be. Within seconds, I returned to my parking space at the curb. It was almost as if I hadn't left at all. Jim carried the printer out of the lab immediately. I would have been more thankful that he was so accommodating if I didn't want to beat his candy ass into mulch right then.

"Thanks for coming back, Calvin."

"My pleasure, Jim," I said, opening the hatchback of the station wagon, almost gagging on my own lies..

After loading the printer, he walked back around to the passenger window and said, "So you'll be sure to bring back the old printer, won't you?"

"Of course."

"Hey, nice rose you have there. Is that for your wife?"

Suddenly embarrassed, I played the comedy card.

"Uh, no. Actually, it's for you," I kidded.

"I'm flattered, but I'm married," Jim laughed, exposing his entire set of pearly whites.

"So am I. I won't tell if you won't!"

My sides, my sides... I kill me.

"Oh, one more thing," he added.

Damn me all to fuck. I waited too long.

"I really hate to impose, but can you possibly take a stat out to County Hospital? Julie's in kind of a bind and I have to be in Sacramento for a meeting. I'm really running late."

"Sure!" I said a little too enthusiastically that it startled Jim momentarily. I guess he hadn't remembered that I too was running late.

"I'll be right back, " he said, dashing back inside.

Some things were just not meant to be. Some things were pre-destined, like my impending stroke.

Again, Jim trotted out the back door to my car carrying a blood vial sealed in a red plastic stat bag.

"Here you go. I apologize for the inconvenience, Calvin," Jim stated with all the sincerity of a man with a crystal-clean soul.

"Like they say, it all pays the same," I explained, unfortunately quoting Terri's earlier remark. It made feel all dirty.

"Have a safe trip."

Jim patted the top of my car and sent me on my merry way. Nice guy, that Jim. What would Mr. Clean do if he knew what demons were lurking within me at that very moment, demons that would have torn him apart like rabid pit bulls and devoured his very soul? How would you have protected yourself, Mr. Clean? Huh? Where's your savior NOW?

"Sorry, Calvin," Julie regretted over the radio.

You want to make it up to me, Julie? I wondered. You know what you have to do. When you're ready to repay your debt, maybe I'll introduce you to my demons too. After they're finished with Jim, they'll want dessert. I'm sure they'd want to start with your toe nose...

Out of the parking lot and headed for the freeway, I calculated my time loss and sought ways to regain at least some of it. I had to resign myself to the fact that my last day in the hills would be hectic. What I needed to do was keep my eyes on the prize and remember that the rose was the key to the kingdom.

At the last traffic light before I hit I-5, I found myself staring across the street to see Terri and her equally bulbous buddy Bonnie returning from grazing, or lunch, as the case may be. They appeared to whooping it up. It must have been All You Can Eat Pudding Day at the Fat Cow Trough Buffet Barn. That's always a cause for celebration amongst the bovine.

When I glared at Terri's car, my eyes heated up. Blood red beams of light shot out from the both of them, causing her automobile to glow white-hot. It blew up into a delicious fireball and their bodies were both ejected in the blast, Terri headed north, Bonnie to the south. Their charred corpses plopped to the street like two burnt, overcooked Butterball turkeys. Traffic didn't slow one bit as cars sped over their carcasses giving them the status of just some more road kill.

"If looks could annihilate," I grinned and drove away when the light turned green.

Recalling the previous day's speeding ticket caused me to keep myself in check in my mad dash down the freeway. My head whipped around in search of any trace of law enforcement on the roads ahead, behind and to the sides. I couldn't screw this day up anymore for myself. This side trip was already a guaranteed thirty-minute delay in the day's proceedings without an unscheduled stop by Mr. John Law.

Once at the hospital, I began to figure out a way to buy myself some time. Well, maybe not buy. Steal was a little more like it. It was a risky proposition because it involved shucking and jiving Thelma if I could and that meant putting my testicles on the line. If she discovered that I was lying to her, she's castrate me with a rusty tin can lid and wear my nuts as earrings. Trust me. She'd do it without batting an eye.

I shoved a handful of change into a pay phone and dialed up the Jackson draw station. Thelma's lilting sandpapered voice rasped on the other end.

"Healthfirst. This is Thelma. How may I help you?"

"Thelma! It's Calvin. I've got a flat tire. I'm going to have to start my route as soon as I get into town. I won't be able to deliver any reports you might have but if you have any pick-ups, let me know now. Otherwise I'll be in before you close," I explained. Lying was becoming too easy for me.

"Is that when I can put my boot in your ass?" Thelma rejoined in a rather sincerely colder fashion than her normal patter, instantly putting me on the defensive.

"It's not my fault."

"No, *yesterday* was your fault."

"What do you mean?"

"You missed your pick up in Pioneer yesterday. They had to re-draw the patient and I had to hear about it. I had suggest you go there first."

"Shit!"

"Shit is right, numb nuts. If you don't pick it up this time, they're going to carve me a new asshole. Then do you know what I'm going to do to you?" she threatened.

"Okay! Okay! I get your point. By the way, I've got your printer too."

"I don't need it."

"What do you mean you don't need it?" I argued.

"Do we have a bad connection or are you just deaf? I don't need the printer. I fixed the old one myself. No use in waiting for help if no one's going to give any."

I rested my head on the pay phone and considered ripping it from the hospital wall.

"I have to go now."

"Pioneer Med Clinic closes at 2:00. You'd better get a move on. How's that flat tire now?"

"It's all fixed," I said quietly.

"Good. Don't ever lie to me again."

Gulp. She was good. She was scary good. Thelma could have been Yoda's white trash girlfriend.

Though I missed my 2:00 deadline by eight minutes, it was still a remarkable achievement in driving if I do say so myself. I'm not even sure how in the world I made it to Pioneer in that short amount of time, but there was no denying that I did. I used every shortcut imaginable and even found a couple more along the way. There would be no way to recreate this amazing path I blazed across Northern California that afternoon because to me, it was all just a blur. Two things propelled me along. First off, I took my Secret Weapon out of The Collection: my James Bond mix tape, combining all the great chase and action soundtrack music from the 007 films composed by John Barry. The other? The rose was a big clue. Then again, perhaps the fear of death by Thelma's withered up, nicotine stained hands was at the core of this Herculean feat. Had I been held up at all along the way, I would chucked it all if it meant missing Sarah, still my main motivation despite Thelma's threats. I still had twenty-two minutes to spare and both the clock and my heart were beating.

I almost dove head first into the Pioneer Medical Clinic, causing the antique nurse at the front desk to have a small heart palpitation.

"Goodness gracious!" she croaked.

"Hi. Healthfirst, m'am. I'm here to pick up a specimen."

"You're late."

"I apologize, m'am."

"But you're still late. We close at 2:00. You're lucky I'm still here."

"I know. I'm very fortunate. Again, please accept my apologies. May I please have the specimen?"

"Well, I have to retrieve it for you."

"Or I can I get it for myself and save you the trouble."

"You're not allowed back here. I have to get it for you myself," she insisted, not very mindful of the fact that I had indeed been back there several times in the past to pick things up for myself.

"Do you think you could get it some time soon?" I found myself saying.

She stood in a huff.

"You're very rude…and you were supposed to be here yesterday. We had to re-draw the patient."

"I'm very sorry for both of those things, m'am. Could I have the specimen now please…pretty please?"

"Of course. That's why you're here, isn't it?"

Oh my dear Lord in Heaven. She shuffled. She actually…shuffled. What doctor in his right mind would have a nurse that was this close to death…Dr. Kervokian? Besides that, she just didn't seem to be in the right industry. On her, a nurse's uniform made this fossil look like she should be working the nuts and chews concession at See's Candy. I glanced at my watch. 2:12 and counting. I drummed my fingers on the counter with all of the intensity of the UCLA marching band. Miss Shuffle Off to Buffalo returned when the half time festivities were nearly over.

"For someone who is this late, you're certainly an impatient young man," she scolded, handing me a paper sack.

Bewildered, I opened the bag and spied a single vial of blood inside.

"Uh, what is this?"

"It's blood, young man. Surely you've seen it before"

"You don't have any specimen bags?"

"I most certainly do not. You don't keep us very well supplied, do you?"

"I'll be sure to bring you some on my next visit. Uh… I'm afraid I don't see any paperwork to go along with this. Do you have the requisition form that states what tests you require for this particular specimen perhaps?"

"Well, I have to write it up for you, don't I?"

The frustration was causing me to stammer.

"B…but I…I thought this was all ready to go…to go."

"Well, " she said calmly. "You'll just have to wait for it just like I've had to wait for you."

My arms darted across the counter and I seized her by the throat with both hands. I had meant to strangle the life out of her, but her ancient skin disintegrated beneath my fingers like some much wet cardboard. I ended up ripping her head off of her shoulders, and then spiked it into the end zone. Touchdown!

"I'll just have a seat, m'am," I said, clenching every nerve in my entire body.

Naturally, she typed up the requisition with all the speed of a dying slug buried in salt. Each hard tap of the typewriter key caused another vein in my forehead to pop. When a bead of sweat dropped from my scalp, I was surprised it wasn't a drop of blood-or a tear. She finished by 2:17. Without a care, I snatched the req from her and headed for the door.

"Thank you very much, " I said on the fly.

"Maybe next time you'll be on time."

"Maybe next time you'll be dead."

"What was that you said?" she called as I slammed the door behind me.

My stomach had become the fiery pits of Hades. I had neglected to eat lunch that day. I had apparently suppressed my hunger subconsciously to the point of the absolute denial of personal nutrition. A single piece of toast with a shmeer of peanut butter early that morning had been my only form of real sustenance that day. With all this anxiety, it was beginning to take its toll upon my system. There was an ulcer with my name burned into it in my future. Popping an antacid into my mouth, I persevered.

I knew of one more short cut from Pioneer that would place me almost directly across the road from Dr. Wilkins' office. I didn't take it very often since it wasn't very reliable during the occasional logging truck. Still, with eleven minutes to spare, I had to take the gamble so I bombed down this road with all the agility of a Formula One driver, that is, if they drove Ford Escort station wagons. The lack of any traffic made me suspicious until I discovered the answer.

The first orange sign I spotted convinced me I had been cursed. It read "BE PREPARED TO STOP", followed immediately by its sequel, "FLAGGER AHEAD". The trilogy completed with "EXPECT DELAYS".

I had nine minutes left. This was supposed to cut my time in half. Now it could double it.

A figure that appeared to be the construction worker from The Village People held his stop sign nonchalantly as I grew closer. With his rippling bi-ceps bulging out of his wife-beater tank top, he could have passed for either a male stripper or as spokesmodel for a gay porn web site. Decelerating on my approach, he extended his arm straight out with all the authority of a guy who couldn't be trusted to operate anything more difficult on this job site than that little paddle of his. Therefore, he over compensated by being an absolute asshat.

I stuck my head out and tried to reason with him.

"Hey, buddy. This is an emergency vehicle. I'm carrying blood specimens that have to go to the hospital right away. So can you let me by, please?"

"You jus' stay put, y'hear?"

Y'hear? Did you say y'hear, y'hick?

"Did *y'hear* what I said?" I mocked unwisely.

"Yeah, I hear ya."

"Then let me go!"

"You-stay-put!"

I lurched ahead. He slammed his sign on the hood then pointed his finger at me.

"You run this sign and I got your license number. Traffic fines are *double* in a work zone, y'hear?"

"Look, this is an emergency medical vehicle..."

"Then where's your red lights and si-reen?"

"I ain't got no si-reen!"

"Then this ain't no emergency vehicle and you stay put, y'hear?"

I flew out of the car and snatched the sign from his hands. Before he could react, I bitch-slapped him with it. Then, snatching him by the collar, I jerked him over my knee, giving me a perfect opportunity to paddle his ass. He cried at the first whack. Poor baby! He didn't like to be spanked.

The Flagger's radio squawked an all-clear signal to him. He turned his cute lil' sign about arrogantly to read "SLOW".

"Slow. Slow means slow, y'hear?" he ordered.

"Slow," I repeated. "Is that how I should drive or is that what you are?"

"Jackass!" the Flagger yelled at me as I pulled away. In my mirror, I could see him flick his cigarette at my car.

I had no choice but to heed his request of driving slowly through the gravel these idiots were laying down. Hot tar stank up the entire vehicle as I pulled through all the hustle and bustle of heavy machinery operating on both sides of the road like a gauntlet. Mercifully, it was shorter than the sum of its part and I was out of the area quicker than expected.

The dashboard clock read 2:29 as I flipped a sharp left into Dr. Wilkins' driveway. I became positively giddy knowing full well that I had actually achieved my goal. That self-fulfilling prophecy crap actually worked for a change. Given the rate of speed I was driving when I made the turn, a cloud of dust I had left in my wake followed me all the way to the office. I always tried to avoid that so I was ready, willing and able for an immediate apology for all the dirt I mistakenly brought with me. I could take the heat. I was a man with a mission, by gum! When this cloud decimated, it was time for me to reap the rewards.

However…

Once the dust settled, nary a soul was in sight. No vehicles other than my own sat in the driveway, off to the side or even in the back. The place looked deserted.

Rose in hand, I stumbled out of my car, not wanting to believe what I began to suspect was to be true. I walked up to the porch and read what looked like a new sign in the window.

NEW OFFICE HOURS
MON-THURS 8-5
FRI 8-12
CLOSED 12-1 LUNCH

No fair, I thought sitting on the porch steps, not mindful of the dirt. I was here on time. I made it. I played the game. Why do you keep changing the rules on me? Quit moving the bar out of my reach.

"I was here on time, GODDAMN IT!" I bellowed. It echoed out into nowhere with nobody to hear.

I guess it wasn't meant to be. To be. To be or not to be? That really is the question, isn't it? I guess not to be then is the correct response. Maybe not to be at all is what it's all about. To end it, once and for all, right then and there. I could have slashed my wrists with my car keys. It might take a while but I could do it. After all, now I had time to kill, so to speak. I could just sit there and bleed to death on that porch, rose in one hand, note card in the other. Then Sarah would know. She'd get the message.

Yeah. Good plan, except for one thing.

It was Friday.

Who knew what Sarah would find Monday morning once the furry little forest critters had finished with me over the course of a weekend? Surely they'd find my corpse to be such a delectable treat they could have gnawed on my decaying flesh to their little hearts desire, picking my bones clean just in time for Monday morning. The way I felt, that didn't seem so unappealing, but I really couldn't do that to Sarah.

I stood and placed the rose in the doorjamb with the card just above it. It was probably going to wilt into oblivion in a couple of days without water and care. I just didn't have the heart to throw it into the garbage.

In fact, I felt as though I didn't have a heart at all.

I had my answer.

Not to be.

CHAPTER SIXTEEN

PASSING LANE

U pon returning to the Jackson draw station about an hour and a half later, I was greeted unceremoniously by Thelma's coldest of all possible shoulders, her own subtle way of letting me know I had done her wrong. I took it in stride, not really wanting to engage anyone in conversation anyway. When I gathered the specimens she had accumulated that day and got ready to make way down the hill for the last time, I told her this would be my last day. Her resentment toward me began to fade as she began a whole new tirade.

"Well, shit fire," she bitched. "I don't want anyone else up here. I hate that goddamn J.B. You may be a fuck-up, but at least you're a fuck-up I can put up with."

"I'll be back some day."

"Maybe sooner than you think. I'm gonna run that asshole so ragged when he gets his fat ass up here, he's gonna beg to come back down to Stockton," Thelma threatened.

All I could do was shrug my shoulders and head for the door. Thelma followed me out to the parking lot, firing up a cigarette on the way. I felt I should try to make amends with her, so I turned and told her that I was sorry I had lied to her. She blew smoke in my face.

"Fuck you…and get your ass back here soon," she sneered.

The time had come to beat feet out of Jackson. I couldn't help but feel I was retreating. The war was over and I had lost.

I specifically drove down Main Street one more time. The good townsfolk who once greeted me with open arms and cheers now stood with their arms folded, faces stern with disappointment and smoldering anger. As if on cue, they began to throw things-bottles, produce, eggs, whatever they could lay their mitts on. When they pelted my car with rocks and garbage, I didn't bother to roll up the windows. I deserved their scorn. Passing the cemetery, the corpses rose from their graves and tossed dirt clods in my general direction. One of them tried to give me an Italian salute, the old "up yours", but his arm broke off, sending it sailing skyward in the effort. A black storm cloud followed me out of the town limits as an enormous iron gate closed behind me.

Heading down the hill, my reluctant trip homeward was slowed by the appearance of a tractor ambling down the road ahead of me in the same lane like there was no yesterday, today or tomorrow. I could tolerate it for only about thirty seconds and began to get frustrated that this numb-butted farmer didn't have the decency to pull over and allow me to pass like he should instead of holding up traffic. This was after all a two-lane highway. It became necessary to go around Farmer Numb Butt.

Any attempt to drive around him was met by oncoming cars heading in the other direction at a decent rate of speed, not the 10 miles an hour my new traveling companion and I were moving. I blew my horn at him, only to have him react by throwing his arms in the air as if to communicate that he had no room to pull over. Veering to the left, I spied an open spot and took it. Gunning my vehicle from 0 to 60 was a major effort and by the time I worked up enough speed, here came another car, a gray Toyota, flying down the road toward me seemingly out of nowhere.

Though I had contemplated death earlier, my natural survival tendencies kicked to life as I cut the steering wheel to the left to avoid the Toyota death car headed right for me, blaring its Japanese horror like a shriek of terror. It missed me by inches, but I was still headed toward a ditch. I immediately steered back to the right, slipping across the other side of the road in a turnout. I skidded the Escort into an abrupt, panicked halt. Sitting transfixed for a brief moment, I then screamed at the top of my lungs in a culmination of complete angst and total fright.

Farmer Numb Butt loped on by in his handy dandy red tractor, staring directly at me, then shaking his head in disdain. *The Tortoise and the Hare Redux.*

Once at home that evening, I found it difficult to open the front door since one of Karen's packing boxes had blocked it. She apologized as she scooted her belongings aside to allow me entrance into my own house. She looked rather fetching in her *Cats* t-shirt and her long brown hair pulled back into a ponytail.

"Are you hungry? I bought some fried chicken from Manny's. You can have some if you want," she offered.

"Thanks. Maybe later," I sighed. "You just do what you have to do."

"Bad day?" Karen asked with a trace of hesitant sympathy.

"Bad life," I replied as only a martyr can.

Now it was her time to sigh.

"Calvin… What am I supposed to say to that? I mean, every day… Are you ever going to snap out of it?"

"I don't know. Let's see what happens when you leave."

As if I had just pulled the plug on her, all the blood drained out of Karen's face. The last straw had officially been delivered. She had every right to spit on me at that moment. Instead, she turned her back and began packing at a more determined speed. I suddenly realized I had a future as a motivational speaker.

Needless to say I had just forfeited my chance for any fried chicken, but that was the sacrifice I was willing to make. How else was I going to react? Was she expecting me to help her pack if she paid me off with a little poultry? Screw that. Besides, on the way home, I ate a microwave burrito from 7-11 that had turned my stomach every which way but loose. The bottom line was that I had been miserable for so long that day that I had gotten used to it, so I shut myself up in my room and just fell asleep. Frankly, I was exhausted. If I dreamt at all, I was mercifully spared any memory of it because I'm sure they would have been psychotic…and not in a good way.

My slumber became disrupted the next morning by the hustle and bustle of Karen's moving day. While I lay on the sofa trying to regain consciousness, Hal, my father-in-law entered the room and hovered over me as he had many times before. A large man who relished the opportunity to use his size to his advantage whenever possible, there was nothing Hal enjoyed more than intimidation. I always found that with all that posturing he did, he never left any lasting impression on the world, certainly not on mine.

"Good morning," I said groggily.

"Calvin," Hal replied, no doubt relishing the fact that he would never have to see me ever again..

"I'll get up and get out of your way," I said, rising on not very steady legs.

"Going to lend a hand?" he asked, already knowing the answer.

"The best way I can help is by leaving."

"Typical," he snapped as he snatched up Karen's sewing table and carried it out
of the room.

Since I fell asleep in my work clothes, all I really had to do was slip on my shoes and hit the dusty trail. As I laced up my hiking boots, Joyce, Karen's mother popped her head in and smiled.

"Hello, Calvin," she chirped. "Did we wake you?"

"I obviously had to get up anyway. How are you, Joyce?"

"Much better thanks."

I didn't know how to take that. Had she been sick recently or was she just glad her daughter was getting away from me? Joyce always spoke in riddles and not the kind that required answers. I always did like her much better than her pantload of a husband. Whether she was sincere or not, at least she feigned an impression of civility toward me. In private, she probably toed the company line and agreed with Hal that I was a useless piece of bird dung unworthy of their daughter's affections. They'd probably drank a toast when they found out our marriage was kaput.

Making a hasty once over in the bathroom before I decided to leave, with included an extremely necessary brushing of the teeth, I stepped out to stand toe to toe with Mr. Intimidation again. He seemed like he was going to call me out for a gunfight. That would have been apropos given the western attire he always wore, giving him that very fashionable LBJ look. After a five second stare down, I tried to make light of this awkward situation.

"'Scuse me, pardner, but this bathroom ain't big enough for the both of us."

Surprisingly, he wasn't amused. Instead he turned and called over his shoulder, "Karen, are you taking the bed or would you like me to take it somewhere and have it burned?"

Karen stomped in from the kitchen wearing her glasses with the Hubble Telescope lenses.

"Dad, stop it. This is difficult enough as it is," she admonished.

"Hal, come on. Let the kids say goodbye. It's all they have left," Joyce said, handing Hal a box as they both walked outside to give us some privacy.

"For once, I agree with your mom," I grinned rather painfully. "I'm...uh...out of here. I'll be gone all day so take as much time as you need."

"Okay. Thank you. You're still wearing your work clothes."

"Yeah. I'm breaking them in for a friend."

I blinked uncomfortably at her, still trying to wake up but coherent enough to feel the gravity of this situation. I didn't want to face up to this at all and turned to go when Karen grabbed my shoulder to stop me. I slowly turned back to her.

"Calvin, wait. This isn't right, but...you are. You were always right about everything. I'll change. You'll see. I have to change. Otherwise, I'll lose you forever. Oh, Calvin, hold me. Hold me and don't let me go."

I shook my head in disbelief and asked, "What?"

"I said goodbye, Calvin. Good God! You didn't even hear that, did you?" Karen said annoyed and annoyingly. She removed her glasses and rubbed her eyes in exasperation.

"No…uh…I'm sorry, I didn't get much…"

"I know. Sleep. I have to get moving here…"

"Yeah. So do I. Uh…take care of…yourself. Bye."

In that moment, Karen and I stood opposite each other transfixed. We could have been prisoners of a freeze frame or even a snapshot that somehow summed up it all up for us, an easy explanation of why it was necessary to dissolve our relationship right then and there. Almost not wanting to do so because it might have been construed as a sign of weakness, we locked eyes anyway and suddenly grew ill at ease, knowing full well we might be on the verge of an honest emotion.

Now what? Should we kiss? Shake hands? Or maybe we should just walk away without another word as a symbolic gesture of how we decided to end one of the great love affairs of recent history in such a feeble fashion without any effort to try to salvage it at all.

No. I made a decision and moved on it.

I threw my arms around Karen and hugged her. It hadn't been more that a couple of seconds, but it was enough to make me reconsider everything. Just as I had imagined her saying to me, I didn't want to let her go. She returned the gesture, but I broke off as swiftly when she started. As I pulled away, I threw in a quick peck on the cheek, then brushed the other with my hand ever so affectionately. I smiled faintly, and then walked out the front door.

Hopping into my work vehicle, I sped away from my own home, not wishing to have anything more to do with the move, the day or even the marriage. I drove only a couple of blocks around the corner to the east side parking lot of Oak Park just behind Billy Hebert Field. Almost immediately, the tears poured out of me in a last ditch attempt to wash the pain of this failure in my life. After about ten minutes of continuous bawling and blubbering, I was spent. My tear ducts came up empty. I sat quietly allowing my levels to return to normal when I came to the realization of how therapeutic this emotional release had been. The pressure from the intense stress I had been buried under, while not disappearing entirely, at least afforded me some much needed breathing room for a change. I had purged my system.

Now it was time for a new beginning.

With that thought in mind, I drove to Denny's for a Grand Slam breakfast. I had sausages instead of bacon.

CHAPTER SEVENTEEN

DO OVER

With a bellyful of Denny's, I set out back in the world for some major wanderin' and ponderin'. Instead of moping about on what started out to be the darkest day on planet Earth, I had to do some serious thinking about my immediate future, namely what happened when I returned to an empty house. I felt it best to maybe get out in the open air and perhaps take in what passed for a little nature in Stockton instead of taking a nice long drive to clear my head. For one thing, a nice long drive to me was just another day behind the wheel. Why would I want to do that on my time off? For another, I was driving a company car off-duty, not having one to call my own. Karen and I shared one car and since she brought it into the relationship, she took it with her. Therefore, whatever driving I could get away with that day had to be done away from the main thoroughfares and on as many back roads as possible. Using a company vehicle for personal use would be grounds for certain expulsion or fired on the spot, if you will.

What I settled for was a walk through Dentoni Park, located on Stockton's north side. Back in the mid 1960s, the area where Dentoni Park now sits was the main location for the Paul Newman film *Cool Hand Luke.* In those days, no housing developments existed for miles around, only oak trees and peat dirt and looking vaguely reminiscent of Mississippi where the movie was set. As I wandered through a basketball court, I could almost hear Strother Martin's familiar refrain, "What…we have here is…failure to communicate." (Sounds like my marriage. Ba-dump-bump!) It positively rankles me that there isn't any acknowledgement in that entire park of that influential film being shot there. I would think people would want to be aware of that fact. I mean, where the hell did Luke eat all them eggs anyway? More importantly, where did Lucille wash that car of hers? Once again it just proved my point that there is no sense of history anymore. How are we ever going to know where we're going if we don't know where we've been?

Maybe the real truth of the matter was that I dwelled on the past far too much. I had a tendency to focus on what might have been which caused me to harbor so much regret that it had brought any further mobility to a grinding halt. It weighted me down like an anchor to the world. Of course, the very thought of this only served to add to the pile because I didn't know how to not feel sorry for myself. How could I when every one of my days had been filled with enough disappointment to depress a birthday clown?

I began to face up to what I had become and had come to the crystal clear realization that I hated this version of myself with every fiber of my being. This brooding, intolerant and hateful psychopath could kill the person I was truly meant to be if I continued to allow him to survive. No wonder Karen left. This wasn't the guy she married. And what about this nonsense with Sarah? When did I turn into a stalker? My mind reeled as what I perceived to be the reality of my situation began to sink in. I had to question whether I was overstating my case as I usually did or had I actually hit the nail on top of my head. Psychopath seemed a tad radical, didn't it? And what about that stalker accusation? My feelings for Sarah felt so genuine. On the other hand, I could just as easily been so delusional that it was entirely possible I could no longer see the forest for the trees because I was lost in the fucking woods. I grew more confused than ever. At least I knew why. It all stemmed from pain, the ongoing onslaught of constant pummeling to my very soul. I was bruised and battered. Now it was time to heal. Then maybe I could sort it all out and come up with some sort of coherent answers somewhere down the line. I only hoped I had the strength to allow that to happen before I surrendered completely because I was wearing out fast. I could feel the life draining out of me and became afraid I'd soon be too tired to do anything about myself at all.

Requiring a little nurturing, I decided to call on my mother, something I had put off for longer than I could remember. It had been almost two months since we had any semblance of a conversation. Lately, I was given to just drop the rent check for the house in the mail without even a note. She and Karen had never really gotten along and I, being the good hubby, always took my wife's side until I declared myself Sweden so they'd both leave me the hell alone. The other thing that kept me away was that I hadn't been so crazy about her current living situation.

After my dad passed away, Mom became a virtual recluse, leaving the house only for work and returning home to shut herself into her hard candy shell until it was time to leave again. Fortunately, her friends rallied forth and dragged her off to her old haunts, places she and my father would frequent on a regular basis. Before long, she became a social butterfly again and stepped out on the town quite regularly. Her favorite spot had been The Maraca, a quaint restaurant/bar in downtown Stockton, kind of like *Cheers* with chips and salsa. It was there that she met and fell in love with Andy Gardea, a former dock worker who had been on permanent disability after an on the job forklift accident screwed up his right knee more or less permanently. With nothing else to do, this afforded him more free time to spend at The Maraca and con mi madre. After what I considered to be too short of a period of time, Mom moved out of the house she lived with my father and into what could only be called Andy's digs. My mom…living in sin… Oh, the shame of it all…

Physically, Andy could have passed for a Latin version of my dad, Sam. His slight build and angular features were right out of the Sam Wheeler Handbook, though Sam would never have worn any Vitalis in his hair. Who even knew that they still made Vitalis? Personality-wise, Andy couldn't hold a candle to my pop. For one thing, he didn't have the brainpower. Also, as gregarious as he tried to be, Andy always managed to come off abrasive. If they ever had met face to face, my dad would have cleaned Andy's clock just for being a dildo.

But I didn't have to like him. My mom did. As long as he treated her okay, then it was okay for me too. I just didn't want to be around them, that's all. It didn't seem quite right to me.

Still in all, I really wanted to see my mom, so I kept my dislike for Andy in check as I pulled up in front of the house they shared which, coincidentally enough, was just around the corner form The Maraca. Yes, their favorite watering hole was just within staggering distance. How convenient. As I walked to the porch, I saw Andy's burgundy mint condition '77 Chrysler Imperial sat in the driveway. I never could imagine my mom sitting inside it. Delores del Rio maybe, but not Alice Wheeler. The front door was open behind the screen door, so I decided not to knock and just peek in with a holler.

"Mom?" I called. "You home?"

"Who's that? Calvin?" I heard Andy say. Peering in to the left, I could barely see him lying on his hideous turquoise 1970s Naugahyde couch watching a baseball game on TV.

"Yeah, it's me, Andy."

"Come on in, man. You don't need no invite," he invited.

Reluctantly, I stepped inside Casa Gardea, squinting as my eyes adjusted to the darkness. Andy had always maintained a cave-like atmosphere in that house, not unlike a garishly decorated wine cellar. He made no attempt to rise from his undoubtedly comfortable position, on his back sans shirt so that I wasn't spared the sight of his bony, shriveled, hairless chest. I tried to shake the image out of my head of my mom, upon seeing this dehydrated chipotle lying on the couch, saying, "That's my kinda man!"

"Alice! Hey, Alice!" he yelled loudly and loutishly.

"What?" Mom replied from the kitchen area.

"Come see your son!"

My mother walked into the living room wearing a black T-shirt with an airbrushed image of some obscure hip-hop artist, a pair of forest green stretch pants and her curly brunette hair impeccable as always. She appeared to be shorter than the last time I saw her. Maybe living with Andy had shrunk her. The look on her face seemed to suggest she had expected someone else and I was right.

"Oh, Calvin. I thought it was Jason," she declared, walking over to kiss my cheek.

"Why would it be Jason? He hasn't been around for about five years now," I said.

"It's not like I see you much either, you know. Give me a hug," she admonished as I complied.

"What's with the shirt?" I asked, wondering if my mom's musical tastes had changed. "I thought you were into heavy metal."

"Oh, this belongs to one of Andy's nephews. I'm just doing laundry. What about you? Did you work today?"

"No. Why?"

"You're wearing your uniform."

"I like it. It's comfy."

"What did you do, sleep in it?"

"That's crazy talk," I pshawed.

"Don't you own an iron?" she smirked back.

"Yeah, but it's in the shop."

I missed this give and take with my mom. It reminded me of better times.

"Calvin!" Andy suddenly exclaimed, breaking whatever mood had been set. He always seemed to chime in at inappropriate times to draw attention to himself.

"Yeah, Andy. I'm right here within range."

"You want a beer?"

Even though it was before noon, I decided to be sociable.

"Sure. I'll have a beer."

"Hey, Alice. Go get your son a beer. Get me one too. C'mon, chop-chop!" Andy ordered.

"Chop-chop?" I wondered aloud.

"Yeah, you gotta know how to treat a woman," Andy smiled with a wink. "Let's go, woman!"

"Forget the beer, Mom. I don't want one."

"I do," he said.

"Then why don't peel your scrawny ass off the couch and get it yourself?" I asked, obviously perturbed.

"Hey, what's your problem?"

"You're my problem. Don't boss my mom around."

"I'm just kiddin' around."

"Yeah, very funny. Why don't you save it for open mike comedy night down at The Maraca?"

"Calvin! Stop it!" my mom insisted. "Is that why you came over here…to cause trouble? I'll get your beer, Andy."

"I don't want no beer now," Andy said like a petulant child.

"Double negative, Andy," I corrected.

"Yeah, well, double…double bubble your trouble too!" he babbled as he fidgeted agitatedly on the couch without rising at all.

"Point well taken," I smirked.

Mom returned with Andy's beer, an open can of Milwaukee's Best, and pounded it on the coffee table next to him.

"Here. Drink the damn thing. And you, come outside with me right now," she said, pulling me by the arm through the screen door to the porch. "Thanks a lot. Now we're probably going to end up fighting all day."

"You let him order you around like a servant girl?"

"That's just his sense of humor."

"Yeah, he's a regular Desi Arnaz."

"What is wrong with you today?"

"You can do better than him. Remember that guy…what was his name? Oh yeah. Dad."

"Andy is a fine man. He treats me like a queen."

"Yeah. A Dairy Queen."

"That's enough!" she said angrily, dragging me even further away from Andy's earshot. "Now you listen to me, Calvin and you listen to me good. I happen to love Andy and if you don't like it, well that's just too goddamn bad for you, mister."

"Then why don't you marry him?" I taunted.

Without hesitation, she replied, "We've talked about it."

Pow! Right into my already hemorrhaging heart.

"Oh, fuck me…"

"Hey! You watch your language. I am still your mother."

"I'm sowwy, Mommy. Wanna wash my mouf out wif soap?" I teased just like the little asshole I could be.

"What the hell are you doing here? Why don't you go home and fight with Karen?"

"Well, I've got ya there, lady. I can't go home and fight with Karen. Would you like to know why? Because she's gone, that's why. At least, she probably is by now."

Mom's face contorted as though I was being a sarcastic prick.

"Gone? What do you mean gone?"

"You know how before, she was here? Well, now she isn't," I answered like a smart ass. Then the words grew thicker as I spoke the truth. "She's gone, Mom. Karen left me."

I reined in my emotions with everything I had. There was no way I was going to let Andy see me cry on my mom's shoulder.

Mom moved closer, furrowing her brow sympathetically.

"Oh, honey... When did this happen?"

"Today. She's packed everything up and took it away," I said, cramming my hands in my pockets.

"Is she coming back?"

I looked at her in disbelief, wondering if she had had a couple of beers herself that morning.

"Only if she forgot something. Did you hear me when I said she packed everything up?"

"Cal, why didn't you tell me?"

The maternal comforting I felt I needed began to have the opposite effect on me. It just made me want to lash out.

"What am I supposed to do-run over here and cry to my mommy even time I have a problem? Are you going to give me a graham cracker and tell me what a good boy I am? That shit does not cut it, Mother."

Coldly, she snapped back, "Then why are you here now?"

"Good question. I'll get back to you," I said, heading for my car.

"Cal! Calvin! Come back here!" my mom called to no avail. I had already started my engine and sped away without looking back.

I floored it as I spied the traffic light at the end of the block turn green. Before I reached the intersection, a beat-up red, white and rust Chevy pickup loaded to the tits with gardening tools and refuse had run the red light and cut me off, missing me by mere millimeters. I stomped my brakes with both feet, causing the back of my car to rise up and bounce as it came to a merciful halt before I got creamed. I sat transfixed and unable to move forward. I couldn't make out the driver, so I had no face to pin any blame to. The truck had turned off onto another street in a blur as if it hadn't existed at all.

Had I not been so shaken up, I might have followed. It had happened so quickly that it rattled me right to the bone. In my rear view mirror, I saw my mother standing on the curb, her hand covering her mouth in shock.

Another life lesson learned in the wink of an eye. This how fleeting this all this at any given time. Had my reflexes not been so keen right then, I could have been broadsided and, at the rate the pickup was traveling, possibly killed instantaneously. If not, perhaps I'd be crippled for the remainder of my days or, best-case scenario, severely injured, never to lead a normal life again. Besides that, I was driving a company car. Worst-case scenario, I'd be dead AND fired. That's what I get for talking back to my mother.

I could see her scurrying down the street toward the intersection, more than likely to see if I was all right. I stuck my head out the window and waved back to her to signal that I was okay. Since it seemed safe to move on, I did, leaving my mother to wonder what the hell she had ever done to make her son hate her so much. Of course that wasn't true, but it sure would have sucked if that truck had killed me before her very eyes and that stupid argument were the last words we had spoken to one another.

I guess I should have had that beer after all.

By five o'clock that afternoon, I felt it was time to return home. Karen was nothing if not efficient and I probably could have gone back by noon, but I wanted to give her enough space in case she needed more time. Besides, we already said our goodbyes. When I turned onto my block, Karen and her folks were long gone.

The house was pretty much of a hollowed out tree trunk without Karen's belongings. She was extremely generous in the items she left behind, various pieces of furniture she no doubt thought she could do without or just reminded her of the life we had shared.

Still in all, she brought a lot into the marriage and certainly was entitled to anything she took away. I wouldn't have begrudged her a goddamn thing. The only item that gave me a little twinge was our wedding album, which she left on the sofa in the sewing room almost purposefully in plain view. I suppose I should have thumbed through it and had another good cry about the tragedy of it all. Instead, I stashed it in the closet with my board games, right underneath *Sorry.*

I had also been surprised Karen hadn't taken the answering machine, which signaled that someone had left a message. Pressing the play button, my mom's unmistakable recorded voice called out to me.

"Cal honey, I hope you're okay. I couldn't believe my eyes when I saw that truck almost hit you. My heart just stuck in my throat. I wish you had let me talk to you some more. It seems like all we ever do is fight and that just seems so wrong. I know you're hurting right now but I just want you to know…"

I heard Andy calling her in the background.

"Alice! Hey, Alice!"

"Andy, I'm on the phone, for Christ's sakes. Hold onto your water. Anyway, honey, I'm here for you if you need to talk. Please call me back. I love you."

Before the message ended I heard Andy call my mom again. If ever there was a guy that needed a swift kick in the nuts on a daily basis, he'd be near the front of the line.

After I rearranged what I had left in the house and turned it into a bachelor pad in the style of early Unabomber, I decided to take another trip down Memory Lane by reviewing everything I had on *ABRACADABRA.* This became my main focus of the rest of the weekend and the best therapeutic workout I could have engaged in. It turned out to be just what Dr. Wheeler ordered as I dove into the entire saga headfirst and didn't come up for air for the next day and a half. My main problem with *ABCD* was that I had been unable to complete it. There never seemed to be any conclusion suitable enough for this tremendous epic I had concocted. All the pieces were there, but they had never been put together as a cohesive whole. In fact, that's what lay smack dab in the final third…one big hole, an obstacle that I had never been able to navigate around and move forward. I had kept trying to fix whatever had come before when it wasn't broken. Now all I had was a mess.

Suddenly, I found a solution. I had to kill off a major character, one that had driven the plot up until a certain point, but soon became…well, pointless. Kala had to go. As I began to formulate a very touching and noble death scene, it all began to make sense again. The tragedy of her demise was the emotional motivation I had been struggling with for who I consider to be the story's main hero, that being Amod de M'Dau and would give he and Solan Kryne's final confrontation the strength it needed. Finally here was a necessary plot device for both *ABCD* and my own life story. After all, Karen had been the inspiration for the character of Kala. When I placed her into the story, the entire genesis of the story began to take shape. My love for Karen had driven the entire project up to that point. So it wasn't a coincidence that when my marriage began to unravel, so did the storyline. Now that Karen was no longer in my life, this was the inspiration I had been looking for and seemed to be the most logical thing to do. Eliminating Kala allowed me to fully accept Karen's departure. I was fixing two problems in one fell swoop.

This entailed a major revision in both *ABCD* and my own life. I didn't mind a bit. Both required an entire reconstruction, which was necessary in order for both of us to survive. I was up to the challenge. I needed to reinvent myself and perform some internal plastic surgery after all the damage I had incurred in the last few years. The right track had presented itself and there wasn't any way I couldn't take it.

But that nagging voice inside of my head just couldn't shut the fuck up. He had to open his yap and remind me of what had occurred that afternoon. What if it had all come together and, just when I rounded the corner for home base, God snapped his fingers and sent another pickup truck to run another red light. This time, the truck might be a little faster or slower and we'd collide this time. It wouldn't matter if it was the old Calvin or the new improved Calvin. It would be just Calvin the Casualty.

Oddly enough, I found this line of reasoning liberating. I could begin again. I could have a do over. Why not? After all, it could all end tomorrow, just...like...that.

Living in the now can be a little creepy.

Amazingly, I worked on *ABCD* all through Saturday night into Sunday morning all the way through the afternoon and finally calling it quits somewhere around the time *60 Minutes* began. I had fortified myself with massive doses of caffeine and not much else, save for the occasional toast and peanut butter, which, after five slices, tended to get a little monotonous. I had written everything in longhand and ended up with three full legal pads, using both sides of the paper and a wide variety of scrap paper I had at my disposal. By the time the sun that I hadn't seen that day had set, I was an exhausted yet satisfied zombie that need to crawl back into the grave and rest. Even the living dead get tired.

The phone rang but I had no desire to pick it up since it was probably my mom checking in on me again. Instead, I heard another familiar voice, one that struck not so much fear but nausea in the heart of my soul and my stomach. It was Terri. Hearing those dulcet yet flabby tones over my answering machine nearly caused me to lose my toast and peanut butter.

"Hi, Calvin. This is Terri. I need you to come in a half-hour earlier tomorrow since you're beginning your new route tomorrow. Hey, at least you get off work earlier, huh? Also, don't forget that you're riding with Jill, so be on your best behavior."

What the fuck did that mean? Was she trying to be funny?

"Okay, we'll see you tomorrow and I hope you're not going to be late. Have a good evening. Oh, and hi, Karen. Bye."

I couldn't wait to erase that message. If only I could erase my memory of her completely.

As gratifying as the previous twenty hours had been working on my dream project, the nightmare that had been my day job was going to do me in if I let it. I dreaded returning to the lab Monday morning as it was without the added torture of starting the Lodi route and accompanying Jill as I learned it. Too exhausted to fret about it, I collapsed in a heap, deciding to let tomorrow take care of itself. What I had accomplished that weekend was too important for my well being to allow anything to ruin it. I had to persevere, to prioritize, to…sleep, perchance to dream…the impossible dream…to fight the…zzzzzzzzz…

CHAPTER EIGHTEEN

GEE WHIZ

Jill Kemper never stopped talking. In fact I don't think I ever I saw her with her mouth closed. She talked when others were talking. She talked when she ate. She probably talked in her sleep. Death might have shut her up temporarily until she'd latch onto a psychic just so she could talk from beyond the grave.

As much as Jill talked, she never said anything, not of any substance anyway. It was non-stop, nonsensical blather, constant yapping about absolutely nothing. She had zippity-doo-dah to add to any conversation except the sound of her own voice. In the grand scheme of things, she wasn't anything more than a back-up singer.

The women in the lab all loved Jill. Oh, she was everybody's best friend. I'm sure she truly was a nice person. I base this assumption on what everyone said about her. "Jill is so nice." "Isn't Jill nice?" "That

Jill…she's really nice, isn't she?" I concluded that she probably didn't have a mean bone in her whole body. Of course, none of her bones were the least bit interesting, but she might make it into Heaven, boring the crap out of the rest of the angels.

As far as I was concerned, she was totally useless. The woman didn't have a brain cell to speak of. Maybe they all vacated the premises in order to get a little peace and quiet. I had been cordial with her in passing, but that was about it. I suppose she wasn't bad looking and, for her age of just on the 50-yard line of forty, still maintained some acceptable female attributes, like what J.B. termed "sweet sweater meat", but then again, he'd get a hard on passing a dairy farm. I had no attraction to her at all. She gave me the impression of a substitute English teacher who couldn't spell. I suppose what really rankled me was that Jill was such a dishrag. While I only picked it up in passing, she seemed to be bringing passive-aggressive behavior to new heights. Everyone stepped on this woman-men, parents, kids, and friends alike. Anyone and everyone could take a shot at her and she'd let them. Then she would talk about it all…endlessly.

This is what I had to look forward to in the next couple of days. Much ado about absolutely nothing. In other words, a slow, lingering torture.

Before I drove into work that morning, I vowed that I would suck it up and stick it out for the duration of the workday so that I could get back to what I really wanted to do with my life since that was the most important thing to me. As soon as I opened the employee entrance door and heard that rapid-fire nasal twang that was Jill's voice, I immediately reneged on my promise and fell several flights into the Dreaded Depths of Despair. I realized right then and there that I had the constitution of a jellyfish. It didn't help that

Jessica's lisping rejoinders were intermingled with Jill's. It was far too early in the day for carping magpies in stereo.

Upon seeing me, Jessica rushed over to me as I clocked in for the day.

"Hi, Calvin. Howth it going?" she asked with an insipid, anticipatory grin on her face.

"Swell," I answered suspiciously.

"You don't thound thwell."

"What do you want from me-a song? It's Monday. It's morning. It's this place. It's talking to people before I've had my coffee. What do you want from me?" I explained on my way to the break room. Jessica trailed behind me like a puppy.

"I underthtand you're riding with Jill thith week."

"Good news travels fast. What wonderful route did you end up with?" I asked, pouring myself a cup.

"Thtat."

"So you're the new stat driver. Want to trade?"

"Terri won't let uth trade. I already athked."

"That figures. I guess I'm stuck going to Lodi."

"With Jill."

"Yeah. With Jill…temporaily. What's your point, Jess?"

She sat on top of one of the tables, facing me with her itty bitty legs dangling like a toddler on Santa's lap. Sighing sincerely, she looked at me almost sweetly with a broken little smile. If she hadn't been trying my patience, I would have thought she was as cute as a button. As it was, I was about to throw hot coffee in her face if she didn't get to the goddamn point in the next few seconds.

"She thinkth you don't like her."

"Who?"

"Jill."

I rolled my eyes so severely I didn't think they'd pop back into place.

"What's to like?"

"I'm theriouth."

"Okay. I like her. I like her so much I want to carry her books home from school. I'm thinking about asking her to the prom."

"Calvin…"

"Again, I ask you, what do you want from me, Jessica?"

"Juth be nithe to her. She'th a good perthon."

"Yeah, you know what? So am I. So are you. We're all nice. But who cares? I'm still going to Lodi and I don't want to."

"Well, don't take it out on Jill. She'th very thenthitive. I'm theriouth. You hear what I'm thaying? It'th not her fault."

I leaned against the sink and rubbed my face in a slow burn. When I looked at Jessica, those two big brown eyes had widened like a Keane painting. Suddenly I couldn't resist her. Jessie was awful damn cute. I could also look down her blouse from where I was standing.

"I'll be a good boy, Miss Jessie."

"Thank you. That'th all I'm athking."

I walked out of the break room with my coffee and Jessica in tow. Looking across the lab, I could see Jill jabbering to Terri about this, that and nothing at all. From that moment on, I knew I was doomed. Call it a hunch.

Off and running…Jill's mouth, that is, which moved at a faster rate of speed than her driving as we headed down I-5 to Lodi. Safety first is one thing, but this was ridiculous. We weren't just traveling below the posted speed limit. We were damn near coasting the entire way in the slow lane while her mouth was a virtual Autobahn. I, being the trainee, took the undesirable role of passenger. At least I got to ride shotgun instead of in the back seat like Miss Daisy. Meanwhile, the slowest driver on the planet sat behind the wheel of this particular Healthfirst vehicle and babbled on like there was no tomorrow.

"I know this isn't easy for you because it isn't easy for me either. I know you didn't want to switch runs and neither did I. It doesn't make any sense to me to switch runs. Why does Terri want us to switch runs?"

"Because she's an idiot, " I groused.

"You don't like her, do you? I know you don't like her. Even though you don't like her, deep down, she's really a sweet person."

"No, deep down, she's really an idiot."

"Well...she's always been good to me."

I decided to have a little fun.

"You mean even though she thinks you're not doing a very good job?

Jill gasped so severely, she almost sucked all the oxygen out of the car.

"She said that? When did she say that? That makes me so mad. Why would she say that? I do my job. Ooh, I'm mad. Did she really say that?"

"Yep. That's why I'm taking over your route. That way she can keep an eye on you," I explained as sincerely as I could without gagging.

"Is that what she said? Oh! Why would she say that? I do my job, Calvin. I do. I've got a good mind to tell her off," Jill went on.

"But you won't," I offered, mainly because it was true and, well, she didn't have a good mind.

Jill began to weaken. The marshmallow that almost roared.

"Well, I know but… I'm so mad right now. That hurts. I can't believe she'd say that about me. What would make her say that?"

I grew weary of this line of teasing since it was too readily apparent that being simple-minded, Jill would do nothing but talk about this one thing all day. Besides it was too easy. It was like fishing with a bazooka. This woman was fragile to the point of being unstable. Did I really want to hurt her feelings? Not really. I was just being a brat. So I nipped it in the bud.

"Hey, don't listen to me. She didn't say those things. I'm just kidding."

Her mouth fell open like a prize trout mounted on the wall.

"Oh, you're bad. You are so bad. Don't do that to me. Gee whiz. You know how gullible I am."

"I do now."

"Well, don't do that, Calvin. I'll believe anything! Gee whiz. Oh, you are so bad," Jill scolded, relieved but still reeling.

I smiled at Jill but I really wanted to reach over to open her door, push her out of the moving car and onto the freeway, just because oh, I am so bad.

This Lodi route turned out to be a virtual coffee klatch. With each stop at every doctor's office, clinic or medical facility, Jill gabbed up a storm with every receptionist, nurse, physician's assistant, associate, anyone and everyone. And all of them were just like her. It was if she was just talking to extensions of herself. There were Jill replicants all over Lodi and she made sure check in with all of them. Their dialogues were filled with more twaddle, gossip and trivial bullshit you could ever imagine or would want to endure unless you were an aural masochist. As Jill introduced me around, they all hoped I would stop and chat with them just like Jill. One harpy actually told me that I would be required to discuss *All My Children* with her on a daily basis or I would be in "big trouble". Yeah, right, lady. Not as long as I had a working testicle left on my body.

I suppose I should been grateful that her route was such a breeze. But it was evident from the git-go that it was also dull and so very routine. The monotony stared me right in the face by mid-morning and I knew that I would be bored to horrors by Wednesday if not before.

Terri's all too familiar moose call crackled over Jill's radio.

"Alpha base to Jill. Do you copy?"

The perky birdbrain in the driver's seat picked up the mike like a good little drone.

"It's your best friend," she winked at me. "Hi, Terri What's up? Over."

"How's it going? Over."

"Fine. I'm teaching Calvin the ropes. Over."

"Hi, Calvin. Over"

I grimaced and waved slightly.

"Calvin says hi back. Over."

"Jill, Bonjour Convalescent has a pick up this morning. Can you guys get that? Over."

"Bonjour Convalescent has a pick up. I copy. *We* copy. Over."

"Thanks. See you at lunch. Alpha's clear."

"Jill and Calvin clear," Jill said in exaggerated professionalism as she replaced the mike. "Bonjour Convalescent, huh? I should probably warn you that this isn't going to be pretty."

It was the first time that morning that I paid attention to anything she had to say.

Jill wasn't just whistling "Dixie". Though it appeared to be a halfway decent facility from the outside, the interior of the Bonjour Convalescent Hospital had been run down to the danger zone, that being eminent closure if the authorities found one more infraction on these premises. For my money, it would have been a mercy killing. There are third world countries with better conditions that what I saw in that snake pit. The minute Jill and I walked in the front door, my nostrils were deluged with the stench of age-old urine and feces that had probably seeped into the foundation. There was also the unmistakable smell of antiseptic that did nothing to mask this horrid odor of fermenting bodily waste. On each side of the corridor was a gauntlet of forgotten old people forced to remain in this wretched Purgatory praying for the sweet release of death. I wished I could have accommodated them. To make matters worse were the mournful wails of various patients, cries for help that mostly would go unnoticed just as their last remaining hours on earth would be. I had followed Jill down the hall to two locked glass doors in the center of the hospital. She entered a code on the keypad on the wall.

"To get into this ward, you have to punch in a really simple code: 1010. To get out from other side, it's the same number in reverse: 0101," she explained as the doors swung open.

We stepped inside to an even more decrepit group of elders, all muttering at the same time so that there was a constant droning in the room. Some sat and muttered. Some wandered about and muttered. Others still lay in beds and muttered. Occasionally, the muttering was interrupted by a sudden outburst, which no one reacted to except me. The residents of this particular ward seemed more than indifferent with our presence. In fact, they appeared rather angry. Therefore, these folks were pissed off as they pissed on themselves.

"Jill, what the hell is this?"

"Oh, this is the Alzheimer's ward," she said nonchalantly.

She wandered over to the nurse's station as I stood transfixed, frozen in place right by the doors. It was readily apparent I was the center of attention as all near dead eyes were locked in on me. Maybe they smelled my fear, though I don't know how that was possible through all the human waste. The inmates, I mean, patients began to move in on me. I was expecting Michael Jackson to pop out and sing *Thriller.*

Someone…or something…began to tug at my sleeve. I turned sharply to see a liver spot with hair and a torn nightgown sitting in a wheelchair trying to pull me down to her. She reminded me of my grandmother who had been an unfortunate resident in one of these dumps in her final days. I was all but ten years old when I rode my bike over to visit her after school one day. When I entered her room, she shut the door behind me, standing stark naked before my eyes. Grandma had been rubbing her feces all over the walls, a lovely mural of shit, *Guernicaa-caa,* if you will. With her brown encrusted fingers, she reached out to me, wanting to hold and kiss me. I ran screaming the hell out of there, never to return.

The liver spot was determined to pull me closer, but I resisted to the point that I broke free and stumbled into Jill.

"Are you all right?" she wondered.

"No, I'm not. I have to get out of here," I said in a panic. "Can we go now?"

"I have what we came for," she said holding up a specimen bag with three vials of blood. She looked at me with some concern. "We can leave."

I hurried up to the keypad and entered the code she had given me. It didn't work.

"I thought you said 0101."

"That's right. 0101."

"It's not working!" I told her with an obvious note of panic.

"Let me try," she replied, trying the same combination herself.

Again, I felt a tug. I knew who it was and wasn't about to turn around. I just moved round to Jill's other side. Now I was facing the liver spot. She tried to propel herself toward me with her one good foot, but could only manage an inch at a time. Her eyes grew intense with determination. She wanted a piece of me.

"Huh. I wonder why it's not working," Jill said.

"I don't know. Try 1010," I suggested so quickly, it all ran together as one word. "Idon'tknowtry1010."

"Try what?

"1010!"

This time it was a success, causing the doors to fly open, knocking me in the shoulder in my haste to exit. I tumbled into the corridor and exited out the front door as quickly as I possibly could. I sat on the hood of Jill's car and waited for her. She skipped over to me like a starlet in a 1960s beach party movie.

"Calvin, are you okay?"

"No! I am not okay! I will never set foot in that shithole again!" I insisted.

"Well, it's only a will call. They only have a pick up once in a blue moon."

"I don't care. I am not going back in there."

"Okay…okay…um… We should maybe go, don't you think?"

I slid off the hood and back into the passenger seat of Jill's car without a word. Jill very hesitantly joined me and we drove away.

"Are you okay?"

"Please quit asking me that. I'm fine," I told her.

"I hate to say this but…you're not going to like our next stop any better," she gulped.

That next stop in question was Lodi Memorial Hospital. Jill led me straight to the surgery department, which is where we would pick up specimens for the pathology division of Healthfirst. It had been the part of this job I had dreaded most because now, along with the blood, urine and other precious bodily fluids, I had to deal with parts, Kibbles 'n Bits, so to speak. All guts and no glory. Some were bagged in containers, other larger portions like placentas, colons and limbs floated in a formalin solution inside plastic tubs. It could have been a Tupperware party at the Dahmer house. Occasionally there were souvenirs from the sexual deviant collection of greater Lodi, AKA "Foreign objects found in rectum" or 101 things guys like to cram up their butts. This day, it was a dog's chew toy. Apparently, this was a regular occurrence at Lodi Memorial E/R. Who knew?

We began to load the specimens into a plastic storage tote we brought in from the car. I filled 'er up as Jill logged everything in a binder. Everything had been fine until, without warning, she handed me an amputated leg wrapped tautly in even more red plastic marked with the Biohazard symbol. I immediately felt faint and started to lose my bearings. I dropped the leg into the bucket where it fell sticking halfway out.

"Damn it! Tell me you're going to do that next time!" I snapped.

"Sorry. Gee whiz, Calvin. How long have you been working on this job anyway?"

"I haven't had to deal with this crap before."

"Now you get to come here twice a day," Jill smiled faintly. "You'll get used to it."

"I don't want to get used to it," I insisted, snatching up the container off the floor, which caused the leg to kick me up the side of my head. Jill looked away because I thought I saw her start to laugh. You know, there's nothing like a little slapstick to brighten up someone's day.

Stomping back to Jill's car, I could only think how well I had shielded myself from having to deal with all these gutty-wuts in the whole time I had worked for Healthfirst. I had gotten used to hauling blood, urine and pap smears to the point that I didn't give them a second thought. They seemed somehow a little more tangible. Maybe their size had something to do with it. Carrying this plastic container full of shark chum brought it all home to me. Now I had the pleasure of this task twice daily, five days a week. Oh joy. Oh bliss. Oh happy, happy day.

Of course, once back into the car, Jill couldn't stop talking about it. I think she was trying to make me feel better. At that moment, the only way that could be accomplished would have been to shove her in the plastic container with the rest of the dead tissue and close the lid.

"Oh, Calvin, I know you don't want to hear this but it's really not so bad. Sometimes it's a lot worse. What I hate are the abortions. Those are the worst. Poor little guys. And Friday, I had an impacted colon and, wouldn't you know it, the lid wouldn't shut."

All the while she was yammering, Jill drove at the speed of a garden slug on a salt lick. Everyone pulled around us, obviously irritated at our sluggishness. Even a car full of nuns passed our car, shooting us a dirty look. I could feel myself aging by the hour for every second I sat there, helpless to move us along any faster. Thank God we were headed back to Stockton because I needed a break. STAT! We pulled up to a four-way intersection and, lo and behold, no one wanted to go first.

"Oh, I hate this. You can go. Yes, you can go," Jill gestured to another driver, an elderly gentleman in a

195

Pontiac. As he started to pull ahead, a delivery van to his right lurched forward. Then a Datsun full of teenage girls made their move. They stopped together in some sort of Mexican stand off, each one motioning the other vehicle to go first. Again, Jill signaled to Mr. Pontiac. "No. It's your turn. Go ahead, sir. It's okay. Go on now. After you."

It was all's I could stands. I couldn't stands no more.

"Get over!" I demanded unbuckling my seat belt.

I scooted over and swung my left leg over the console, basically straddling the gearshift and pinning Jill to the driver's door. Then, grabbing the steering wheel with my left hand, I stomped on the gas pedal, not realizing that Jill's foot had slid off the brake and underneath mine. We darted through the intersection leaving all those polite people behind to figure out who was next. Jill screamed in pain since I was crushing her foot.

"Ow! Calvin! My toe! You're crushing my toe!"

But I didn't want to listen to her. We raced down the road as Jill tried prying herself from under my left shoulder. She wriggled her arms around me and grasped the
wheel.

"Calvin! You're breaking my toe!"

Halfway down the block, Jill slipped her right foot off the gas knocking mine off in the process and pulled the car over to the right shoulder, braking with her left foot. We stopped in a lurch, the contents of the pathology tub splashing about behind us.

"Calvin! Are you crazy?"

"Were we ever going to go through that damn intersection?"

"What is wrong with you? Gee whiz, I think you broke my toe."

I rubbed my sweating face in frustration and tried to calm her down.

"I'm…I'm sorry. Are you okay?"

"No! I'm not okay! My toe hurts and you scared the beejesus out of me! We could have been killed!"

"No, we wouldn't have been killed," I reassured her.

"Well, we could have gotten in a wreck-in MY car!"

"It's a company car."

"So what? It's MY responsibility. Gee whiz, Calvin. I think you broke my toe," she complained, rubbing her foot.

"Which one?"

"The BIG one."

"I said I'm sorry."

"Well, I know, but gee whiz… Why did you do that?"

"Because…"

"Because why?"

I looked out the window and tried to think of a way not to answer her. I put my hand to my cheek and leaned against the window.

"Because…of everything…the hospital…the damn Alzheimer's ward…the leg… I just couldn't… I'm sorry, Jill. Honest," I said as sincerely as I possibly could.

"But why take it out on me?"

I looked at her pained expression and grew infuriated. Her mopey expression perfectly emphasized her status as the world's dishrag. She was so oblivious to her own weaknesses that it made me wanted to shout. So I did.

"BECAUSE YOU DRIVE LIKE OLD PEOPLE FUCK!"

It was as if a grenade had just gone off in the car. Jill was so startled, she recoiled dramatically, propelling her body against the driver-side door. Her face immediately grew ashen as she turned away from me and stared out the windshield in total shock. I could have pissed on her and not gotten a worse reaction.

My outburst even startled me. I couldn't believe what had just come out of my mouth and how powerfully I had delivered it. Immediately, I went into spin control because I had crossed so far over the line it might not be possible to come back. But I had to try.

"Oh my God, Jill. I apologize. Jesus, I am so goddamn sorry. I didn't mean to do that. I'm under a lot of pressure right now…"

I didn't want to say it but this was an act of total desperation.

"My…wife…left me the other day…"

Jill turned back to face me. The color, what there was of it, began to come back to her face. This sudden confession of mine appeared to be the antidote I needed to defuse this potentially traumatic situation. Her expression grew faintly empathetic. Considering what I had just put her through, it was more than I could ask for right then.

"Really? That's…terrible, Calvin. I didn't know."

"That's because…I haven't told anyone."

"I'm so sorry."

"Me too."

"But, gee whiz, do you have to take it all out on me?" she said slightly sarcastically.

"You just happen to be in the way. I'm really sorry, Jill. Let me make it to you. I'll drive back."

"No way! Do you think I have a death wish?"

"I'll take it easy. I'm…fine now. Honest to God."

"Well, alright, but, gee whiz, Calvin."

"I know."

As we headed back to Stockton, I had to tell her about Karen, but I swore her to secrecy. I knew it was futile because once this Mouth of the South returned to the lab, all bets were off. I don't know. Maybe it felt better for me to open up to an outsider since I found myself answering every single one of her questions concerning our break up the entire trip back to Alpha Base. I knew deep down this would cause even worse problems for me not very far down the road. For the moment, it worked. However, I needed to make sure everything was somewhat hunk-dory, at least for the time being.

"How's the toe?" I asked after a long silence.

"It's okay, I guess."

"So… Terri really doesn't need to know about all this, does she?"

She searched my face for the right answer.

"I don't know what to do. I really feel like I should tell her, Calvin."

I looked into her eyes and only saw a VACANCY sign flashing back at me. Regret began to rear its ugly head into my brain as I realized that I probably exposed myself to this twit for no damn good reason. I fought it back as I tried to convince Jill not to rat me out.

"Look, you know how Terri is about things. Telling her is only going to make matters worse for the both of us. Can we please just put this behind us and start over?"

Of course, I had no idea where I was going with this. I was tap-dancing in wooden clogs.

Suddenly I wondered how many guys in abusive relationships with Jill had given her the same line of crap in the past. But, as it has been the usual pattern in her life, she

caved. I suddenly felt very dirty.

"Okay, I won't. It'll be our little secret.'

"Thank you and again, I hope you will please accept my apology. That never should have happened and I feel like an idiot."

"You really scared me, Calvin."

"I know. I scared the beejesus out of you. What are the beejesus anyway?"

"I don't know, but thanks to you, I don't have 'em anymore."

Gee whiz.

CHAPTER NINETEEN

DOWN SHIFTING

For the remainder of that afternoon, I was the best little boy you could ever imagine. I didn't moan. I didn't groan. I didn't bitch. I didn't gripe. Why, I could have been voted Healthfirst Employee of the Year for I performed my duties with a bounce in my step, a smile on my face and the occasional song in my heart.

My personal charm level had been turned up full blast and from lunchtime on, I didn't let Jill out of my sight. After purchasing a salad bar meal for the two of us at the Round Table Pizza down the street from the lab, I continued to make Jill my new best friend, just like everyone else. Since this tactic seemed to be working, I allowed her to see the inner Calvin Wheeler, the real man underneath that hard candy shell. It wasn't long until I started to openly flirt with Jill and, by mid-afternoon, I even bought her a snow-cone.

All this bullshit was polluting me from the inside out. I had shown some much restraint that I felt my sphincter might explode. I had to keep checking my ears to make sure my melting brain hadn't begun to ooze out as I knew it would if I kept this up any longer. While I loathe the effects of alcohol on my system, I would have paid good money to have a bottle of Jack Daniels handy to guzzle as soon as this day was mercifully over.

Using my immortal soul as a human shield for any collateral damage that might have occurred had been essential to my well-being. My stupid actions earlier that day could have had severe consequences, namely being fired on the spot. I could also be brought up on charges for endangering the life of a co-worker, committing assault and battery on said co-worker and reckless use of a company vehicle. This could also have been compounded with traffic citations with the probability of a license suspension.

I was fucked. Let me rephrase that. I had just fucked myself.

Jill had me completely over the proverbial barrel. She would have totally justified in reporting it all to Terri or anyone else in the company and I would just have to face the frigging music, which would have Beethoven's 5th. However, I was counting on Jill's complete lack of good common sense, minimal brainpower and gullibility to not say a word.

Therefore, I became Rico Suave. I really didn't know what other card to play. I felt bad enough without throwing guilt into the mix. But how far was I really willing to go with this? Or would I chew off my arm to escape the trap?

Perhaps what really bothered me was that this impulsively idiotic act of mine frightened me to the core. My rage was about to spill completely over and its containment became doubtful. The frequency of these outbursts had increased and I began to lose stability. It was as if I had a fault line in my psyche. The rage continually fed off of me and grew stronger by the day. It seemed to nurture itself off my inherent fears. I suppose I was scared of loss more than anything. One thing after another, I had lost the most precious things in my life. I lost Karen. I lost the Hills. I lost Sarah. I even thought I had lost my mom. Now I could lose my job. I couldn't stand another mark in the loss column because it was causing me to slowly, but very surely, lose my grip.

By the end of my shift, I had convinced myself that this five-hour snow job-or snow-cone job, as it were-had a positive effect on Jill. She had seemed content that she had gotten to know the Real Me, even though the Real Me was a complete lie. But, the Real Me apparently made up for stomping on her big toe that morning and verbally abusing her. As she left the lab, she even turned to give me one last smile. I thought she looked rather giddy. I had pulled it off, or so I thought until I actually noticed her limping out to the parking lot.

Heading home, it finally dawned on me that that I hadn't thought about Sarah all day long, not even fleetingly. In my panicked state, it's no small wonder why I didn't. But now, away from the facade of the Real Me and my dumb bunny co-worker, I could now only speculate what happened when Sarah saw the rose I left for her and read the card. I only hoped she smiled, however sadly. I'm sure that, without water the entire weekend, the flower was in pretty sorry shape by then, not unlike the condition I had been myself the same day I left it for her.

The phone rang as soon as I walked into my front door. I had gotten in the habit of screening my calls with my answering machine, but maybe here was another new leaf I should turn over. Perhaps I needed some more human interaction.

"Hello?"

"May-I-speak-to-a-Mr.-Way…Way-el…Wailer, please?"

The voice on the other end could have belonged to a recent immigrant who used English as a second language that he hadn't mastered yet. Instead I gathered it was a telemarketer with little or no rudimentary telephone skills. Why I didn't register my name on the Do Not Call list is beyond me.

"Wheeler. There is no Wailer."

"Is-this-Mr.-Wailer?"

"Wheeler. The name is Wheeler, not Wailer."

"Oh. I'm-sorry. Is-this-Mr.-Whee-ler?"

"Maybe."

"How-are-you-this-evening, sir?"

His sincerity was completely non-existent. This jamoke was so very obviously reading everything from a prepared script including both the greeting *and* the apology. Something about this little pest prompted me to pursue this further. Maybe I just felt it was time to have a little fun at someone else's expense for a change.

"It depends. What are you selling?"

"Sir, are-you-satisfied-with-your-long-distance-provider?"

"Yes, I am. Are you happy with yours?"

Uh oh. Curve ball. There's dead air on the line.

"Ummm… What-would-say-if-I-told-you-that-you-could-cut-your-long-distance-bills-in-half?"

Gasp.

"In half?"

"Ah, now-that-I-have-your-attention, Mr.-Wailer…"

"Wheeler.'

"Wheeler. Sorry. You-can-save-35-to-50-per-cent-that-you-normally-spend-on-your-long-distance-phone calls."

"I don't call anybody long distance."

Another pause that refreshed. This was too pathetic. I began to grow weary of this game.

"Ummm…but-if-you-did…"

"But I don't. Look, Junior, I really don't want to play today."

"You-don't-want-to-save-money?"

"No, I don't. You see, I don't need to save money. I am extremely wealthy. In fact, I'm so rich, I poop quarters. By the way somethin'…why do you care?"

"I-am-trying-to-save-you-money."

"Don't do me any favors. Oh wait. There is one favor you can do for me."

"What's that?"

"Hang up!"

This time the silence was interrupted when I heard him sniff. Please don't tell me that I made the poor little chump cry.

"You know…"

"Yes?" I answered smugly.

"You don't have to be such an asshole."

I don't think he read that off his cheat sheet.

"What?"

"You heard me. I'm just trying to do my job and you're stepping on my dick."

Damn. Mr. Hesitation sounded like he just acquired a pair of brass ones.

"Really now?"

"That's right, man. You got no reason to disrespect me like this. I gotta good mind to look up your address and come over there to kick your ass."

"Whoa! That's bold talk for a minimum wage earning phone jockey!"

"I could kill you with one finger, motherfucker!"

"Would that be your dialing finger? Bring it on, tough guy!"

"Don't think I won't!"

"Where are you calling from?"

"Your mama's pussy!"

"Really? Good acoustics in there. Seriously, where are you?"

"Atlanta, motherfuckin' Georgia."

"And I happen to be in Califuckingfornia, you stupid little bastard. I'll be waiting for you when you get here…oh, say…next week?"

"I'm gonna poke out your eyes and skull fuck you!"

"What's the matter…can't you get a girl?"

"Die, motherfucker!"

With that, he hung up. I ended up really liking his sales pitch. Little did he know that I was *this close* to changing my long distance provider.

Between kissing Jill's ass all afternoon and the high level of internal paranoia I put myself through had taxed me to the limit by the end of the evening. After dinner, I decided to forego the TV and started to work on my manuscript when I nodded out at my desk, resting my head on a pile of notes. Several hours had passed when the phone rang again. Mortified by the interruption of my beauty sleep, I snatched up the receiver before the second ring.

"Yeah?"

"I'm gonna kill you, man."

"What?"

"I said I'm gonna kill you, man."

I woke right up, almost pleasantly surprised in the process.

"Is this the kid that wants to skull fuck me?"

"Yeah. That's right. I'm coming to get you and I'm gonna kill you."

"Can't this wait until morning, Skullfucker? Death threats are one thing, but in the middle of the night? That's just plain rude."

Apparently I got through to the young man if the dial tone was any indication .I managed to crawl onto the couch that I called a bed and finished my evening's slumber. I didn't bother to set an alarm and paid the price the next morning, awakening twenty minutes before I was supposed to be at work. As I rushed about in my mad dash to get
myself ready, the phone interrupted me again and, like a schmuck I picked it up.

"Yeah?"

"It's morning."

"Skullfucker?"

"It's morning and I'm gonna cut your throat."

"Good. Then I won't have to wear this stupid tie anymore."

"Fuck you, man."

"Junior, get a life, okay?"

"I am. I'm gonna get yours."

"You can have it, pal. Let's go, you little son of a bitch. Come on! What else you got?"

"Your name is Calvin Wheeler. You live in Stockton, California. Your address is 330 East Knoles Way. That's where I'm gonna find you. I'm gonna find you and I'm gonna get you, man. I'm gonna get you good. See you soon, motherfucker…"

Click.

Oh.

Well, that's a fine how do you do.

Seems like I'd just made a new friend.

CHAPTER TWENTY

LIVING HELL

Talk about persistence. I really had to hand it to the little bastard. He actually looked up my information before he set out to harass me. I had a good mind to report him, but I had no idea what long distance service he worked for since we never got that far on his first call. I thought of casually bringing it up in our next inevitable conversation, then contacting his company. This wasn't just idle paranoia on my part. Theoretically, I supposed he could have traveled all the way to the West Coast...

Giving more than a moment's thought to that little twerp and his what empty threats pissed me off. I certainly had more pressing matters to attend to that morning, like the events of the day before and what repercussions I might be facing once I showed my face at work...late, once again, albeit no more than five minutes.

Wouldn't you know that the first person I would run into would be my dear old friend, J.B., loading up his vehicle with supplies for the day.

"Hey, how's it going, man?" he asked in that cheerful tone that suggested he was moving on with his life even though I still had issues…nay, volumes!

"You tell me. How's my route?"

His face fell…both of them. It was all too obvious that I was carrying a grudge.

"Why don't we sit down and talk about this?" he offered.

"Oh, gee, I'd love to do just that very thing but…" I stopped my bitchy sarcasm to pull an imaginary knife out of my back. "Here. You might want this back."

He looked at me almost condescendingly.

"I'm sorry you feel that way."

"What, betrayed? I guess I should have expected it. After all, it's the Nature of the Business."

On that sanctimonious note, I breezed past my former friend and into the lab. Elsie spied me out of the corner of her eye as she prepared a stack of petri dishes.

"Good morning, Mr. Calvin. Miss Terri requests the honor of your presence in her office," she smiled, fully anticipating my predictable nauseated reaction when I received this news.

Swiping in, I considered making a run for it and into morning rush hour traffic, but instead, I took it in stride.

"Thanks, Elsie. You take such joy in my pain, don't you?"

"It's the little things in life that count," she grinned.

To my surprise, Terri was actually doing something productive, taking inventory in the storeroom.

"You wanted to see me?" I asked.

"Yeah. I wanted to tell you that I'm riding with you today. Jill won't be coming in."

One gulp was worth a thousand words.

"Why not?"

"She broke her toe."

"Oh?" I said almost too innocently. "That's too bad."

Terri put the clipboard down and asked me point blank, "What happened yesterday?"

"What do you mean? We went to Lodi. Jill showed me her route. Why do you ask?"

"Jill said she doesn't want to ride with you again. Ever."

Trying not to ham it up, I appeared taken aback, however coolly.

"Really? She said that? Huh. That's funny. Did she say why?"

Terri crossed her arms over her gigantic knockers like she was resting them on a fireplace mantle.

"Jill said you got very upset. Did you yell at her for some reason? You have a very bad temper, y'know?"

Thinking fast, I had to offer something up.

"Did she tell you that I bought her a snow cone?"

"Why did you do that? Were you trying to make up for something?"

"I don't feel much like dancing this morning, Terri. Why don't you quit beating around the bush and get to the point?"

"All she said was that you got really mad about something. Is it true?"

"What do you think?"

"I'm think I'll be riding with you today."

And that was all she wrote.

Swell. Just what I needed…a fucking chaperone and a corpulent chaperone at that. Apparently, I couldn't fly solo on my new route just yet even though I learned everything I was ever going to know about it the day before. Company policy. What a bunch of crap. I could have run that route with my eyes closed, which I had planned to do the very next day once I got out on my own again.

I guess I should have been grateful Jill kept her motormouth shut as much as she possibly could. She actually didn't file a formal complaint against me. Still, spending all day with Terri was cruel and unusual punishment. I owned up to my fate like a man, knowing full well I deserved it after the way I treated Jill. It did cross my mind to appeal to Amnesty International the first chance I could.

On the way out of the lab, I had to incur the wrath of little Jessica who marched up to me on her itty-bitty muscular legs and stared straight up at me in an outright glare, planting her hands on her hips.

"I thought you thaid you were going to be nithe," she spit.

All I could do was shrug and walk away. Looking over my shoulder, Jessica remained where I left her, shaking her head at me in disdain.

Looked like Jill didn't keep her promise after all.

Terri insisted that she drive while I brooded in stony silence in the passenger seat for hours on end. I had difficulty breathing, more than likely a knee-jerk psychosomatic reaction. But then again, I could attribute it to Terri's girth taking up valuable air space. Or there was the distinct possibility that since Terri herself was an absolute vacuum of a human being, she just sucked the life out of everything she came in contact. Whatever the reason, I had to crack open the window in order to survive. Occasionally, I would nod my head or grunt as we reviewed what I learned already about the Lodi route. It was obvious she was uncomfortable being with me as well, but she became convinced early on that I knew what I was doing. At first, she followed me into offices to observe my performance. By mid-morning, she didn't bother to get out of the car any longer and even allowed me to drive. The day was sheer torture for the two of us. For me, it was obvious. In her case, this had been more physical activity than she could probably stand in one day. She probably couldn't wait to go home that night and soak her weary bulk in a nice, hot bathtub full of gravy.

But, by day's end, Terri began to loosen up, feeling a need to have an actual conversation on our final departure from Lodi at the end of the day. I would have preferred the uneasy silence.

"It's really not such a bad route. It used to be mine, y'know, before I took over as lead. Remember? I miss it. Everybody's so nice. I really like Lodi too. My husband and I were going to move up here but the prices for new houses were just too high. We got a good deal on our place. Do you and Karen own your place?"

"No" was all I could manage to utter.

"I thought you did. We do. I wished we lived in a better neighborhood though. Well, I don't mind it so much but my husband doesn't like all the Mexicans."

I looked over at a passing car and mouthed the words "Please kill me" to the driver.

"Calvin, do you think you could handle the route by yourself tomorrow?"

I could have handled the route today, you ignorant sow was what I wanted to say but instead just nodded my head affirmatively.

"Yeah. I know you can. I just had to be sure. You're a fast learner. You're a good worker too. I just wish we got along better. I try my best but you just seem so mad at me all the time. Y'know, you can always come to me with your problems. My door's always open. I just want to be your friend again."

"Again?" I asked in mild astonishment. "Terri, we were never friends. We're just people who work together and that's all we'll ever be. I'm sorry if that's blunt but it's
true."

"Well, I liked you. I got you and Karen a Christmas present. "

Recalling the awful office holiday tradition of the Secret Santa, I winced at the memory.

"You drew my name. Besides, isn't Secret Santa supposed to be secret?"

"Yeah, but we all tell everyone anyway. I got something for the both of you that I thought you would like."

She sounded hurt. Like a fool, I almost let down my guard.

"Karen and I…"

My inner voice was pissed. *Shut up, you fucking idiot! It's none of her goddamn business!*

"…really appreciated it," I finished in an almost desperate tone. I nearly choked on the next words out of my mouth. "That was really nice of you. I know you went over the ten dollar limit."

"What did I give you again?"

"The Cheese Wizard."

It was some sort of awful As Seen on TV piece of plastic crap that cut cheese into different shapes, kind of like a Play-Doh Fun Factory for dairy products.

"Oh yeah. I almost kept that for myself," Terri said rather proudly.

Mercifully, the lab was within spitting distance. I pulled the car up to the loading zone near the back door and could not get out of the car quick enough. I felt like kissing the ground.

Terri pried herself loose from the passenger seat as I handed her the keys to her vehicle.

"Calvin, I hope we can get along…"

I cut her off before her parting words could finish by walking inside and straight to the bathroom. I puked up my unsettled lunch. I had hoped against hope this would have exorcised me from that day. All it did was stain my shirt.

Receiving my reprieve from the governor, my sentence had been served and I returned to society a free man. I had considered visiting my mom again, but once I turned the corner, I could see Andy watering his lawn, so I passed on by. I had no concern whether he saw me or not. I could only speculate what my own mother, an otherwise intelligent woman, saw in this massive tool. Maybe he had a massive tool….

You sick fuck! That's your mother you're talking about!

That crassest of all possible crass thoughts caused me to cover my eyes and shake my head in frustration when I stopped at the stop sign, the same intersection I was almost creamed by that pick-up truck a few days before. Maybe I sat for a split second too long, but that still didn't give the nimrod in the gray Honda behind me to blare his horn.

Indignant, I stuck my head out of the window and yelled, "Take it easy, jack off!"

Was this my unlucky intersection or something? As I pulled away, the guy in the Honda sped after me. Catching up to me after I turned the next corner onto El Dorado Street, he rode along side in the opposite lane. Once again, another Angry White Man had joined the fray and snarled at me. He would have spit bile on me if he could.

"What is your problem, buddy?" I asked him.

"Were you waiting for the stop sign to change colors? Pay attention or get the hell off of the road!" he snapped back like a pit bull with a driver's license.

"Congratulations, sir! You just won Shithead of the Day!" I called over to him, clapping my hands as I steered with my knee.

The Angry White Man turned his car into mine, not enough to hit it, but enough to intimidate me and grab the steering wheel again.

"Whoa! What the fuck is wrong with you?"

"Who's the jack off now?" he challenged.

Now furious, I began to scream every obscenity in the book and a few more that weren't at this maniac and he in turn repeated the gesture. Back and forth without any intelligible dialogue at all, we sped neck and neck down El Dorado, bellowing at each other, swear words and spit a'flyin'. I fed off his anger as he fed off mine. Passing through intersection after intersection, the intensity of this battle grew to such an extent, I became aware that a transformation was occurring. The Angry White Man began to take on my very features until he became an exact duplicate of myself. It was almost identical to that other Angry White Guy at the gas station a few days before, but this time, it was so vivid, so clear, so very real. In seconds, I saw that the person I was raging against was me. When that image pulled into sharp focus, I felt the madness immediately begin to subside as the realization of what it meant punched me right in the middle of my psyche. I started to decelerate and let the Angry White Man go on his crazy way. I stopped in front of a Lutheran church and sat staring straight ahead, watching the lunatic's taillights disappear, hopefully forever.

I drove cautiously home, still whirling from my hallucination and somehow felt safe enough enter my house. The phone rang, but I made no effort to grab. I tossed my car keys in the bowl that that used to be on the table that Karen took. They fell to the floor and I let them be.

The answering machine message began, "This is 555-7773. Leave a message…or don't."

And just who was it on the Wolfman's telephone? Why, my new best friend, Skullfucker.

"Hey! Are you home? Huh? Why don't you answer your phone, bitch? You scared? You should be. Guess where I am right now. Texas. That's right. I'm coming to get you, Wheeler. Wheeler, Wheeler, little potato peeler…That's right. I'm gonna fuck you up, man. I'm gonna fuck you up, then I'm gonna fuck you, bitch! You hear me, motherfucker! You are dead!"

As he hung up, I noticed the answering machine had 27 messages recorded on it that day. Either I suddenly became very popular or they were all from the Skullfucker. They were. I listened to each and every one of them. Then I disconnected the phone.

Sudden inspiration suddenly overwhelmed me. My hallucination on the streets with the Angry White Man du Jour and my budding relationship with Skullfucker became a creative fusion that allowed me to create a new character to add to *ABCD*, albeit a minor one. I couldn't justify using the name Skullfucker, so I adapted it to read Skullcrusher. It seemed to be a little more family friendly. Skullcrusher is a persistent little demon that will not die. Each time he is apparently slain, he returns from the dead, more vicious than ever. Torsius discovers the best way to deal with Skullcrusher is to have him deal with himself. He creates a doppelganger of the demon to battle to the death. Skullcrusher runs himself ragged and eventually tears himself apart, limb from limb until there is nothing left at all.

Jotting all this down way past the midnight hour knocked me on my collective ass. It seemed that I had run myself ragged as well and passed out on the floor.

A ray of sunlight honed in on my face as I lay, wrapped up in my throw rug I used for a blanket. I felt as though I had been in a coma for the past twenty years. As consciousness barely registered on any of my brain waves, I rolled over to get my bearings and propped myself up on one elbow. The clock on the computer read 8:38.

Startled by the lateness of the hour, I leapt into the air and ran to find another clock to confirm the time. Unable to find my watch, I stumbled into the kitchen. The stove clock, perennially five minutes slower for some reason, read 8:43.

With that piece of bad news, I dove onto the phone. I had forgotten I had unplugged it and cursed the phone company until I realized my faux pas. Pumping adrenals, I fumbled with the cord but finally found a connection. With a dial tone at my disposal, I somehow managed to call the right number for the lab on the first try.

"Healthfirst Clinical Lab, Julie speaking."

"Julie, it's Calvin! I'm very late."

"You're also in very deep shit. We tried calling you all morning."

"I'm on my way. I'll go straight to Lodi."

"Okay, Calvin, but…"

"But nothing! Gotta go!"

Within three minutes, I was ready to go, more or less. As I headed out, the phone rang and I answered it because I never learn.

"Yeah?"

"Hey, bitch, where you been?"

"Not now, Skullfucker!"

Slamming the receiver down, I zipped out the front door and heard the phone ringing yet again behind me. I had to admire the little bastard's persistence. With that kind of dedication, he could have gone far in this world.

Nah.

Thus continued the world's longest losing streak. I had to resist beating myself to death that morning as I figured out a way to make up lost time. Knowing that the best way to Lodi from my place was the back way down Highway 99, I sped out of my neighborhood around Oak Park and all the way up Alpine until I could enter the freeway from Wilson Way. In the meantime, I turned on my two-way radio and made an attempt to extinguish any flames before they burned out of control.

"Calvin to Terri. Calvin to Terri. Do you copy?"

"Calvin, this is Jill. I'm in Lodi. Terri's on my new route."

"Listen to me, Jill. I'm on my way up there, so you can go do…what you have to do, okay?"

"Calvin, Terri's really mad."

"I…copy."

I wanted to ask Jill about the condition of her injured toe as I fantasized stomping on all the rest, but decided to let it pass. There were other fish to fry that day and I was the prize flounder.

Struggling to get though the morning, I handled my tasks in the best way, most efficient way I could, even though I was way off schedule. Had it been anywhere else, I probably wouldn't have been able to catch up, but since it was Lodi, everything evened out within an hour. The route was just so damn cut and dried that I had no trouble remembering where I had been the past two days without the distraction of my two traveling companions. My only obstacles were the residents of this little burg. Lodi had become quite the ultra suburbia in the past decade. It was as though an army of soccer moms were stationed there and they all drove super-duper sized SUVs. When did these things get so goddamn big? A sports utility vehicle by itself is bad enough but these monstrosities are ridiculous. Who needs that much room? What do you do-give steroids to your minivans? Why you just get yourselves a school bus ala *The Partridge Family*? Then there are those stupidly huge 4 X 4 pick-ups that these families feel that they need for suburban driving. Do they have their own monster truck rallies in their cul-de-sacs? "SUNDAY! SUNDAY! SUNDAY! BIG TRACTOR PULL AND TAG SALE!" Those little housewives can barely see over the steering wheels of their giant vehicles let alone anything smaller on the road than a semi-truck, not to mention taking up twice as many parking spaces as should be legally allowed. Then of course there are the elders of Lodi, those who have lived in the area before the invention of dirt. Legend has it that Eskimo families deposit their elderly on ice floes, leaving them there to die. In Lodi, they stick them in cars and have them drive around until they croak. Then there was the swarm of smarmy pharmaceutical reps that picked this particular day to infest every doctor's office in town like the drug-pushing pests that they are. But even with these human obstructions, I caught up with my work in no time flat. I even made it to the hospital to pick up a glorious abundance of lovely surgical specimens, enough human insides to make a nice steaming pot of menudo. Lucky me. I had another amputated leg to deal with as well. What better way to stir the stew? I'll be damned if I didn't return to Alpha Base five minutes ahead of the day before.

  As I opened up the back hatch of my Escort to remove the storage tote full of body parts, Terri stomped out of the lab. She planted her feet and crossed her arms dramatically, almost like she wanted to challenge me to a wrestling match. Before I allowed that thought to sink in, I decided to speak first.

"Terri, it's not easy for me to say but…"

"I don't want to hear it."

"You came outside not to hear me?"

"Calvin! I am fed up with you!" Terri barked, leaning so far forward I thought she might keel over from the weight of her teats.

"Terri, I'm sorry but I'm on schedule. No clients were missed. It will not happen again."

"You're right. It won't happen again because this is your last warning."

"My last warning? Did I get a first warning? What did you do, post it in the break room?"

"I'm tired of putting up with you."

"*You* put up with *me*?"

Why was I allowing this to continue? Couldn't I just shut up for a change?

"I thought after yesterday, we might have worked this thing out, but it just gets worse. I bend over backwards to be nice to you."

"That's an image I could live without."

"I'm dead serious. One more problem, if you're late one time, ANYTHING…and you're gone," she said, emphasizing her point with a meaty finger.

"What's the matter…can't say the F word? It's called fired!"

Terri breezed past me toward her car. "I can't talk to you now. I have to leave."

"Yeah, I thought I heard the lunch bell."

That did it. Terri turned sharply and screamed at me at the very top of her lungs.

"Make fun of my weight! Go ahead! It's just going to make things worse for you. This is your last warning! I mean it!"

With that, she stampeded to her car but since I wasn't finished with her yet, I followed close behind carrying my treasure chest of pathology specimens. As angry as she was, she had some difficulty trying get behind the steering wheel without maneuvering her mammoth chest to one side and then the other. I stood looking down at her through her open sunroof. Then, as if on cue, it happened.

I lifted the plastic container up over my head and deposited the entire contents of the bucket through the hole, completely covering Terri in placentas, lungs, intestines, blood and formaldehyde. Terri squealed as though she had just fallen into a cesspool and opened the door immediately, drenched in red goo. She stood on shaky legs looking like Sissy Spacek in the Jumbotron version of *Carrie*. Gasping and choking on the deluge of crimson liquid, she stared at me in total disbelief.

I held the amputated leg in my hands. Just I had done before, I pointed to right field again, repeating my tribute to the great Bambino. Then I whomped her right in the mush with my leg bat. It clocked her right across the chin, causing her to bounce against the car door and then down to the ground. As she squirmed on the pavement, I smacked her again, this time with an overhead slam across the stomach. She actually made the sound "Oof!" Not stopping there, I beat her back the other way against her skull and again and again and again and…

"Calvin!"

I had been gazing down at her through her sunroof, plastic container in hand.

"I said I can't talk to you now!"

She started her car and backed away as I leaned against Julie's black Passat. I felt so drained all of a sudden that I needed to rest right then and there. Plopping straight to the ground, I cradled the plastic tote in my arms, but once again, I was greeted with a kick up the side of the head by the amputated leg. I probably should have let it kick my ass as well.

Why not? Everybody else was.

CHAPTER TWENTY ONE

HAZARDOUS CONDITIONS

I might as well have tattooed a target on my chest the way Life had been taking potshots at me. There is nothing more I could do anymore without being the whipping boy for the entire world. The punishment had been so constant, it became numbing, especially since whenever everyone wasn't taking his or her frustrations out on me, I'd continue the beating from the inside. My spirit began to resemble a cauliflower ear.

Some say to remain active on the job was excellent therapy for it keeps your mind off your troubles. But if your job is the source of all your cares and woes to begin with, it just adds injury to insult, doesn't it?

Not helping matters in the least was a confrontation I had that afternoon with Dr. Roberts, the lab's resident pathologist who kept an office at Lodi

Memorial Hospital. Part of the daily duties of the Lodi run was the delivery of slides made from all the pathology specimens that the good doctor could read for interpretation.

On this fine day, the eminent Dr. Roberts had misplaced the slides I had delivered to him right after lunch. Elsie had called me on the radio to tell me to stop whatever I was doing and search the car for the missing slides. Insisting that I delivered them, I began to doubt myself. Had I only imagined I completed that task? Were my fantasies moving from the outrageous to the merely mundane? Turning up zilch, I returned to Dr. Roberts' office.

I found the normally mild-mannered resident pathologist in the midst of a full-blown panic attack. Not only is he normally calm, cool and collected, he is also absolutely meticulous about his appearance. One would say the man is natty. When I entered the room, his tie was all askew, shirt sleeves unevenly rolled up and his fading hair tussled as though he had pulled both sides out with aggravated hands in a rather stereotypical mad scientist coif. He had been frantically tossing papers about in an apparent futile search of his missing work. Now he was on the phone to Alpha Base in a total rave out.

"I've looked fucking everywhere! I can't find the fucking things! I'm telling you that incompetent fucking moron didn't deliver the fucking things!"

The crazed doc jumped almost comically when he discovered my presence until he could focus his anger on yours truly.

"Where the fuck are my fucking slides?" he growled, a dollop of spit resting on his chin.

"I placed them right there where I'm supposed to, Dr. Roberts," I explained, pointing to his empty wooden IN box. I wondered what time that Mr. Hyde here would be going off into the night to kill prostitutes.

"Well, why aren't they fucking here? Did you look in your fucking car?"

After my blow-up with Terri, I kept calm but I wasn't sure how much of this insane asshole's shit I could stand.

"I don't have your slides. I brought them to you not forty five minutes ago."

"Well, why didn't I fucking see you?"

"I don't know. Maybe you were pre-occupied."

"Where did you say you fucking put them?"

"Right here," I said, again pointing to the IN box.

"Here? Well, they're not fucking here now, are they?"

As Roberts leaned forward, he had his hand on an open travel magazine. Peeking out from underneath, I spied the cardboard slide folder he was looking for. I stepped forward and pulled it out and presented it to him.

"Like I said, right here."

He snatched them away from me and spoke into the phone.

"We found them," he said haughtily.

"I found them," I corrected.

"Yes. The courier found them."

He then slammed down the phone without another word, then sat back in his chair removing the rubber bands that held the folder together

"Don't you mean the incompetent fucking moron found them?"

Dr. Roberts glowered at me. How dare I try to take him on? He could buy and sell me cheap on E-Bay.

"What do you want-a fucking medal? A fucking apology perhaps? Here!"

He stood again and slammed the slide folder to the floor, shattering the glass slides everywhere. Then with all the histrionics of a Little Rascal on Ritalin withdrawal, he stomped up and down on top of it in a full blown, grand mal temper tantrum.

Finished, but still fuming, he snarled, "How do you fucking like that, huh? Are you fucking happy now?"

"To tell you the truth, I'd have to say…no," I said.

He looked at me in bewilderment, completely out of breath. Observing the aftermath of his destructive act of immaturity, he grinned very weirdly at me.

"Get the fuck out of here and never speak of this to anyone," he quietly.

Yeah, sure, I wanted to say. *We'll keep this between us, you sick fuck. Just remember…I know your secret. You ain't so goddamn special after all, are you…Doctor Demento?*

Instead, I just nodded and backed out of his office slowly. No sudden moves here.

This little tête-à-tête might have come back to bite me square on the ass had Dr. Roberts not decided to take a few much needed days off and never mentioned it to anyone upon his return. Therefore, I remained the only eyewitness to his freak out and, if it came down to it, it would have been just my word against his anyway. But at least I knew the real truth. For once I had a minor victory to claim. Too bad I couldn't really see it that way. As far as I was concerned, it was just another encounter with an Angry White Man and it just made me depressed. If this malady could affect someone with the status of a doctor, how long before it overtook me? Who said it hadn't already?

Piling on. That's all it seemed to amount to for me. It was just one more thing to add to my load. I suppose I had to consider myself fortunate that I remained unscathed for the rest of the afternoon. Recovering alcoholics talk about taking things one day at a time. The way my luck was running, I had to take it one hour at a time. Along with getting punchy, now I was getting gun-shy as well. The Sword of Damocles became my traveling companion.

Returning home to the sanctity of my cave, I proceeded to do absolutely nothing productive, leaving the writing alone for the time being. My complete lack of energy and desire had transformed me into a useless lump of flesh with hair and teeth. Therefore, I decided to live out my role by indulging in yet another frozen dinner and engage in the most useless act I could think of, that being channel surfing on the tube known as boob.

I had no interest, passing or otherwise, in anything on the small screen as I clicked through each and every channel on my cable system, which, at last count, offered 85 different options. It spanned the whole gamut from local crap to basic crap to premium crap or even pay-per-view crap. I may have been totally lethargic but there really was nothing on my television that night. I don't care how many TV channels you have, whether it is 10 with an antenna, 100 from the cable or 500 if you have a satellite dish. When there's nothing on, there's nothing on. However, given the current state of television as a whole, even something is nothing anyway.

The one oasis I discovered in this cathode desert had been Droid, the all science fiction network that occasionally broadcast some content worthy of my attention. I used to enjoy their anthology series entitled *The Gray Area*, kind of a *Twilight Zone* rip-off that dramatized urban legends, which had just aired not minutes before I switched on the set.

A promo for the program coming up next on Droid caught my eye like a fishhook to a wide mouth bass. The advertised show was the two-hour pilot episode of Droid's new fantasy spoof, *Areola, Barbarian Queen* starring the voluptuous Alanna Morgaine whose perfectly round, surgically enhanced breasts were totally exposed in her costume with the exception of two strategic straps crossing her chest and barely covering her nipples. How she swung a sword without total exposure would have made the show worth watching all by itself. But something else miraculously interested me more than her glorious globes. This preview, condensing the entire two hour premiere, plot and all, into a thirty second blurb, complete with some well chosen action sequences, made sure this was Must See TV for me and it wasn't because it promised to be so damn good.

The commercial opened on a medieval festival in some unknown small town. An actor dressed as a wizard utters what he thinks is a fake incantation, which accidentally opens a tear in the fabric of space and time. This causes an evil sorcerer and his demon army a chance to escape into the world of today. The only person who can save the world is Areola, Barbarian Queen who follows them through the portal. With the help of several characters from the medieval festival, Areola sets out to destroy the evil wizard and close the dimensional passageway once and for all before time and space cease altogether.

I could not move. My jaw had dropped and locked into place. With the exception of the occasional blink, my eyes did not leave the television screen. My only purpose, my only resolve was to stay put in front of that set and maybe say a prayer, perhaps just a little one, that what was about to occur had only been a figment of my imagination. It had to be, right? After all, I had been daydreaming and fantasizing quite a bit these days, hadn't I? This could not be real. My paranoia had begun to spin my perception of reality way out of control, off the charts, so to speak. There was no possible way that this idiotic piece of absolute garbage could be so close to my life's work. Could it? No. There's nothing that could make me accept that. Denial. Total denial. I refused to believe this. If there was any resemblance at all, it was just a coincidence. Right?

What I was so desperately hoped would not happen started to unfold before my very teary eyes. The grand sweeping and complex epic known as *ABRACADABRA* that took seven years of my life had seemingly been adapted, reduced and trivialized into an insignificant steaming pile of total shit that probably took an afternoon to slap together. Clumsily directed, horribly acted, pathetically produced and, worst of all, poorly written, *Areola* managed to take a man's life- THIS man's life-and snuff it out like a cigarette butt. Ashes to ashes, dust to dust, all up in smoke, I was a goner-and that was all before the first commercial break. Maybe *ABRACADABRA* had been conceived first, but since it was unfinished, that was only in my head. By the time my story was ever completed, it would have the stigma of being a rip-off of a loathsome tits and ass extravaganza, thus rendering my work, regardless of the quality, null and void.

Not being able to stomach another second of this abomination, I stood from my chair as if in a trance and lumbered over to the television. I grabbed the set without switching it off or disconnecting the VCR, DVD player or cable box and pulled the TV off its stand. Hauling it across the length of the kitchen with the rest of my entertainment system dragging behind, I headed out the back door and straight to the garbage can. I kicked off the lid with my knee and dropped the set inside. I threw the VCR on top of it, followed by the DVD player and finally the cable box, shards of plastic, metal and glass sailing all about, one piece scratching the side of my forehead. For punctuation, I kicked the trashcan over, spilling electronic debris across the driveway.

I opened the gate to the outside world and loped into the night, lumbering about like the distraught Frankenstein Monster throughout the neighborhood. I didn't even bother to use the sidewalk as I ambled down the street with no rhyme or reason, right or wrong, good or bad, left or right, light or dark left in me. The only thing left was one big rotten cavity, an empty hole devoid of any substance. I couldn't comprehend the meaning of anything. I felt as though I had been the recipient of an unsuccessful lobotomy.

Everything became a question. Who-what-when-where-how-why…Yes, why? Tell me why! I want to know why. And how… How and why? How did this happen? Why did this happen? Did this really happen? What happened? Where am I? Who am I? Why am I? And most importantly of all…WHAT THE FUCK AM I GOING TO DO NOW?

The only answer I could muster up that made any sense out of this horrible mess was the harshest truth of all and I had to force myself to admit it. *Areola, Barbarian Queen* may have been total and absolute dreck, but what was painfully obvious by watching it was that if you boiled down the essence of *ABRACADABRA,* that's what was left. My masterpiece was in reality just low grade, run of the mill, pedestrian and commonplace CRAP, nothing more but something less. I had just spent seven years of my life in the belief that I had created a classic that would span the ages, inspiring generations to come when all I had just been living a lie. This was the fact I could not ignore. Even if

I continued on and kept everything intact, all the detail, all the complexity, everything that made my story so very special and released it to the world, I would always know that I was a fraud because I knew the truth and the truth was a bloody lie. The last thing I had left in my pitiful existence that I could hold onto and keep me from falling into the abyss had just shown its true face to me and it turned out to be just a mirror. *ABRACADABRA* was crap. Therefore, I was crap. Anyone with a millimeter of foresight could have seen that my lot in life, not the one that I had deluded myself into believing but the real deal, was that I would eventually become my very own punch line.

Ba-dump-bump.

The hateful thoughts that rattled in my head like a demonic drum machine were interrupted by the exaggerated sound of someone hocking up a mouthful of spit. This caused me to stop in my tracks and look toward the source of that disgusting noise. Sitting on the porch of his tract home was the kid that loogied on my car a couple of days before. Gazing at me defiantly, he unleashed the contents of his phlegmy endeavor out of his mouth, leaving a small puddle of his own vile saliva on the ground before him. Attempting to ignore him, I took another step when coughed up another, even more pronounced than the first. I hesitated again and stared back at him. He propelled this next wad of human goo out of his mouth into the air like a space shuttle full of spit. Then, he cocked his head and smirked at me. This little pissant was taunting me.

On the ground, I spotted a tree branch about the size of a broomstick probably cut from an earlier pruning. It seemed to be just the length for me as I bent down to pick it up. Suddenly I felt an energy surging through this piece of wood and into my entire body. In my hands I held the Janus Stick, the wondrous staff that contained all the magical powers of Enatar, the Dimensional Circle. As I grasped its firmness, the fog immediately lifted from my head as a sense of purity and clarity filled my soul. Suddenly I realized who I truly was in this world. My name was Amod de M'Dau, the warrior wizard and guardian of Montei, the planet Earth. I spun the Janus Stick in my right hand with a dexterity I had never known before but now felt so right. I was prepared for battle.

Before me was The Expectorator, a follower of Woraxas whose weapon of choice was the acidic and poisonous mucous it spit from its diseased mouth. The Expectorator had challenged me, Amod de M'Dau, to a duel to the death. I, Amod, complied and stepped toward the demon as he rose from the porch in anticipation of a fight to the finish. What I, Amod, did not see was The Expectorator's mother watering the lawn on the side of the house.

"What the hell do you think you're doing?" she shrieked.

Surprised by her appearance from out of the shadows, I turned to see who had screeched. A witch perhaps? Well, close. As she stepped into the light, I saw that it was Marie Chamberlain, a girl I remembered from the neighborhood. We knew each other only in passing since we lived in the same vicinity, but her reputation certainly preceded her. Marie had always been easy, but not necessarily on the eyes. Still, she had a brood of kids that she had managed to squeeze out over the years, including, it seemed, The Expectorator. She stomped across her yard, her drooping braless tits bouncing underneath a dingy white t-shirt nightgown emblazoned with a Nike swoosh and the slogan "Do it". Her limp flat blonde locks were pulled back into such a severe ponytail that looked like it probably hurt.

"I said what the hell do you think you're doing? Are you comin' after my kid? Stan! Get out here!" Marie hollered.

Stan the Man threw open the screen door and plodded onto the porch behind the kid. A man of large girth wearing too small of an undershirt to cover his hairy jelly belly, Stan yelled,

"What? I'm tryin' to watch the game!"

"This asshole's comin' after Kevin with a stick in his hands," she explained, planting her hands on her formidable childbearing hips.

For a big ol' fat guy, Stan moved rather swiftly off the porch and right for me. I dropped my guard immediately and took a few steps backward. That sudden insurgence of power I felt from the Janus Stick evaporated instantly. It wasn't the Janus Stick after all but only a goddamn piece of wood. And I sure as hell wasn't Amod de M'Dau either. Now I was just some guy threatening a little kid.

"Is that right? Huh? What are you gonna do with that stick? Huh? You a tough guy? Huh?" Stan interrogated me with each step he took, backing me away.

I lost my footing and fell to the street, dropping the stick in the process. Stan reached down and snatched it up. He threatened to beat me with my own weapon, causing me to cover up and cower like a disobedient dog.

"Pickin' on a kid with a stick, are ya? Huh? Say somethin'!" Stan ordered, kicking me right square in the ass for emphasis.

Trying to cover up, I couldn't say a word. Words just weren't forming. Instead, all I could utter were whimpers.

Marie wandered over to stand over me as well, dangling her gnarly nipples in my direction like a pair of fleshy gun turrets.

"I know this piece a'shit. His name's Cal Wheeler. He's the neighborhood freak. He's always been fuckin' weird," she sneered.

Kevin the Expectorator joined his folks, smiling at me with a look of pride that only a punk could who just watched his parents de-humanize someone.

"You want me to call the cops, weirdo? Huh?" Stan threatened. "Maybe I should just beat your ass with your own stick. What do you think of that? Huh?"

Stan made like he would club me with the stick, faking me out and nearly causing me to ball up into a fetal position.

"Kevin, you tell us if you ever see this asshole even come near you again," Marie told her son.

Kevin said nothing. He just spit on me, nailing me right on the left cheek.

"Yes!" the Expectorator cheered, thrusting his arms in the air victoriously.

"Nice one, honey," Marie congratulated her son.

"Stand up!" Stan demanded, kicking my ass and leg a few more times as I struggled to my feet. "Get the fuck outta here and don't ever let me see you again. You got that? Huh?"

I couldn't stand on my own two legs, only managing to crawl away from them as I cowered in abject terror and humiliation.

"You heard him! Get outta here, you fuckin' freak!" Marie snarled. "I know where you live, asshole!"

"Yeah, so do I!" Kevin added.

"You hear what I said? Huh? I told you to get outta here!" Stan barked. "Move!"

As I struggled to my feet, Stan chased me away, swinging the stick back and forth, cutting the air behind me. I ran away, arching my back in anticipation of a whipping that never occurred. I heard the stick hit the street, assuming that Stan had dropped it. When I reached the end of the block, I started to slow my pace when something struck my right shoulder. Wincing in pain, I turned to see Kevin jumping up and down triumphantly.

"I got 'em! Mom! Stan! I nailed that sucker!" Kevin celebrated. "I rule!"

Whatever object had hit me lie in the shadow of a mobile home parked at the curb near the stop sign. Grasping my shoulder, I ambled over to see what Kevin had used for ammunition. Lying near the back tire of the mobile home was what I foolishly believed just a couple of minutes before to be the mythical and legendary Janus Stick. I picked it up and stood in the streetlight, looking at the happy family down the block. As a bold gesture to show they hadn't gotten the best of me, I took this piece of wood in both hands and set forth to break it in half over my knee. The branch was too thick. It didn't break, but my knee almost did in the attempt. This caused my audience of three to give me a collective horselaugh that echoed throughout the neighborhood. I let the stick fall and limped my way home in a final concession that the only thing broken around there was yours truly, in every way possible- physically, mentally and spiritually.

Maybe I should have left the TV alone and hopped in the garbage can myself.

CHAPTER TWENTY TWO

FLAME OUT

O nce I was mercifully home, I dragged myself inside. I suppose it was fortunate that I left all the doors wide open since I didn't bring my keys, though I would have just broken in anyway. Unaware of what I was going to do, the phone rang and, out of pure habit, I answered it even though I wasn't sure I had a voice in which to speak. Maybe I would have just listened.

Wouldn't you know it? On the line were the dulcet and comforting tones of my ol' pal, Skullfucker.

"Hey, motherfucker. Did you miss me? I'm coming to see you. When I do, I'm gonna make you my lil' bitch. Then I'm gonna kill you."

At first I didn't answer him.

"Did you hear what I said? I'm comin' to California to kill you, motherfucker. How do you like that, bitch?"

Again I said nothing. My silence agitated him.

"Did you fucking hear me? I said…"

"When?"

The question seemed to faze him.

"When? What do you mean when? When you least expect it, man."

"No. I want to know when. When are you going to kill me?"

"When I see you, motherfucker! That's when!"

"Please."

"Please what, you little bitch?"

"Please kill me."

"What?"

"Please kill me. I want you to kill me like you've been saying. Look, I don't know you and you don't know me but I'm telling you…I'm begging you to find me and kill me. I'll even give you directions. Please. I want to die. I want you to fucking kill me! Please!"

There was that pause that I hadn't heard since his initial phone call.

"I…I said I'm gonna kill you and I am! You just wait and see!"

"No! I can't wait! Listen to me, I'll pay you to do it. I can't do it myself. I'm too much of a fucking coward. Shoot me, slit my throat, strangle me with your bare hands… I don't care! I want you to kill me, you stupid little shit! Don't you understand? I'm giving you my permission! KILL ME!"

Skullfucker hung up. I guess he couldn't take it. You just can't depend on anyone anymore.

This was no shuck and jive to get rid of him. I couldn't have been more serious. Suicide really wasn't a viable option for me. I hadn't been able to pull it off in the past and nothing had changed since then. Besides, somehow, some way, I would fuck it up and I'd manage to live the remainder of my miserable existence even more tortured than before because I would have to contend with the physical ramifications of my botched suicide attempt. I'd be brain dead, comatose, crippled, mangled-anything else but what I wanted to be which was stone cold dead. Somebody had to do it for me. Maybe I could have asked my mom's boyfriend. Surely he would have obliged.

That's when it hit me. If I couldn't do myself in, how about a surrogate instead? I could kill *ABRACADABRA.* It had been such a part of me that destroying it would be just like doing myself in, so why the hell not? This all encompassing, one true thing that I had built my entire being around for seven wasted years had just become my greatest and most formidable enemy. It was either it or me. I chose it. It had to go. Besides all it was doing now was taking up space.

Heading out to the garage, I found a shovel and stepped into my backyard. I dug a pit right in the middle of my poorly maintained lawn. This was no mere hole in the ground but a grave rather. Satisfied with its size, I headed back inside.

Tearing through my office and everywhere else in the house, I gathered up every single, solitary piece of material relating to *ABRACADABRA* I had and took it to the backyard in armfuls. There were notebooks, legal pads, files and floppy disks. Reams of scratch paper and scribbled napkins and matchbooks filled one box alone. I emptied my file cabinet of all of its contents including character biographies, costume designs and promotional material including extensive material for the inevitable action figures. Oh, what a pile it all made in the pit I had dug. After all, it had been seven years in the making. Just for shits and giggles and to make this an even more festive outing, I added all 5442 pages of *Myself 'til Now.* What the hell. Might as well make it a party.

For fuel, I grabbed the self-starting charcoal briquettes I used for my barbecue. The foul gassy smell from the black bricks wafted over me as I dumped them over the mound of paper that lay at my feet. I knelt to the ground and lit them with a wooden kitchen match at several strategic spots. Within seconds, the flames began to ignite the paper gathered in the hole and soon, my love became a funeral pyre.

The fire hypnotized me with its antics, catching aflame the green notebook that contained the love story of Torsius and Melayna Ro. The floppies started to melt, those filled with the background of the Circles of Being and the apprenticeship of Solan Kryne. A loose-leaf binder filled with the evolution of Forevertime popped and sputtered away. This entire universe and all of its characters-Woraxas, Dulee, Kala, Fred Muggs, and finally my supposed hero and savior though probably my true albatross, Amod de M'dau-burned, becoming embers floating and evaporating in the night sky. *ABRACADABRA* was flaming out of existence. Funny, but for such a large bonfire, I couldn't feel its warmth at all.

I sat on the dirt mound I made from the hole, front row center of this punk dramatization of the hoary old cliché "watching my dreams go up in smoke". How pithy. But the more the fire destroyed my work, the more a soothing calm swept over me, which I felt to be a sense of relief. *ABRACADABRA* had been controlling my life. I believed it to be a comfort zone where I could be safe and sheltered from the outside world when it had actually been a prison of my own making. What I had just done was not destructive, but totally necessary. This had been a mercy killing. In order my soul to survive, *ABRACADABRA* had to die. Here was my reprieve from the governor. I was being released on parole.

From the midst of the flame, an image began to materialize, the figure of a human being writhing in pain from the tortuous incineration of its body. As the vision grew into focus, it took the form of a woman wearing a white dress and tied to a stake like some sort of Joan of Arc scenario in reverse. When her face became clear, I dropped to the ground on both knees in utter shock.

Oh my dear God in Heaven.

It was Sarah.

She too had been a part of *ABRACADABRA* and now she would be no more.

"Calvin! Calvin! Please!" she begged in agony. "It hurts! You're killing me! You're burning me alive! Why? Why? I love you, Calvin! Please make it stop! Calvin!"

I covered my mouth in horror, staring as flames began to envelop the love of my life.

"Sarah! No!" I screamed, helpless. Panicking, I ran to turn on my garden hose full blast, then pulled it to the fire in a dead run, But, the damn thing was too short and flew out of my hands just before I reached the other side of the yard.

"Calvin! Help me! I'm burning! It hurts! Please!"

I picked up the hose and sprayed it from where it fell, about ten feet away from the blaze. Trying to extinguish the inferno with water, I wasn't able to stop Sarah's white dress from igniting, engulfing her in its fury. Her cries of anguish tore through my soul like razors while her flesh grew scorched by the inferno, raising blisters instantly across her entire body. Struggling in vain to break herself free from her fiery trap, her hair sizzled off her head and that face of an angel charred to a blackened skeleton, smoldering in the fire's wake.

"Calvin! Please! Why? Why are you killing me? Why? Why?"

I dropped the hose and dove into the pit. The charcoal burned my hands and arms as I batted away at the fire and tried to disperse it, scattering burnt paper and ashes away while searching for Sarah in the process. I called her name over and over again in pure desperation. Tearing through the cinders with no regard for the burns I was sustaining, she was nowhere to be found. The fire had been extinguished, but Sarah was gone.

My mind swirled in a heady mixture of exhaustion and confusion as I lay in the muddy pit of ashes, half-burnt soggy paper and red-hot smoking briquettes. Here I thought I was slaying the Beast when the Beast turned out to be me. Perhaps I should have set fire to myself.

Roast Beast.

How amazing it was that in the midst of a complete mental breakdown, I could conjure up an obscure Dr. Seuss reference. Any other time I might have at least grinned in acknowledgement. But there were to be no more smiles, laughs or any sense of joy to speak of for me. The only emotion I had left was grief and it had been set so deeply within my being, my bone marrow was in a state of mourning. I had officially finally fallen to the absolute lowest point of my life and now the grieving could begin. But unlike the day Karen left me, this time I couldn't cry. That seemed like a luxury I couldn't allow myself. Instead I internalized my sorrow so severely that I curled up into a complete ball, lying in this hole in the ground that very well could have been my own grave. I tensed up every muscle in my body as though I were trying to create an implosion, just wadding myself up like a discarded piece of paper. Reaching out with my left hand and tried to pull some of the dirt into the pit with me in a lame effort to bury myself. When I grabbed a white hot piece of charcoal along with the dirt, I stopped and just continued to lie there. Then I started to rock back and forth in this fetal position and didn't stop for several hours. In that entire time, I didn't shed a single tear. I didn't have it in me. I didn't have anything left at all.

CHAPTER TWENTY THREE

YOU TURN

I eventually pulled myself out of the ground and staggered indoors like a re-animated corpse. Once in the bathroom, I gazed at the image staring back at me in the mirror but he was totally unrecognizable. Who the hell was this guy? Was he a performer in traveling minstrel show? A member of Red Adair's team just back from fighting an oil fire? A slab of Cajun spiced blackened salmon? Whoever this was certainly had his share of burns on his body rooting around in the embers. While none appeared serious, there were obvious reminders that this guy should not go barbecue diving again anytime soon.

I removed my filthy clothing where I stood and stepped into the shower. After I turned on the water, I sat down at the far end of the tub and just let the water rain upon me, washing the cremated remains of *ABRACADABRA* and whatever life I had made for myself off of me and down the drain where they belonged. Reluctantly, I slowly rolled a bar of soap over me in a rather lackluster fashion, cleaning myself as feebly as only I could right then. After about an hour, I finally turned off the water, which had grown cold by then anyway. I remained in the tub for the rest of the night, both damp and damned.

At first light, I removed myself from the bathtub and managed to dress myself for work. I didn't know what else to do. I hadn't slept and certainly had no inkling that I might be anytime soon. So the creature of habit possessed me and caused to stick to my daily routine. Maybe someone had hooked me to some remote control unit and was guiding my every move. What did I know? Absolutely nothing. I knew nothing. I felt nothing. Maybe that was best for everyone concerned. The best way to get through what was left of this thing called Life was not to think, not to feel, not to care, just be a robot. Fuck the Tin Man. I don't care what he said. He didn't need a heart.

I have no recollection of how I arrived at the lab. I wasn't even sure that I brought my car. For all I knew, I could have walked there. I didn't bother to clock in since time was relative but not really related to me. I spoke to no one and just gathered up my reports and supplies for the day, shuffling about with all the swiftness of an octogenarian loaded up on stool softeners. Elsie attempted to engage me in conversation but I chose to pretend that I didn't hear her. As I ambled back and forth, she called my name in order to get my attention to no avail. I wasn't having any interaction at all.

Upon my departure, the back door of the lab swung open and I stood face-to-face with Terri. We both didn't budge as if in freeze frame, gawking at one another. Neither of us was able to move for that brief moment. She tried to maintain a stern glare at me, perhaps suggesting I let her pass. But I held my ground. I wasn't exactly in a gentlemanly mood. I wasn't in any kind of mood at all. I couldn't even hate her like I always did. All I could see was a big red headed blur. Terri was just an obstacle in my way, blocking my path. In seconds, her expression weakened and so did her resolve. She backed down and let me through. Why, she even held the door for me. I didn't thank her though. As I said, I was no gentleman.

Jim Banner and J.B. were having some nonsensical discussion out in the parking lot as I headed to my car. Had I not noticed them initially, I might have run them over when I backed out of my parking space, accidentally of course. I'm not sure, but I think Jim might have wished me a good morning. If he only knew…

Avoiding the freeway, I opted for the solitude of the back roads into Lodi. It was probably in the best interests of everyone in that morning commute that I chose this alternate route, leaving the other drivers on the road to fend for themselves and not having to deal with a man who didn't care whether he lived or died, therefore would not have given one single shit about them either. Much like I did in the lab, I pretty much ambled my way through the farmlands that lie between Stockton and Lodi, staying on Davis Road for the most part of the drive.

My uncaring state of mind included my lack of concern for traffic laws, namely the posted speed limit. I heard a sudden burst of a siren behind me and my eyes lackadaisically glanced into the rear view mirror to see the flashing lights of a motorcycle cop behind me. It didn't compute at first, so I continued on at the same rate of speed. The cop hit me with a double shot of his siren this time, an almost comical sound effect reminiscent of how a gazelle might react during a rectal exam. The message was finally delivered to Cranium Central as I turned the corner of a side road and pulled over to the side directly in front of a large ditch. In my numb state of mind, it registered that yet another speeding ticket had just appeared in my immediate future and so was a reservation in the unemployment line. There wasn't much to take right then but somehow the all mighty Powers That Be decided to take it all away from me. Not like it really mattered after all I had been through. However, in a momentary reflexive action, I punched the visor above my head and heard a crack. I opened the lid to see that I had broken the mirror. Observing my cracked image gazing back at me, I traced my face in the glass, cutting open my index finger. I let it bleed.

Any other time, this particular incident would have caused me to melt down to an ooze-like consistency, a puddle where a man used to sit. This would have been IT-the last straw. El finito. The farm had been bought. Elvis had left the building and headed out for funnel cakes. My life was officially over. Roll credits.

But, you can't hurt someone who is already dead. I had nothing left, nothing to give and certainly nothing to lose. Therefore, I could now do something about it.

As the officer began to dismount his motorcycle, I popped the car into reverse and stomped on the gas. The back bumper of my car slammed into the front wheel of the bike, causing it to bounce into the air on its back tire, just like an out of control wheelie. It catapulted the policeman off his seat and backwards into the ditch. The motorcycle fell to the road and into the ditch on its second bounce. I heard a sudden groan of pain when it finally landed.

The emotional fog bank I had been engulfed within since the night before made me question what had just occurred. I didn't think my imagination could conjure up such a vivid fantasy again since I banished it from my life once and for all. I became both aware and unaware of the situation, barely keeping afloat within a sea of doubt. Before I could accept what I think I had just accomplished, I hesitated before I stepped out of my car to assess any damage I might have caused...or if it was just all bullshit. I looked out the open window and couldn't see any evidence of a motorcycle cop. Maybe it did happen after all. I stepped out of the car cautiously, listening for the familiar cry, "All units...officer down!" When that didn't occur, I walked gingerly to the ditch when I heard the faint sounds of rustling and an engine cooling from the hole below. As I stood at the edge, I could actually see with my own two eyes that the motorcycle had fallen right on top of Officer Down.

So much for the daydream theory.

Pinned underneath from his upper torso down as well as his left arm, the cop appeared to be alive since he was still wriggling, undoubtedly attempting to free himself. Operating on what was probably pure adrenaline, Officer Down seemed to be fumbling for something on his hip. He was reaching for his sidearm. Of course he was. What else was he going to do at that point-write me ticket? I immediately rushed down to him and grabbed it before he could. He tried to knock my hand away. I can't say I was very proud of the fact that I had to stand on his only free arm to get him to stop, but I had to have that weapon. Once I removed the pistol from its holster, I stepped off of him as well

Unfamiliar with guns, the policeman's sidearm seemed odd to me. I believe it was a Glock, but it could have passed for one of those toy pistols that fire little plastic discs. I had no idea what caliber of this gun would have been, a .45, a 9mm perhaps? Ya got me. I knew it was some kind of automatic, that's all. As I inspected it further, Officer Down became suddenly more agitated.

"Don't shoot!" he pleaded.

The thought hadn't even occurred to me. Why was he putting ideas in my head? The answer to that was obvious. The balance of power had now been shifted.

Blood rushed into my head with all the intensity of an oil gusher. This moment of clarity opened up a whole new world of possibilities for me. The ninety-eight pound weakling had just become the Hero of the Beach. My normally supple hand was now a Fist of Fury. For all intents and purposes, this very well could have been the Janus Stick, the source of all power, but that was a mere fairy tale. This was the Real Deal. I had discovered strength that I never knew existed. Suddenly I had a purpose in life. I
didn't just belong in the world. I *was* the fucking world. The boy had at last become the man.

Again, the traffic cop pleaded for his life.
"Don't shoot me!"

"Take it easy," I assured him. "I'm not in the mood."

That didn't exactly reassure him since he remained covered up, peering at me over the top of his wristwatch.

I bent down and ripped the microphone off the headset on his helmet so he couldn't call in. I'm surprised he didn't try to bite me. Obviously not a Monty Python fan.

"Are you hurt badly?" I asked without that much concern. I guess I was just being polite.

"I can't tell. See if you can get this bike off of me," he ordered.

"Uh, I don't think so."

"You're in big fucking trouble!" he barked.

"Speak for yourself," I said, climbing out of the ditch.

"Where…where are you going?"

"Like I'm going to tell you?"

I walked to the corner and looked both ways down Davis Road. The lack of traffic was unusual for that time of the morning since that was a well-traveled route, but didn't faze me a bit. Besides, the trapped officer and his motorcycle weren't easily visible unless you right over him. The flashing lights clicked off when the bike hit the ground. Still, I grabbed a couple of nearby tumbleweeds and plopped them over Officer Down in a half-assed attempt of camouflage.

"You son of a bitch!" he cried back.

I stood my ground and pointed an accusing finger at him.

"Hey! You shut your mouth! Be goddamn grateful this is all I'm dong to you. Just remember, this is your fault as much as it is mine," I admonished him. "Take some goddamn responsibility for your actions. Maybe you should think about that while you're lying there."

I couldn't see his face through the tumbleweeds but I sure he wasn't staring at me with admiration. More than likely, he was probably still thinking I'd shoot him with his own weapon. Why would I do something like that? That wouldn't have been very sporting of me.

As I left Officer Down to fend for himself, I got back into my car and shut the door. Okay, now that I opened up this can of worms, what the hell was I going to do with them? The two-way radio answered me.

"Alpha Base to J.B. Alpha Base to J.B.," a familiar voice called.

"This is J.B. Go ahead, Elsie."

"J.B., Sarah from Dr. Wilkins' office in Pine Grove just called. You have a pick up there this afternoon."

Sarah…

"Okay. Write it on the board for me and I'll be sure to get that later today," he replied.

"Will do, J.B. Alpha clear."

"I'm clear."

So was I.

Don't bother, J.B., I thought. *I'll be picking that up this afternoon.*

I pointed the car in the direction of the foothills and drove away. I suppose it was a little inconsiderate of me to kick up gravel as I left, pelting my friend, Officer Down in the ditch below, with rocks and dust. Oh well, add it to my growing list of grievances. The best course of action I could have taken at that moment was obvious. I had to put as many miles between me and the cop in the ditch as possible. Besides, I had a job to do and really didn't want any distractions.

Unfortunately, no one told the daffy old dame in the green Plymouth in front of me on Lower Sacramento Road. She was probably driving into town to deposit that all-important egg money she earned to pay off the farm. She sat so far ahead in her seat that she and her steering wheel seemed to be as one. This Daffy Ol' Dame just ambled along at the speed of a candle. I supposed I just should have zipped around and not given her another thought had she not committed an unpardonable sin. Her left signal had been flashing continuously without any hope of ever switching off. Whatever turn she had made was somewhere back in another county and there was no way she would ever notice it until years after she passed away. After her spirit is summoned during a séance, maybe then she'd remember, "Oh, yes…and please go out to the old

Plymouth and turn off my turn signal." Certainly, not before.

Yeah, like that was going to happen. It's been said that you can't teach an old dog new tricks, but I thought it was high time to disprove that myth right then and there.

As I began to pull along side the Plymouth, I grabbed the Glock and aimed it at the offending light. Fortunately, the passenger window on my car was down. What a lucky quirk of fate that was. Not having handled such a weapon before in my lifetime, I struggled a bit to release the safety, a rather difficult maneuver to figure out with one hand while steering with the other. Feeling it unlock, I pulled the trigger and fired. The red signal light was extinguished in an explosion of sparks and plastic. The blast from the gun caused me to weave momentarily, the sharpness of the shot screaming through my ears painfully but somehow necessarily. I shook it off as I accelerated past the Plymouth and blew out the front signal as well, freaking out the D.O.D. to no end. Her car swerved back and forth haphazardly until she just stopped dead in the middle of the road. I too braked to a halt, then backed up beside her.

"M'am?" I called to her. "I hoped you learned a valuable lesson today. Don't leave your turn signal on. Pass it along to your other…old friends. Good day to you"

I left my student in the road as I sped away to lose myself in the confines of the countryside. I can't say that I enjoyed scaring the daylights out of that Daffy Ol' Dame. But life is hard enough if you don't bother to pay attention. I felt confident that I did a good thing out there. It'll be a long time before she made that faux pas again. More than likely because she won't ever get behind the wheel ever again. If that was the case, so be it. Maybe it was time. The world needed someone like me to come along and fix a few outstanding problems in the world. Yeah, that was me, alright.

The World's Handyman…and a damn good natural marksman, if I do say so myself.

And I just did.

CHAPTER TWENTY FOUR

BREAKING NEWS

I couldn't get Peter Falk's voice out of my head as I cut back and forth across the upper San Joaquin Valley in my attempts to avoid and elude any law enforcement officials. The entire time, all I could hear was Falk yelling at me like I was Alan Arkin in *The In-Laws*.

"Serpentine! Serpentine, Sheldon! Serpentine!"

The calm I exuded really impressed me, considering the fix I was in. My nerves had previously been worn to frazzled split ends like a teenage girl's goldilocks. Once upon a time not very long before, I would have stopped by the side of the road, stripped off my clothing and ran into a cornfield screaming for mercy and Moon Pies. Why the hell was I so damn cool and composed with this current situation? Here I was, a potential candidate for a tri-state killing spree who had just assaulted not only a police officer but also a harmless little old lady in the course of only about ten minutes and I never felt so relaxed in my life. I thought that I wasn't going to shoot the policeman, but how as I really so sure, especially when, not very long afterward, I threatened a senior citizen with the same gun? The answer to that and other introspective questions were easy to explain. They didn't cross my mind. I didn't analyze anything because I couldn't. Everything had just fallen into its exact place. The puzzle had just been solved and I had a course of action to undertake. Casting any doubt at this juncture would have aborted the entire mission and this was my last chance, one that had literally fell right into my lap. I acknowledged this to be a once in a lifetime opportunity because after all, brothers and sisters, this was a matter of Life and Death.

So I didn't worry about it.

Not one teeny-tiny bit.

Besides, it was time for The Don Olsen Show.

"Good morning, everybody. Don Olsen, The Don Olsen Show here on KGY. We've got a hot one today and we're just to jump right in. On the line is our old friend, Calvin Wheeler and he is indeed the man of the hour. Calvin, are you there?"

"I'm here, Don. Good morning."

"What's going on, Calvin? You're on the run. What the heck are you up to today?"

"Well, Don," I laughed almost embarrassed as I answered. "I…uh…I've finally taken over my own life."

"And what does that mean?"

"It means that I know exactly what I have to do right now for the very first time and I'm not going to allow anyone or anything stop me. I have a loaded gun sitting on the car seat beside me that's going to guarantee that."

"Calvin, what happened? Last week, you were a writer. Today, you're a criminal."

"I'd be considered a criminal only in the lowest common denominator. In the abstract, it all makes perfect sense. I'm a hero and I'm going to prove it. All my life, I've had to prove myself for everyone's benefit but my own. I never got anywhere. I was held back because I was made to feel weak. Now things are a little different. I'm going to be in charge and I'm going to show you all what I'm really made of."

"I'm sorry. I don't think I quite get it."

"And you never did, Don. How could you be expected to grasp this concept at all when your only interests are ratings and exploitation? Complex thoughts don't fit into your demographics. You've used me and now I'm going to use you in return to get my message across to everyone in your audience. Just know this. When everything is said and done, this will all make complete sense, even to you, Don."

"So what happened to *ABRACADABRA*?"

I felt a sudden twinge at the very mention of its name, but I shook it off like so much dandruff.

"*ABRACADABRA* is dead. It was taken away from me so I went ahead and killed it. I found it to be a liability. So, like a cancerous tumor, I surgically removed it."

"I'm sorry to hear that," Don spoke, struggling for empathy in utter vain. "I really thought it had some potential."

My face grew warm as my emotions began to rise. I wanted to suppress them for I couldn't afford a loss of control now that I had finally obtained it.

"You're lying," I told him in measured tones. "You know goddamn well that you believed *ABRACADABRA* would have been, at best, a flash in the pan or, worst case scenario, a total failure. That's because not only do you embrace this ephemeral world of ours, you encourage it. You fan the flames because that's what keeps you and your ilk alive. You don't want anything to last, that way we all just keep on buying. It's all disposable, isn't it, Don? This is the world you people have created. And it is because of you and your world that *ABRACADABRA* became what it did-just a magic trick, a slight of hand. There's no way you could ever discover its true meaning because you never bother to recognize the truth in anything. It's all just a big lie."

"But I thought you said without magic, there is nothing."

"I was wrong. There is no magic. That's the real trick. By the way, thanks for remembering."

This diatribe of mine served to keep me in check. I didn't lose my balance at all and therefore came out ahead. It did prove to unnerve the erstwhile talk show host though. To fill dead air time, Don cleared his throat and struggled through the next part of the interview.

"What now, Calvin? These so-called daring exploits of yours can't last forever. Let's face it. It's time you deposited that reality check of yours. You've committed some mighty serious acts of felony here and now you're on the run. Surely you must have a goal in mind."

"Sarah. I'm going to see Sarah."

"For those of you who are new to the program, Sarah is the love of Calvin's life…such as it is. Okay, you're going to visit Sarah. I assume that it's not just a social call. Then what?"

"Then I'm going to get back what I lost and yes, that includes Sarah. Here's something else you are never going to be able to understand, Don. I told you that I have a destiny to fulfill. Do you know why? I said it before and I'll say it again. I am special. I wasn't put on this earth to fritter away to nothingness. My life has meaning. I have always had a purpose. The dull monotony of everyday existence that you and everyone like you perpetuate has brought me to this very moment in time. But, like the old spiritual, once I was lost and now I'm found. With Sarah, I'm going to get it all back. She is my muse. She is my life. We belong together. Amazing grace, how sweet thou art."

Devil's advocate time, just before traffic and weather together. Here's Don Olsen.

"What if she doesn't want to go? What if she has no interest in a life on the lam with you-or just no interest in you at all? What if she doesn't get it? What if..."

"What if? What if? What if I turned the car around and drove to San Francisco to blow your fucking brains out, you stupid mealy-mouthed cocksucker!"

"Okay, I had to hit the dump button..."

"Shut up! Just shut your stupid ignorant mouth RIGHT FUCKING NOW!"

As I bellowed at Don Olsen, a black Chevy Monte Carlo pulled along side me. Its occupants, three low-grade punks were pointing and laughing derisively at me. I stopped my tirade and suddenly focused on my surroundings. I had stopped at an intersection on a frontage road running parallel to Highway 99 near Galt. The jackasses in the car had their bass driven music cranked to the max, pounding my chest and giving me uneasy heart palpitations. The only thing I could gather was that it was a slow day at the zoo and these chimps decided to leave Monkey Island for some playtime at my expense.

"Hey! Who you talkin' to over there?" a clown from the back seat yelled over the thundering music.

Boom-boom-boom-boom!

I looked ahead and sighed, hoping this was not a long traffic light.

"Are you crazy? Hey, answer me? Hey, Looney Toon! I'm talkin' to you!" the driver chimed in.

Boom-boom-boom-boom!

I guess I shouldn't have looked at them and smiled, but I did.

"What are you, a faggot? Huh?" the driver charmingly asked.

Boom-boom-boom-boom!

"Hey, faggot! You want some'a this?" the simian in the backseat yelled, grabbing his crotch, prompting more whoops from his chums.

Boom-boom-boom-boom!

I ignored them and drove away the second the light changed to green, only to have this barrel full o' monkeys follow me. Attempting to intimidate me for their fun and amusement by lurching the car up a little at a time, they finally cut me off altogether just before the next light. Amazingly, the three of them actually got out of their car and started to head for me. I couldn't believe how short they were, probably not more than five feet each. They could have fit twelve more of their friends in that Chevy without any crowding. Not matter how tall they were, their swagger, overall demeanor and the number in their party gave them their tough guy status. Now it was time for some serious fucking around totally at my expense.

Boom-boom-boom-boom!

Fortunately the light turned green and since I obviously didn't feel like playing, I slammed the car in reverse and sped around them. In order to ditch these bozos, I headed for the nearest freeway on-ramp another block down. True to form, they followed and entered Highway 99 right behind me. Since their car was faster than mine, they easily caught up to me and stayed directly on my bumper. I could see in my mirror that the driver feigned bumping into me a couple of time, much to the delight of the other monkey boys. He repeated the same gesture as he pulled beside me on the left, swerving over ever so slightly. The white t-shirted punk in the passenger seat lunged toward me in a stupid attempt to psyche me out, as if he could really reach me from the car. What was he going to do, jump in my car? Go ahead, Cheetah! I'd like see you try.

Boom-boom-boom-boom!

I slowed to let them pull ahead and tried to avoid them but moving into their lane in back of them, But, the Barrel Full O' Monkeys caught on fast and fell behind me again, flashing their lights and honking their horn, howling in delight with each moronic act they performed. Ahead of us in the far right lane was a twin trailer semi truck, loaded with gravel. I stepped on the gas full bore and pulled in front of the truck, angering the driver enough to give me a blast of his air horn. The Barrel Full O' Monkeys chased me down and flew up next to me. The kid in the back seat threw an empty bottle at my car, smashing it against the driver's door. The other passenger in the front seat cackled and flipped me an extreme middle finger.

That was my cue. It was then that I reached for the pistol with my right hand, thrust it out the window and pulled the trigger in one motion. I shot that fucker's middle finger clean off. Bingo! The punk howled in pain as he fell back in his seat and sprayed the inside of the windshield with his blood. Leaning against the driver caused the Barrel Full O' Monkeys to veer immediately to the left across the other lane and along the guardrail, spraying sparks the entire length of it. Then, because they had lost pace with me, I could see in my rearview mirror that their car had cut back to the right to get off the rail. But now, completely out of control, it plowed right into the trailer hitch of the gravel truck. The force of the crash caused the back trailer to jackknife into the Barrel Full O' Monkeys, crushing it like a empty beer can. The truck and both of its trailers flipped over to the

side, then began rolling over the freeway, spraying
gravel and dead punks all along Highway 99 like so
much shrapnel and collateral damage. In the wreckage
that ensued, other vehicles, their windshields sprayed by
gravel bullets, joined the fray, crashing into the fallen
truck and trailers blocking the freeway or trying to avoid
them by smacking into each other, punctuated by the
enormous explosion of a detonating gas tank.

Boom-boom-boom-BOOM!

"Oh my God," Don Olsen said solemnly. "You
are serious."

"I told you I was," I replied, trying to concentrate
on the road ahead and not worry about what was behind
me. It was quite a sight, I must admit, though I felt
somewhat removed from it all viewing it in my rearview mirror, kind of smaller than life. This detachment
was necessary though. After all, I had a schedule to
keep.

"We're speaking with Calvin Wheeler, current
Master of the World," Don continued "Let's go to Alice
Garcia in the KGY newsroom with a late breaking news
bulletin."

"Thank you, Don. This just in: A massive traffic
pileup involving several cars and an overturned semi-
truck and trailer had just occurred on Highway 99 south
of Sacramento near the town of Galt. Right now, there
are several unconfirmed reports of possible multiple
fatalities and…"

CHAPTER TWENTY FIVE

RETURN TRIP

M y trek to Jackson took almost three times as normal with the curly cue trail I blazed across three different county lines. I must have hit every point in the compass as I zipped back and forth, up and down, over the river and through the woods to Grandmother's house I went, flying under the radar of detection at any cost. It seemed like I was following directions on a road map that Jackson Pollock had drawn for me.

Along the way, there were several transmissions from Alpha Base on the two-way radio. First, Julie tried without success. Then Elsie got on the horn a couple of times. About a half hour after that, a none-too pleased-Terri, sounding like she had a bellyache from one too many pies, gave it a go. As I headed out of radio range to the sanctity of the hills, Jim Banner even called me in somewhat cheerful tones, which suggested to me that now I was in real trouble. Naturally, I didn't reply. They would just have to be patient for a little while longer, just like everybody else. But now it was official. My non-response solidified the fact that this workday was to be my very last. It didn't really matter. I hadn't swiped in that morning anyway, so technically, I was off the clock. This was my time. As such, I happened to glance over to the passenger seat where the Glock lay and noticed The Collection. My potpourri of inspirational music served no legitimate purpose to me anymore and only reminded me of my broken past. I didn't bother to examine the titles, choosing to grab the cassettes by the fistful and chuck them away forever behind me like so much litter on the roadside. I hesitated only once when I recognized Mahler Symphony No. 1, but I dropped the tape to the road without regret. It was high time to remove the clutter in my car anyway. I wanted Sarah to be comfortable for the long road ahead.

After three hours of solid driving, I had reached a side entrance to town past Jackson High School and turned onto Highway 4 on my way to the draw station. My plan was to tell Thelma I was filling in for J.B. that afternoon to throw her off my scent. That involved lying to her face, but with my newfound confidence, I knew I could pull it off. I couldn't believe that in this entire time that I hadn't spied one law enforcement official in any shape or form since Officer Down that morning. This streak continued on Highway 4, normally a route where I would pass at least three sheriff's cars in less than a mile. But nary a cop there was to see as I turned into the Healthfirst parking lot.

Damnation. I forgot to check the time. It was the noon hour and Thelma usually closed up shop until one o'clock to eat lunch and pound down another pack o' smokes at the choke 'n puke diner down the street she frequented day in and day out. Even though it was a quarter to one, this was a fifteen-minute wait I really couldn't afford. Now I would have to tread water until she returned and laying low was not in my game plan. As someone who detests all sports and football in particular, the words *game plan* were not in my game plan either, if that's any indication of my sense of sudden frustration. I didn't feel like I could just sit and wait for her but I also couldn't just travel up to Pine Grove right away either. I didn't want to risk being spotted tooling around in a Healthfirst vehicle without explanation. But instead of fretting, I shrugged it off. The New Me accepted this challenge as an odd sensation of invulnerability had taken me over. Without a single doubt in my head, I was convinced that whatever decision I made from here on in would be the right decision because *I* was right. The true meaning of the term *self-righteous* was so obvious all of a sudden. Therefore I chose to stay the course as planned. Boy, was I ever full of myself. What a nice change of pace.

I had me a powerful thirst, so I drove to the supermarket up the road where I could get a vending machine soda for a quarter. Sure, it was the store's own knock off brand- Cocoa Cola, Dr. Pecker, Mountain Dude-but hey, a drink's a drink when you're parched. Besides, for the rock bottom price of twenty-five cents a can, the soda machine could have been filled with carbonated beef bouillon and I would have bought it.

Walking back after my selecting my choice of beverage (the aforementioned Mountain Dude, for all of you completists out there) and back to my vehicle, I saw a brand spanking new latte colored Audi pull into a handicapped spot. I couldn't help but notice there weren't any of the required tags or stickers that would authorize the use of this prized of all parking spaces by this fuck you car. The driver, a golf shirted belly boy in smart looking khakis bounced out of his car with all the grace of an aquatic park walrus popping up leisurely out of his tank for some sardines from the friendly crowd. His features indicated that with his bushy mustache and burly demeanor, this analogy wasn't far off the mark. Koo-koo-ka-choo.

"Excuse me," I inquired. "Are you handicapped?"

"What?" he asked indignantly, stopping dead in his tracks, ready to back me down like the bully I immediately imagined him to be.

"I asked if you were handicapped."

"What's it to you?"

I pointed to his car. "That's a handicapped parking space."

"Are you a cop?"

"No. Just a concerned citizen."

The Walrus took a step toward me in a lame attempt at intimidation and said, "Mind your own bee's wax."

As he strode inside the grocery store, I realized that it was high time that this Walrus in question would have to be taught a lesson if not for the use of the words *bee's wax* alone.

I sat in my car with the engine running, laying in wait for this human turd to return to his Audi so that I could open my lesson plan and give this good ol' boy some necessary schoolin'. It didn't take long for my student to leave the store with his purchase in hand, a twelve pack of a delicious frothy beverage. Out of my parking space, I pulled forward and up the next row to gain some momentum. Then I turned swiftly around again with the Walrus dead in my sights. That's when I gunned it, giving him no time to react. I veered the car away at the last possible second so that only the right front bumper would clip him, catching him just below the abdomen. I stopped as I watched my reluctant pupil propel backwards into the iron shopping cart rack, spine first. Amazingly, he still held his beer, protecting the most important thing in his pathetic life. When he hit the metal, the cardboard ripped open and cans flew everywhere, including at his feet. The Walrus, his face contorted in mid-cry as he slid off the rack, fell face down into a foamy puddle of a great American brewski.

"Now you can park wherever you want," I told my portly student. "Class dismissed."

Another job well done, if I do say so myself...

Or do I?

I found myself sitting in the same parking space as before, watching the Walrus walk out of the supermarket, only he was pushing an elderly woman in a wheelchair with a grocery bag placed in her lap. She might have been his mother for all I knew. But that was beside the point.

The point was that I hadn't hit that fucker with my car after all. I only imagined it. My fantasies had just come back with a vengeance...and this time it was personal. Doubt reared its ugly head into my psyche once again and started to slap the New Me around like a pimp taking care of his ho. Had any of this day actually occurred or was it only been a series of very elaborate daydreams? Did I just cross over the line, only to have the line disappear altogether so that I would have no hope in returning...EVER?

I reached under the seat where I stashed the pistol when I bought my soda. Fumbling about an increasingly feverish pitch, I couldn't find it. Oh shit. Oh fuck. I hopped out of the driver's seat and fell to my knees to the asphalt of the parking lot, a rock dug into my left knee, but it didn't matter. Where was that goddamn gun? I couldn't have lost it because that's where I left it unless...it didn't really exist at all. Ramming my arm underneath the seat, the sleeve of my jacket caught on the adjustment and ripped it when I pulled it free. Now a nervous wreck in a matter of seconds, I then stuck my head inside, my face skidding across the perennially filthy floor pad.

There it was. I had shoved it all the way to the back. Again I reached for it and pulled it out from its hiding place. Holding this weapon in my hand once again was the tangible evidence I needed right then and there. As for what else had happened that day…well, fuck it. Time will just have to tell. The New Me blocked Doubt's next slap and kicked him right in the nads.

"Don't you ever lay a hand on me again, " the New Me threatened.

The only possible explanation I could have for what had just happened-or what hadn't-was that I was going through a period of adjustment. After all, I had only been the New Me since that morning. The previous mess of a human being I had been was several years in the making. I wholeheartedly admitted to speaking to Don Olsen, but I always did. Maybe I just needed to verbalize my intentions right then. I always knew that our dialogues were all bullshit. I found it therapeutic and he was the only one willing to listen to me. As for everything else, I had to sort this out. Obviously I had the gun, which I believed came from the cop known as Officer Down. Shots had been fired. That too was evident. My ears were still ringing. The freeway incident? Well, it sounded pretty far-fetched, but then I took a look where one of the punks had tossed that bottle and sure enough, the dent and scratched paint confirmed it. I suppose I could have turned on the radio since news of that nature surely would have on every channel. I didn't want the distraction. No, I had to do this my own way or at least the way of the New Me. With a satisfied look on my face, the New Me gripped the pistol and knew damn well this all the proof I would ever need. As for the Walrus, well, it turned out I was wrong. That could be another reason I went into fantasy mode and not acted on my every whim. Maybe the lesson to be learned right then was for me alone…or the New Me anyway.

Looking up, I spied Thelma's beige Jeep heading down Highway 4 back to work. That was my cue and not a minute too soon. Driving back into the drawing station lot, I parked next to Thelma and smiled. She didn't seem too pleased to see me. I holstered my firearm in my belt and zipped up my jacket before getting out the car. The charade had to go just as planned.

"Hey you," I greeted.

"Well, look what the cat drug in. What are you doing here?" she asked rather stiffly.

"I'm filling in for the day. Thought I'd just get up here a little early and take advantage of it for a change. I miss it up here," I said, walking with her to the door.

"Uh-huh," she sort of answered.

"Something wrong?"

"No, no. I gotta goddamn sinus headache is all. How are things down in Shit City?"

She looked up at me as she was searching for something, some sort of recognition that escaped me. There was a faint look of concern that looked just plain alien on her rawhide face. Did she know something? Hard to tell. Her sinus headaches usually altered her already hard bitten personality as it was, so I paid her no mind.

"Eh, you know. Same ol', same ol'. Look. My lip cleared up."

"I see that."

"That stuff you gave me really worked. Are you going to open the door already? I've got to use the can," I told her.

"Shut your piehole or I'll make you piss your pants," she groused. There was the Thelma I knew.

It had been the first comfort break I had taken all morning. That soda was the only thing I had in my system since the night before and the caffeine it contained recharged my battery immediately. No wonder I felt so light headed. I shook it off as a sign of weakness and stepped out of the bathroom. The phone had been ringing since we first walked in the door. I wondered why Thelma hadn't answered it.

"Hey, are you going to let that thing ring off the hook or what?"

I stopped when I saw her speaking on her cell phone with one hand while digging around in her purse with the other. She mentioned my name to whoever was on the other line. Seeing me, she dropped the phone and pulled a nickel-plated .38 revolver out of her handbag, pointing it right at me. She pursed her lips tightly in locked determination, looking ready to blow a hole right through my larynx. This was a first for me. I've never had a gun held on me before. I didn't much care for it.

"Thelma! What the fuck!"

"Calvin, you stay right where you are. The police are on their way."

"Goddamn it, Thelma. Put that down!"

"Uh-uh. No way. I don't know what you did and I don't really give two shits. All I know is that this gun is loaded and I will shoot you if you move. Do we understand each other? I will not hesitate to shoot you if you move. Tell me understand, Calvin."

"I understand."

This was the Thelma of legend, the same Thelma they sing about up in them thar hills, the same Thelma whose name the kids whisper in the schoolyard, the same Thelma who made love to a mountain lion after kicking a grizzly in the nuts just for shits and giggles. In that frozen moment in time, she became Calamity Jane, Dirty Harriet and She-Ra all wrapped up into a scrawny strip of rawhide with hair and glasses-and she was ready to blow my head clean off.

"Thelma... I have a gun too."

"Leave it alone. Keep your hands where I can see them. I don't want to shoot you but don't think that I won't. You know me."

"I thought I did. I thought we were friends."

"Don't go there. We ain't friends. We're just two people who work together. That's all."

Goddamn it to snot anyway. I hate when my own logic gets thrown back in my face.

"What have you heard?" I asked.

"Terri just called me when I was at lunch."

"Don't you mean Her Blubberness?"

I was looking for a common ground but Thelma wasn't having any of it.

"You are in such big ass trouble."

"Let me go. You never have to see me again."

"Calvin, you need help."

"You pull a gun on me and I need help."

The front door swung open as the pale tattooed giant entered for his weekly hepatitis test. Seeing Thelma with a gun, he immediately fainted and collapsed to the floor in a heap. This distracted Thelma enough so I could run into the next room and slam the door behind me. I grabbed a metal stool and tossed it out the sliding glass door. Glass crashed all about me as I dove out, rolling over onto the ground as the Glock dug into my groin. Ignoring the pain as I got to my feet, I pulled the pistol out and ran for my car. I heard Thelma fire her weapon, the bullet pounding into the roof of my vehicle. I reluctantly returned fire, not watching where I shot. Thelma took another turn, this time blasting out my side mirror.

"Thelma! You stupid bitch! Cut it out!" I screamed, firing once more to get her to stop. It did. The bullet struck her in the hip and dropped her to the ground. I immediately ran over to her.

Being the determined Harpy from Hell that she was, Thelma tried to find her pistol where she dropped it. I kicked it out of the way before she could. She hit me in the shin with her fist.

"Thelma! Look what you made me do!" I complained.

"Oh yeah…it's all my fault," she groaned, grabbing her hip.

I sighed heavily. "I'm sorry. I really am"

"Sorry don't stop the bleeding, you stupid asshole…"

"What can I do for you?"

"Give up!" she snarled at me right between the eyes. "Or just get the fuck outta here. I mean it. Go! Just fucking go!"

I kicked her pistol again, this time down the driveway far enough so she wouldn't be able to reach it all.

"That's so you won't shoot me in the back."

"I wouldn't miss on purpose like I just did either," Thelma winced, probably more pissed off at herself than she was at me. "Will you get outta here already?"

As if on cue, I heard a siren in the distance and took her advice.

"Calvin..." Thelma said one last time. "One way or the other, you're gonna die. You know that, don't you?"

I looked her straight in the eyes, first with regret with what I had done to this woman that I more or less respected, but then with the suddenly calm resolve of the New Me..

"Not right now. I've got a pick up to make."

I left Thelma bleeding in front of the draw station. Somehow I imagined the tattooed giant reemerging from the office, seeing Thelma on the ground and fainting all over again. I only hope he didn't land on her.

CHAPTER TWENTY SIX

QUE SARAH

Well, that didn't go very well, did it? In retrospect, it would have been so much easier for me to have not waited for Thelma at all and gone straight up to Pine Grove. That way I would have avoided the totally absurdity of getting into a shootout, of all damn things, with a co-worker. I mean, how much sense does that make? Keep in mind that running a policeman into a ditch, scaring a little old lady and causing a major traffic accident with several fatalities was just fine and dandy with me up to that point. But a Gunfight at the O.K. Draw Station? That's where I crossed the line.

The really weird part is…it really happened. That wasn't a relapse into Fantasyland like I had just experienced at the supermarket parking lot. I had concrete, solid evidence this time. For one thing, my clothes were dirty. It was obvious that my gun had been fired again. Then there was the matter of Thelma's blood on my hands. Steering with my right knee, I hurriedly washed the stains off with the remainder of my Mountain Dude, drying them with some paper napkins I had stashed in the console. Realizing I wasn't dreaming this all put me back on the right track. Now every second was critical and I needed every wit I had left in me in order to win the rest of the day as I intended to do.

The Jackson Police must have all been out to lunch when the call came into the station about the heated gun battle occurring on the outskirts of their sleepy little town. Too bad they had to tear themselves away from their chili sizes and Sloppy Joes in order to perform some actual police business. In the extended time it took them to respond, I was long gone, flying down another back road headed toward my final destination, that being Pine Grove and my Damsel in Distress.

Passing through the community known as West Point, I kept my speed steady but not excessive so as not to draw any more unnecessary attention to myself. Of course, this recent turn of events announced my presence in the Gold Country with all the fanfare of a brass band in a monastery. Now every law enforcement official in the state knew approximately where I was and my capture appeared imminent. Little did they know that they were dealing with a man who had a destiny to fulfill. Unfortunately, this afforded me even less time to complete this holy quest. Again, my old nemesis, Time, worked against me. Time was running out. Therefore, I had to travel double time. Soon I'd be into overtime. What if I ran out of time altogether? Could I live on borrowed time? And if I borrowed time, wouldn't I have to pay it back eventually? What are the interest rates on time?

Sarah. There'd be time with Sarah. With Sarah, I could just start over, I believed. I had to believe. It was too late not to believe. Too late… Time. Again with the goddamn time.

The oncoming orange road signs alerted me that some attempt made be made to delay my destiny even further. The words BE PREPARED TO STOP and FLAGGER AHEAD were messages I chose to ignore, especially when I discovered who the flagger in question was when I approached the roadwork site. It was the same dipshit from the last time I had been in the area, holding his stupid little sign as if his life depended on it. Little did he know how true that was as I tried to drive right past his station. Naturally, this gave my ability challenged friend pause, to explode into a Yosemite Sam style temper tantrum.

"Stop!" he cried, thrusting his arm forward forcefully as he pounded his sign on the hood on my car and shoved it toward my face. "Can you read? This means stop, y'hear?"

"Oh really? This means go," I replied, firing my pistol and blowing a hole right throw the T of his sign. "Y'hear?"

With that, I stepped on it and immediately found myself headed into oncoming traffic. I fired another round in the air, causing those drivers to get the hell out of my way. Road workers scattered as diverted vehicles drove through their area. One pick up veered off toward the back of the tar truck, causing hot tar to spray inside the cab and onto the driver, his screams of being scalded to death overpowering even the sounds of the heavy machinery. A station wagon full of what looked like migrant workers narrowly missed an asphalt roller but failed to skid to a halt before disappearing off into a ravine. I plowed right through this mess without a hitch. This was called demanding the right of way, something the Old Me would have condemned in traffic school.

Any hope of salvaging any anonymity went right out the proverbial window as I flew further on up toward Pine Grove, just a hop, skip and a jump now that this most annoying of all obstacles was out of my way. I left a road full of gawkers and supposedly innocent bystanders in my wake. I wondered if they realized how insignificant they were to me because I would have run them over without a care. Other than myself, there was only person in the world that truly mattered and she was right around the corner. The expectation of seeing Sarah became such a vivid reality that it became a booster rocket that propelled me toward my final destination quicker'n a wink. Before I even knew it. I had made it to Dr. Wilkins' office. I took that sharp turn into the driveway with all the confidence of a man in total control of his being. You look in control, you are in control.

The trees surrounding the office provided excellent camouflage for me as I slowed to a crawl. I didn't want to kick up any noticeable dust clouds as I usually had in my past visits. Despite my reckless abandon the past hour, I needed to remain hidden for a short period of time in order to finish business here and be on my way before I got totally boxed in by the various constabularies that would be closing in on me at any moment. I parked in a shaded area near the garage, near the gray Mitsubishi that I had assumed to be Sarah's.

I took the gun with me, concealing it under my jacket. As the warm weather increased in the afternoon sun, this was a particularly conspicuous fashion choice for a summer day, but I wasn't exactly carrying a derringer. I shoved the pistol behind me, the barrel uncomfortably holstered between my butt cheeks. Now not only did I look weird, but I walked funny too. At least I remembered to dust myself off before I entered.

The office was silent and appeared empty as I stepped inside. After the hustle and bustle of that day and particularly the past half hour, this was an eerie, almost unsettling quiet. I knew that Dr. Wilkins seemed to prefer his surroundings to be devoid of any ambient sound of any kind, pleasant or otherwise. Therefore, no background music played to soothe the nerves of an anxious patient awaiting the diagnosis of that mysterious lump in her breast or the reddish hue of a middle aged man's urine. All I ever heard were the persistent keyboard hammering of Janice the receptionist or the clod-hopping footsteps of Dr. Wilkins on his wooden floors. This time, not a creature was stirring, not even a mouse.

"Hello?" I politely called.

"Back here," I heard Sarah answer and the world all fell into focus.

Stepping into the kitchen, I discovered the source of those lilting tones and there she was, the Woman of This or Any Other Hour, looking as though she had, as the song goes, walked out of my dreams and into my heart. Her manner of dress at first seemed out of character since, other than my fantasies, I hadn't seen her out of her nurse's uniform. This day she wore a pale pink t-shirt and blue jeans, giving her the impression of a sweet country gal that had just gone into town for some gingham and molasses down at the general store. The only thing that contradicted that image was the fact that she wore latex gloves as befitting any healthcare worker. She had been writing a lab requisition for the blood she had drawn on a long gone patient. Looking up, her broad smile suggested that she seemed to be pleasantly surprised to see me.

"Well, hi there. Long time no see."

You remember me.

"Hi, Sarah. How are you?"

"I'm very well, thank you. And you?"

"Fine thanks. I've never seen you out of uniform before."

"Once and awhile I wear my own clothes. What about you? Aren't you…hot?"

Suddenly recalling I was wearing a fleece jacket in ninety-degree weather, I fumbled for a clumsy answer.

"Me? No. It's…comfy," I said, feeling a ball of sweat trickle down the side of my head.

"I just have to finish writing this patient's insurance information and this will be all ready for you."

"Take your time. I'm in no hurry. I'm early actually."

She smiled with some concern in her eyes.

"Are you sure you're not hot? It's pretty warm out there."

"I'm fine, It's nice in here though."

Especially where you're here, my love.

"Well, can I get you a glass of water?"

You really do care, don't you?

"Honest. I'm fine. Really."

"Okay. I won't be long."

This is it. The moment of truth.

"Ummm, Sarah… Did you get my… note?"

She looked up again, mildly confused.

"Note? What note?"

Uh oh.

"I left it the last time I was here, a week ago. You were closed so maybe you saw it…Monday? "

"No, I'm sorry. I didn't see a note. Where did you leave it?"

"In the…in the door."

"I'm sorry. I didn't receive it. What did it say?"

You genuinely want to know what I have to say.

"Well, I wanted to tell you that I wasn't going to be your courier any longer," I began as the words clogged into my throat in a log jam.

"You're here today," she smiled almost wistfully. After sealing the blood vial and paperwork in a plastic bag, Sarah suddenly pulled off her rubber gloves abruptly but with all the seductive grace of a classic striptease artist. The spontaneity of this action took me aback with an audible gulp. "Are you sure you wouldn't like a glass of water? It's no trouble."

You really do want to take care of me, don't you?

"Sure. That would be great," I agreed as she filled a Styrofoam cup from the sink. "Thank you so much."

"You just seem rather…overheated."

You have no idea.

"Anyway," I continued. "I'm just filling in for the day. The other driver is out sick."

"Oh yes. What's his name… J.J.?"

"J. B. That's him. You didn't see a note though, huh? I left it in the door with…a flower."

"Was it a rose?" she asked with some recognition. "Janice found a rose. I think she thought it was for her. Janice?"

"Yeah?" came the reply from one of the back rooms, sounding as though a smoke alarm had suddenly been triggered.

Startled, I whipped about to catch a glimpse of Janice in the space between the kitchen doorjamb, opening the door of the bathroom but making no attempt to walk toward the kitchen.

"Do you remember that rose from the other day?"

"What about it?" Janice snidely answered her question with another.

"Was there a note with it?"

"Yeah. What about it?"

"I believe it was meant for me," Sarah explained, grinning at me rather shyly.

"The note or the rose?"

"Both."

"Oh," Janice honked in her goose voice as she finally decided to haul her pear shaped body out of the can so that Sarah wouldn't have to raise her voice any longer. She gave me the snide once over when she noticed me standing there. "I couldn't make it out. The handwriting was pretty bad. I think it said 'Thank you', so I just figured it was for me. The rose was dead anyway."

"Well, the note and the rose were from…I'm sorry. What was your name again?" Sarah asked.

"Calvin," I replied, drawing my pistol from behind me and shooting Janice point blank in the chest. As Dr. Wilkins' ex-receptionist collapsed to the wooden floor, I turned back to Sarah. "The rose was meant for you. The card clearly had your name written on it. She should have told you."

Dropping the cup of water, Sarah covered her mouth and nose with both hands in absolute shock and immediately shivered in terror. Her eyes widened to such a degree that they almost popped out of their sockets and instantly filled with tears.

"Oh Lord Jesus, please protect me. Please. Please. Please don't kill me, " she quivered backing away toward the sink.

"Oh. No, Sarah. No. I'm sorry. I guess that explains the jacket, doesn't it?" I smiled anxiously but it was obvious I had scared the Love of My Life half to death. I removed my jacket and dropped it to the ground next to Janice. The change in my body temperature was refreshing. "Whew. That's better. You're right. It is hot."

"Don't kill me…. Please… Dear Lord, please protect me…"

"Sarah, don't be scared. It's okay. I would never hurt you."

"No…please…no…"

"You don't have to say please. Honest. I'll put this away," I tried to reassure her as I tucked the gun into my belt, burning my stomach. "Ow! Shit!"

As I pulled it out again, Sarah jumped and fell against the refrigerator.

"Please!"

"Sarah! You don't have to say please. I'll put it here on the counter. Guns are scary. I know. You should see how other people react when they…"

"What…what…do…you…want? Money? I have some…. Not much but…"

What a frightened little rabbit, absolutely terrified. Damn it. I didn't want this to happen. I had to make this better. I wanted to reach out and comfort her in my arms but it probably was too soon. Talk about getting off on the wrong foot.

"Money? No! I don't want your money. Look, this is very confusing, isn't it? Uh, where to begin…"

Janice's body began to convulse on the floor, apparently going through her death throes. Between the thumping of her limps on the hardwood and the gurgling sounds of her choking on her own blood, Janice's actions became very distracting. Even her final moments here on Earth were annoying.

"She's a little noisy, isn't she?" I admitted. "I don't want to shoot her again. That wouldn't be right. Can we just go in another room?"

"Yes…yes… I'll do anything you want…just please…"

"Sarah! Stop saying that!" I demanded. It was the first time I raised my voice to her.

"I'm sorry! I'm sorry! Whatever you want…"

After grabbing my pistol again, I took her by the arm and led her gingerly around the flopping Janice and into one of the examination rooms. Sarah shook even more when I touched her. Not a good sign. Boy, did I ever have to exercise some damage control but quick.

This is it. There's no turning back now.

"Sarah, just hear me out, would you please? I don't have the luxury of time to really say everything that's on my mind so I'll be as brief but concise as I can, given the circumstances. I really hate to edit myself, but I guess I'll just have to blurt this out," I said, then swallowed hard because here came the big reveal. "I love you. I am in love with you. I have been since the moment I laid eyes on you. You are the most beautiful, captivating woman I have ever seen in my entire life. You're kind, sincere… Your heart is so full… Look, we don't really know each other in the traditional sense, I mean, this is more than just a little unorthodox to say the very least but I know you. I've always known you. You've been living right here in my heart always and when I first saw you, I knew it was you and you all along. You are the one. Sarah, I want you to…"

The sound of someone pulling into the driveway had just rudely interrupted the single most important monologue of my entire life. I spun about to see a Ford Bronco with what appeared to be a man and a small child inside pulling up behind the Mitsubishi. I grabbed the gun off the counter.

"No! Please! That's my husband and baby! Don't shoot them! I beg of you!" Sarah cried.

281

Sarah's words slapped me right across the face. Now it was my turn to be shocked.

"That's your what and your what?"

"My husband and my daughter. They've just come to give me a ride home. Don't hurt them. Please. I'm sorry. I won't say please again, just don't hurt them. They're everything to me. I'll do whatever you want just leave them alone," she pleaded.

"Husband? You're…married?" was all I could muster as the inner workings of my entire being came to a grinding halt. I turned to Sarah and grabbed her left hand, sopping wet with what I assumed to be nervous sweat. As I gazed at her ring finger, a simple gold wedding band that I swore had not been there before had suddenly materialized. I dropped her hand and turned away in disbelief.

"Calvin?" I heard her say, uttering my name for the very first time. "It…it's Calvin, right?"

"You don't even know my name," I declared. I turned and pointed the pistol directly at her, right between the eyes, then pulled the trigger as she screamed. The gun clicked empty.

Oh no. What had I just done? I just killed the woman I loved…or I would have had a bullet remained in the chamber. This was an act on pure reflex against the only person who truly mattered to me. At least I thought she did. Maybe she hadn't after all. It was too easy to just eliminate her, snuff her completely out of my life by snuffing her out altogether. Was this self-defense because she had just stabbed me in the heart? But no, it wasn't me. It was the New Me. The Old Me would never hurt Sarah. The New Me is a cold-blooded son of a bitch. How could I have allowed this to happen? Scaring myself almost as much as I had Sarah, I recoiled against the door of the examination room.

"I didn't mean to do that! I did not mean to do that! I love you! Sarah, I…love…you…"

I pictured her in my arms with the top of her head blown off. Tears fell out of my eyes in a downpour of grief as I embraced her, her brains spilling over my hands. I wanted to wail at the absolute tragedy of it all, only the cry wouldn't release, as if it came from a very long distance which would have been the depths of my wretched soul. Instead I stood in strained silence, my mouth agape as I tried to scream as hard as I possibly could but not a sound came out.

Footsteps on the porch snapped me back to whatever reality this was as I heard what should have been a strong masculine voice calling Sarah's name. Instead, it almost sounded like the croak of pubescent teenager.

"Sarah? Are you okay?"

"Tim!" Sarah yelled.

I grabbed her and covered her mouth to shut her up. If I was going to be the stereotypical crazed gunman, I figured I might as well go all the way with it. Besides it was pretty much a foregone conclusion by now that I had completely blown it with Sarah. Scaring her was bad enough, but trying to shoot her as well too closed the deal.

Peeking out to see who Sarah picked over me confused me even further. I thought Tim would have been a strapping lumberjack type in a short sleeve work shirt with bulging biceps and Levis that looked like he was poured into at the stud farm. That's a Tim I could have accepted. But the Tim that stomped inside the office as Sarah's Knight in Shining Armor appeared to be just an androgynous non-descript little schlep who could have easily have passed for Sarah's younger brother. As he rushed to his wife's rescue, he tripped right over Janice and tumbled to the floor.

"Oh my God…Sarah!" he called as he clumsily scrambled to his feet in the pool of Janice's blood.

I had to get out of there fast so I pulled Sarah down the hall with my empty gun to her head, my hand still over her mouth. Time for a little bluff action.

"Easy, Tim," I warned him

"Sarah, are you alright?"

"She'll tell you later, okay? Just back up so I can get by. And watch out for that lady down there."

"Sarah, it's going to be okay," Tim told her, waling backwards with his arms in the air and stepping over Janice's body. "Jesus will protect you."

Jesus would do a better job that you, pal. Boy, Sarah, can you ever pick 'em.

Sarah began to resist as I tried to walk with her. She tried to grab my hand away from her mouth.

"Hey! Stop that! I've got a gun here!"

"Sarah! Don't struggle! It might go off!"

Pulling free, Sarah exclaimed, "It's not loaded! It's empty!"

"Here!" I barked, shoving her into Tim, knocking them both to the floor. What a nice couple they made. "You deserve each other!"

With the front door wide open, I scrambled out of the office but made the idiotic miscalculation of leaping off the porch. I fell knees first into the gravel. Tim was right behind me and almost on top of me when I tossed the pistol at him, striking him right in the mush. As he grabbed his face, blood squirted out between his fingers. I must have broken his nose.

This bought me enough time to get to my car and make my escape. On the way out, I caught a glimpse of Sarah's daughter sitting in the Bronco, body pressed up against the window watching the action. She was a miniature scale model of Sarah, the daughter we should have had together. I saw the three of us standing together before our castle on the beach. My arm is around Sarah as I hold our daughter, the ocean splashing at our feet. First our daughter disappears, then Sarah. I'm the only one remaining as the castle behind me explodes and is totally destroyed. I find myself in the rubble in the remnants of all my broken dreams, gone as the tide carries it away until there is nothing left at all.

In the rearview mirror, I could see Sarah caring for Tim as their daughter rushes out of the Bronco to them. The dust cloud I leave behind me engulfs the three of them and now they too gone forever.

Que Sarah, Sarah.

Whatever won't be, won't be.

CHAPTER TWENTY SEVEN

RED ASPHALT

Now what?
I had no plan. Nothing had existed in my mind beyond this point. Sarah and I were to drive off into the sunset, living happily ever after. The End. There was no alternate ending. That was it. Now with Sarah gone and the surprise introduction of a new character in the final act, her flitty little husband, everything was FUBB-Fucked Up Beyond Belief. I had nowhere to go, nothing to do, no one to be.

Aimlessly I drove throughout the foothills in all directions of the compass, my only intention being escape, but from what? The sirens wailing all about me were the only things I tried to avoid and evade. I had to keep moving. Hiding seemed a futile gesture. Sooner or later I'd be found, so if I just had some forward momentum, I'd have some kind of an out when I needed it.

For no apparent reason, I flipped on the radio, channel scanning as I always did. Moldy oldies, country crap, hip-hop garbage and endless blah blah blah spewed out of the speakers in mind numbing monotony just like any other day of the week. Abortion…unemployment… illegal aliens…women's rights…gay rights…civil rights…taxes…terrorism…crime…AIDS…SIDS… AFL-CIO…NFL…NBA…MLB…BLT…DNC… GOP…CIA…HBO…E-I-EI-O…

"Calvin, things haven't worked out too well for you, have they?" Don Olsen said.

"No, they sure haven't, Don. I guess that's it for me."

"What are you going to do?"

"I don't know. I guess I never really did know anything at all."

"Well, cheer up. Maybe you could go to the Wizard and ask him to give you a clue," he quipped.

"Yeah. Good one. Clueless. That's me, alright. Maybe I'm the Wizard, Don. Don't look behind the curtain. It's just me. There's nothing there. I'm a fraud, a complete fake. It was all a bluff, Don. I raised the stakes…I went all in and Life called my hand. Look at my cards! Garbage! I had nothing! Nothing!"

"Our guest has been for the very last time Mr. Calvin Wheeler, Pitiful Soul Extraordinaire. We'll be right back, but he won't. Never again. This is The Don Olsen Show on KGY," Don signed off.

"Don? Don, wait! I need help, man! Help me!" I pleaded. When I realized my broadcast buddy wouldn't answer, I gave the radio a good kick with my right foot, causing me to momentarily lose control of the car and scuffing up the countryside in the process before I was able to regain my rightful place on the road.

Here came the waterworks, as my mom used to say. Tears poured out of me, making it difficult to see. With them came the obligatory snot and the requisite whimpering which soon became nearly uncontrollable.

My grief would be my undoing if I let it consume me, which was a distinct possibility. I couldn't help but notice that when I cried, I didn't sound any different than when I was a child. I didn't cry like an adult. I bawled like a baby. Baby gonna cwy? Cwy-baby! Cwy-baby!

"J.B. to Calvin. J.B. to Calvin. Do you copy?" the familiar voice on the two-way radio called.

I hadn't realized that I had left it on all this time. No one had called since that morning and there usually wasn't any radio reception in the foothills. Maybe it was another bad hallucination in the series. Whatever it was, it made me stop my blubbering long enough to respond.

"This…is Calvin," I spoke into the mike. "Over?"

"Hey, bud. How ya doin'?"

"Oh, you know. Same shit, different day. You?"

"Yeah, me too. Say, what's your location?"

"Oh, I'm around. Are you in the hills?"

"Yeah, yeah, I am."

"I thought so. There's not a lot of static. You sound almost clear."

"Uh-huh. So, you want to…uh…get together?"

"Oh, I don't know. I'm kind of busy right now."

The long pause that followed made me think I had insulted him and he hung up.

"Calvin?"

"Yeah, I'm still here."

"It's all over," he said in utmost sincerity, if a little too dramatically.

"That's the general consensus. Say, are the cops all listening in right now?"

"Yeah, yeah, they are. Why don't you just give up, man?"

"Give up?" I asked, looking at the radio quizzically. "What the hell is that? Good idea though.

No, I've got to do this myself. Do you understand? No collaborators. I work alone. How do you think I got this far?"

"Calvin, come on now. Give it up. Don't be an asshole."

"Wow. I think you missed your calling in life. You should have been a motivational speaker, you know that? Thanks anyway, but I gotta do what I gotta do."

"What does that mean?"

"You got me, pal. Do you what really sucks in all this?"

"What?"

"I still don't have an ending. Ain't that a pisser? I have no idea how this fucking thing is going to turn out. It is the hardest thing in the world to come up with. Do you know that? A goddamn ending! You know what it is, don't you?"

"Yeah…yeah, I think so."

"Of course you do. Like we always said, it's the Nature of the Business."

"Calvin…"

"Forget it, J.B. I'm out."

With that, I tossed the mike across the passenger seat and flipped the two-way off once and for all. I didn't need anymore unnecessary distractions while I was running for my life. As my head swam with uncertainty, focusing in on a decision concerning my immediate future was an arduous task to say the least. I decided that I needed a crutch, so I fell back on the What If game. The What If game gives you several possibilities to choose which way a story or a character will go and it came in handy right then and there.

What if I did give up? I'd become an instant celebrity and a cause celebre. My face would be featured on every news outlet around the world. The court trail itself would make all others pale in comparison and my death sentence would be challenged by the biggest bleeding hearts in the land. I could get married to one of those lunatic women who fall in love with serial killers. Charlie Manson could be my best man.

OR

What if I ditched my car and hiked up deep into the woods, never to be heard of again? I could live by my wits alone eating berries, leaves and small pebbles for fiber until I caught my own food with a pointed stick. I'd be able to live out the rest of my days in a mud hut that I built myself and legends would told about the Crazy Old Hermit of the

Forest.

OR

What if I barreled straight down Highway 12 at maximum speed, knowing full well I would meet the biggest road block the state of California had ever seen? All weapons would be directed at me as I rapidly approach. On command, they'd open fire. Bullets would rip the car and myself to shreds but they couldn't slow me down in the least. I'd plow right into their roadblock in a blaze of glory, taking everyone with me in the process.

OR

What if just before I'd reach the roadblock, I'd hit a hard right and flip my vehicle over and over, end over end until it landed right at their feet?

OR

What if I drove straight off a cliff?

OR

What if…

They were heading right for me on the road ahead, three sheriff's cars, lights a' blazin', sirens a'blarin. No matter what scenario I could come up with, it didn't matter for this was the one they had chosen for me and now I had to wing it completely. The What If game was over. Now it was time to play Hot Pursuit and I was It.

The only thought that came to mind was the most logical. RUN! This is what cowards do and this was no time to debate the issue. I had to flee and fast. Try as I might, I just couldn't turn 180 degrees and head in the opposite direction. Instead, I cut into a lumberyard and hoped for a way out on the other side. I don't know how I managed the maneuver, but it worked as I ended up exiting out a back driveway, just beating a semi about to pull in.

I couldn't sustain this for very long. Why should I believe that I could get away when everything about my life pointed in the direction of failure? I wanted this to end, to have it all be over and done with once and for all but I didn't want to be caught either. I'd never be able to face up what I had done. Sorrow and shame possessed my spirits as I recalled the day's events from Officer Down to the D.O.D. to the Barrel Full O' Monkeys to Thelma to the Flagger to Janice to Sarah…Oh, God, Sarah… What did I do? What did I do to you? I'm not a killer. That wasn't Me. It was the New Me. Bullshit! It's all a goddamn lie! There is no Old Me. There is no New Me. There's just Me. It's always been Me. I am Skullfucker. I am Dr. Roberts. I am The Angry White Man. I am a cold-blooded murderer. This is what I've become. It's why I have to run away. Or have I been this person all along? Maybe this was my true destiny. This is the real reason I was put on this Earth. I'm not a writer. I'm not a creator. I'm not an artist. I am what I have always been…a total fuck up and at that level, I am a total success. To think that I ever could have been anything else is and always has been pure folly. No wonder I never could face the real truth about myself. I had completely pulled the wool over my own eyes. The bottom line is so very plain, so very simple and oh so devastatingly obvious. It was all just an illusion…

Abracadabra.

One of the patrol cars had almost caught up to me from the lumberyard, so I turned off toward West Point, back in the same direction I had just traveled not fifteen minutes before. Flooring the accelerator, I attempted to steer my car the best I could at such a high rate of speed but I found it difficult to concentrate on the road ahead while catching the progress of my pursuer in the rear view mirror. As I whipped around the next bend, I clipped the BE PREPARED TO STOP sign, cracking the windshield as it bounced off.

I found myself right back in the same roadwork site as before. The crew scattered, either recognizing me or noticing this was a high speed police action or both. Whatever the reason, they fled the area immediately, even those running the heavy machinery, hoping off their various tractors and equipment to safer grounds, which was anywhere but there. The driver of the dump truck pulled ahead and accidentally cut off the sheriff's vehicles, which would have given me a reprieve, had I not begun to lose control in the gravel. As I skidded toward the giant asphalt roller, the operator dove off as his machine continued to roll on without him. My car went into a spin and slid backwards into a ditch, slamming into the side of a hill. The car stalled when it hit and suddenly I was a sitting duck. Restarting the engine, I tried to drive out to no avail. The car was indeed stuck, wedged in tight. The back wheels spun sending up an instant cloud of rubber burning smoke. I wasn't going anywhere.

On the other hand, the asphalt roller was traveling right for me. Slowly and methodically, it rolled toward my car, relentlessly. It loomed before me in mere seconds as I desperately tried to drive the hell out of that death trap I had just created for myself. The front drum of this behemoth started to roll over the front bumper. Giving up on driving out, I concentrated on just getting out as the hood became crushed in the onslaught of this rolling behemoth. Panicking as it my lot, I struggled with my seat belt until I hit upon the bright idea of unbuckling it. The door wouldn't open, slammed up against the hill. When I tried to crawl out the window, it was too late. The roller had mashed over the engine and pinned the steering wheel to my legs. I held my arms up in hopes of, what…stopping it with my brute force? The windshield broke over me, showering me in glass as the huge roller loomed over me, engulfing me in its shadow. This thing was squashing me like the bug I most certainly was. In just a couple of seconds, I wouldn't even be a memory. I'd be only a stain. My clock had just run out. There wasn't even enough time left to have my life flash before my eyes because it was now over-right here, right now. I screamed with all of my might, a sickeningly pitiful high pitch screech ripping through my entire being as it was being crushed to complete and absolute obliteration. I had met my Maker…and his name is John Deere.

THIS WAS NOT THE ENDING I HAD IN MIND!

The roller stopped short of squishing out my very existence, the scalding metal of the drum pressed up against my face and frying my left cheek as my hands were pinned against it, as if ridiculously trying to hold it back. The engine quit and this massive piece of heavy machinery sat on my lap, the weight of which cramming me against the entire world. Though it had come to a halt, having this thing on top of me didn't instill a bit of confidence. It could still finish the job. Hasn't anyone ever heard of gravity, for Christ's sake? It is the fucking

LAW, isn't it? There was absolutely nothing I could do at this, what was probably the very last moment in this life of mine but sit tight and await my fate. What else could I do? But I was still in command of the situation. My non-action, not moving a single iota, kept the tractor from squashing me into a puddle of Calvin goo. If I chose to I could have simply scratched my nose and the game would be over. I controlled my destiny. Somehow I found no comfort in that. I was now at the final impasse. I didn't know whether I should live or die. I couldn't make up my goddamn mind.

But I wasn't in charge after all. The person who stopped the roller just in the nick of time had still been aboard. Through what was left of the passenger window, I could see his shadow as he gingerly stepped off, causing me to gulp from my throat to my rectum in anticipation of the weight shift. The seconds that followed waiting for the big splat to occur seemed to last forever, whatever that meant. As far as I knew right then, forever could have lasted only a few seconds. For once in my life, I had absolutely no concept of time.

Peering inside to check on me, I saw that my savior had turned out to be my old friend, the Flagger. He knew me just like I knew him. Staring directly at me, he narrowed his eyes in disparaging recognition.

The Flagger then shook his head back and forth derisively, in judgement of me.

ABOUT THE AUTHOR

Born and bred like a fatted calf in Stockton, California, Scott Cherney is also the author of *In the Dark: A Life and Times in a Movie*, *Please Hold Thumbs: A Not-So-Round Trip to South Africa* and his collection of comedy sketches entitled *Now THAT'S Funny.* As a playwright, his works have included *The Song of the Lone Prairie, The Legend of the Rogue* and *La Rue's Return* (with Edward Thorpe). In his lifetime, Scott has also been a stage actor, a film critic, a weekend cowboy, a stand-up comic and even a raccoon. He currently lives near Portland, Oregon with his wife, Laurie.

CPSIA information can be obtained at www.ICGtesting.com
Printed in the USA
LVOW092132130812

294224LV00002B/71/P